P9-CBY-249

Kissing Caleb Tanner was good.
Very, very good.

But mere kissing wasn't enough. Not nearly enough. Crystal felt a feverish need for more. Crazy thoughts cartwheeled through her brain. She wanted to explore all that heat and muscle held in check by the cloth she twisted beneath her hands.

Caleb hauled in a ragged breath. "Oh, baby," he muttered. "Where have you been all my life?" Dipping his head, he brought his lips to hers again, and Crystal experienced the sensation of a weightless free fall.

Nothing like this had ever happened to her. She never lost control around men. Never. Panic reared suddenly, shutting off her intake of air. It made no sense. The faces of people she'd loved, people who'd left her, beat at the back of her eyelids. Her mother and now Margaret Lyon. Her dad. Her fiancé.

She couldn't breathe. Words of warning shrieked in her ears. *Back off! Back off! You're nothing to Caleb Tanner. You're a fool to fall for him!*

But maybe some men were different.... Crystal willed the panic to subside. They each eased back a little. Crystal released his shirtfront, wishing he'd say something. But why should he? He might have laid the fire, but she'd struck the match.

Dear Reader,

I've loved reading family sagas since I picked up my first Edna Ferber novel quite some time ago. And I think many people enjoy reading about complex families playing out destinies of power and conflict and—of course—love.

It's been a wonderful challenge to be one of three authors privileged to take Superromance readers on a fifty-year journey with the Lyon family. From the sultry swamps of Bayou Sans Fin to the lush Garden District of New Orleans, I've helped the family forge one of Louisiana's most powerful broadcasting businesses.

But life is never simple in any dynasty. Fortunately, love is ultimately the legacy that holds the Lyon family together. And up till now, Crystal Jardin, a Lyon first cousin, has had precious little love in her life. But Skipper West, an injured child she befriends, and Caleb Tanner, a hero in every sense, are going to change that!

I hope you enjoy *Family Fortune* and the other LYON LEGACY books.

Sincerely,

Roz Denny Fox

P.S. I love to hear from readers. You can reach me at: P.O. Box 17480-101, Tucson, Arizona 85748

LOOK FOR THE ENTIRE "LYON LEGACY" SERIES:

FAMILY FORTUNE
Roz Denny Fox

HARLEQUIN®

TORONTO • NEW YORK • LONDON
AMSTERDAM • PARIS • SYDNEY • HAMBURG
STOCKHOLM • ATHENS • TOKYO • MILAN • MADRID
PRAGUE • WARSAW • BUDAPEST • AUCKLAND

If you purchased this book without a cover you should be aware
that this book is stolen property. It was reported as "unsold and
destroyed" to the publisher, and neither the author nor the
publisher has received any payment for this "stripped book."

ISBN 0-373-70859-9

FAMILY FORTUNE

Copyright © 1999 by Rosaline Fox.

All rights reserved. Except for use in any review, the reproduction or
utilization of this work in whole or in part in any form by any electronic,
mechanical or other means, now known or hereafter invented, including
xerography, photocopying and recording, or in any information storage
or retrieval system, is forbidden without the written permission of the
publisher, Harlequin Enterprises Limited, 225 Duncan Mill Road,
Don Mills, Ontario, Canada M3B 3K9.

All characters in this book have no existence outside the imagination of
the author and have no relation whatsoever to anyone bearing the same
name or names. They are not even distantly inspired by any individual
known or unknown to the author, and all incidents are pure invention.

This edition published by arrangement with Harlequin Books S.A.

® and TM are trademarks of the publisher. Trademarks indicated with
® are registered in the United States Patent and Trademark Office, the
Canadian Trade Marks Office and in other countries.

Visit us at www.romance.net

Printed in U.S.A.

THE LYON FAMILY

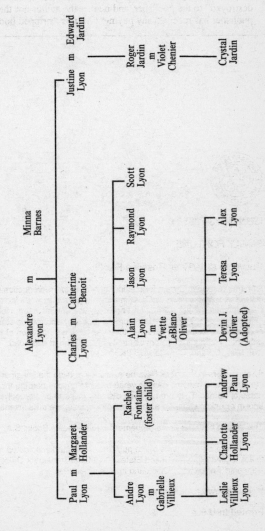

CHAPTER ONE

September 1999

ANOTHER THREE THOUSAND DOLLARS withdrawn from Margaret Lyon's private bank account! Crystal Jardin scowled at her computer screen. In the past two weeks, there had been identical withdrawals from Margaret's bank account via an ATM. Always on a Monday. And from an *unknown* automatic teller. Crystal found that the most worrisome. She wouldn't be as concerned if she hadn't just seen a WDIX-TV segment on a computer hackers' convention. She'd learned that bank officials haunted the convention, hiring the brainy kids who could get into bank systems and putting them to work writing codes to plug this very type of break-in.

The segment stuck in her brain because, in addition to her duties as the business manager for the family-owned, New Orleans-based Lyon Broadcasting Company, she served as personal financial adviser to Margaret, the principal stockholder, and to a few other family members, as well.

Granted, the amount of the withdrawals wasn't particularly alarming. Margaret was an extremely wealthy woman, and prone to shopping sprees. And Crystal hadn't been too concerned when Margaret disappeared without informing the family of her whereabouts. Until today. She recalled that the last time they sat down to go over finances, which they did regularly, Margaret hadn't been herself. Who'd expect her to be? It was just after her beloved husband Paul's death.

Crystal understood that Margie needed time alone. The woman had loved Paul Lyon for nearly sixty years. Losing him suddenly to a heart attack—after doctors had twice snatched him from the brink of death—had shaken the entire family, and no one more than Margaret. Not only that, the funeral had been overwhelming, with half of New Orleans turning out. The many heartfelt eulogies given by colleagues in the broadcasting business for the man known as the Voice of Dixie must have added to the weight of Margaret's sorrow.

At the time Margie went missing, everyone in the family assumed she'd gone off alone to grieve. But when she didn't call or show up at one of the ocean resorts she and Paul had always favored, her son, André, and his wife, Gaby, began to panic. And now, this complete elimination of a paper trail in Margie's bank transactions was beginning to panic Crystal, too.

At seventy-seven, the family matriarch excelled in anything relating to the TV station she'd brought to life fifty years ago. But the woman Crystal loved like a grandmother didn't have the skill to hack into a bank computer system.

So she'd enlisted someone's help. Whose? And why go to such extremes? Crystal racked her brain for other possibilities. She avoided terms like *kidnapped*. André, Paul and Margaret's only child and general manager of the business, had tiptoed around the term at breakfast, too—though Crystal knew it was on his mind today when he'd debated whether or not to file a missing-person report with the police.

André was torn between allowing his mother the independence she'd always demanded and being horribly remiss if anything was wrong. Crystal felt the same pressure now. She wanted to show him the account—except that Margaret insisted on keeping her financial dealings private. Besides, if she'd fallen victim to theft, wouldn't the criminal clean out her account and be done with it? Crystal thought it more likely that Margaret, always a headstrong woman, had bullied a banker friend into freeing her from a cloying family for a few weeks. The days after Paul's death and before the funeral, family members had closed ranks, hoping to ease her pain. "Smothered" was how Margaret had described it to Crystal the morning of the service. So after a lengthy internal debate, Crystal decided to respect her client's wishes—for now.

Just as she finished making her decision, her friend and junior accountant tapped on her open office door. "I'm leaving, boss. Here are the vouchers you asked me to draw up for the news department. All they need is your signature." The perky redhead zipped into the room.

"Thanks, April." Crystal accepted the forms, her gaze straying to the clock. "Yikes. When did it get to be five-thirty? I promised to be at the Tulane Medical Center by five-fifteen."

"Are you playing your saxophone in the children's ward again?" April asked as Crystal hastily shut down her computer.

"Probably. The boy I told you about—Skipper West? He underwent another spinal operation today. His foster mom has four other kids, three of whom have chicken pox. I promised Beth I'd visit Skip tonight since she can't."

"You want a lift? I'm taking the accounting class you recommended. The medical center's on my way."

"You're a lifesaver, April." Crystal gathered her belongings and flashed her friend a smile. "How's the class going?" she asked as they walked out together.

"Great. I'm learning as much as you said I would, if not more."

As Crystal locked her office, a dark-haired, dark-eyed man, at least ten years her senior, stepped out of an office across the hall. He pulled the key from his door before shrugging into a cashmere suit coat. Glancing at the women, he singled out April. "Sucking up to the boss again? Or do you prefer women over men, hmm?"

April's face erupted in red blotches as she sputtered indignantly.

"Watch it, Raymond," Crystal warned coldly. "Your name might be Lyon, but that doesn't exempt you from the company harassment policies."

Ray, third son of Charles Lyon—Paul Lyon's brother and the lesser company stockholder—ignored Crystal. He leered at April, instead. "You'll soon see you've aligned yourself with the wrong side of the family, baby doll. If you're a little nicer to me, I might ask Alain to keep you on when he takes over as general manager."

"If that ever happens, God forbid," Crystal said, thrusting her saxophone case between the two of them, "most of the staff, including me, will volunteer to join our competition. What are you and Alain up to now? Don't you two get it? *Nobody* cares what went on fifty years ago." She was aware, too, that her being promoted over Ray no doubt stuck in his craw.

"Grandpa Lyon shafted my dad when he left Uncle Paul controlling interest in WDIX," Ray said. "That's fact. You should side with us, considering that he excluded your grandmother altogether. Attitudes like yours, cousin dearest, will make revenge sweeter when Iron Margaret's dynasty crumbles at her feet."

He deliberately brushed against her on his way to the men's room, and Crystal recoiled from his touch. "The sky could fall, and I wouldn't side with you," she muttered.

April rallied. "All of Charles Lyon's sons are creeps, except Scott."

"Jason's not so bad, although he's had his moments. Shall we go? I'd rather not be around when Ray comes out of the john. I may kill him and end up in jail."

The two women were in April's car heading toward the university when suddenly April said, "I know I'm fairly new here—but how did I miss hearing that you're related to the Lyons? Alain isn't really going to oust André and Gabrielle, is he?"

"That threat is older than dirt. As far as my relationship to the family goes, I'm a second cousin to Ray and his brothers—my grandmother, Justine, was Charles and Paul Lyon's sister. She never inherited shares in the original radio station. Great-grandpa Alexandre subscribed to the school of thought that women didn't belong in business. At first she had a generous allowance. But even that reverted to the family after she died giving birth to her only child, my dad. He was whisked out of New Orleans to be raised in Baton Rouge by her husband's family, the Jardins. I was more or less estranged from the Lyons, but the rift between my grandmother's brothers is legendary. I grew up hearing all the rumors, and the stories intrigued me so much I applied to work here after I graduated from college. Margaret found out and more or less bundled me out of my apartment and into the family home—Lyoncrest. She and Paul and the others have always treated me as more than a second cousin. In any event, I've never seen a shred of evidence that the old rumors are valid."

"Well, I hope they *are* lies. If Alain took over and

moved Raymond into your job, I'd have to quit, no matter how many college loans are hanging over my head. People say that Ray dabbles in the black arts." She gave a nervous laugh. "Is that true?"

Crystal rolled her eyes as April stopped to let her out at the hospital. "Is Ray smart enough to conjure up a spell? Oh, I'm not saying you shouldn't keep your distance. He *is* a creep. For instance, I know he accesses Internet porno sites from his office." She sighed. "André would love to remove his computer. Unfortunately Paul's sixty percent of the voting stock isn't sufficient to dislodge the other branch of the family. Not that Margaret would let that happen. She's big on family sticking together."

"How can somebody like Ray, born into that kind of privilege, turn out so rotten? I try never to be alone with him." She lowered her voice. "I've heard he smacks women around."

"We can only hope one of them will press charges someday. Hey, if I don't scoot, you'll be late for class. I appreciate the lift."

After closing the car door and giving April a wave, Crystal jogged up the hospital steps. Ray was bilgewater, Alain a jerk. Her own dad wasn't so hot, either. He'd let her down, and so had the only man she'd ever been serious about. Luckily she'd found out *before* the wedding that Ben Parker's real interest had been her contacts in the jazz community—and that while they were engaged he'd slept his way through all the groupies at the club where he played.

Maybe it was because of the hormonal change that occurred at puberty. Little boys were cute and charming. Then they grew up.

Crystal hated to think of that happening to the boys she

was on her way to visit. She'd volunteered to entertain in the long-term orthopedic ward because she'd spent time in one. At twelve, a skateboarding accident had left her hospitalized for most of one school year. She'd lost her mother three years before the accident. Her dad, the busy oil executive, never visited her. Nor did his stern aunt, who considered Crystal's confinement a reprieve from her forced guardianship duties. The only good that came of it was that Aunt Anita had insisted Roger Jardin pay for music lessons to keep his motherless daughter occupied. Music had eased Crystal's loneliness, which was why she made time to bring music into the lives of kids like Skipper West.

That last thing she'd set out to do was lose her heart to this tough but lovable nine-year-old ward of the court. It had just happened. Skip had suffered a sports-related injury, as had the other boys in his unit. If Crystal had any clout, she'd force communities to scrap football and soccer; she considered them dangerous and she loathed the values they taught—the focus on celebrity and the concentration on physical rather than mental skills. She'd love to see them all banned, *especially* football and soccer. "Ha. Fat chance," she muttered, peering into the six-bed room. Maybe she would never let a child of hers get involved in team sports, but most parents, coaches and kids only clamored for more, not fewer.

Crystal didn't blame Skip's coach. The man, like many coaches of kids' teams, was just a dad seeking an opportunity for his own son to play. As usual, more kids showed up than there were teams. So Sam Bingham had let himself be talked into attending a short course on coaching provided by the league—and that was apparently all the qualification he needed.

Skipper looked so small. Encased from chest to knees

in a new plaster cast, he lay in the large bed, clinging to his favorite toy. *A football.* Crystal's heart twisted. Amazing that after everything he'd been through, he still ate, slept and breathed football. He had to be in pain, yet he listened raptly as Randy, in the next bed, described a game Skip must have missed.

Crystal masked her feelings before she walked in. Skip's coach had brought him the football. She didn't begrudge the boy his talisman. Kids in foster care had darned few possessions to call their own. Yet it was football that had landed him here. Crystal couldn't help feeling ambivalent.

Skip's gaze left Randy as Crystal walked into the room. In spite of looking pale, he sent her a wide gap-toothed smile. "Crystal, guess what?" he said excitedly.

"What?" She leaned her sax in a corner and approached his bed. Her heart leaped. Did his joy mean the surgery had been successful? Would he soon be able to walk?

"My new doctor said *Caleb Tanner* is down the hall in the adult wing. Isn't that cool?"

"Who?" The name meant nothing to her.

The boys in all six beds stared at her. "He's practically the best quarterback the Sinners ever had," one of them informed her.

"Ah. A ball player." She lifted a shoulder negligently and let it fall.

Skip tried unsuccessfully to sit up. Pain clouded his eyes, and his fingers clenched the football. He gave up, flopping back against his pillow.

"What do you want, honey? A drink? Some ice chips?" She tried to read the chart that sat on his nightstand. "Is it time for your pain medication?"

He thrust the football toward her. "Would…would you

go ask Cale to sign my ball? Nurse Pam said if you stop at the desk, she'll give you a permanent marker. Cale might not have one. You know what? I think he's had more surgeries than me."

"More? Oh, Skipper, I don't think so. I can't barge in on a sick man."

"He's not sick. Three guys hit him in a preseason game. Cale ain't gonna let a little knee injury sideline him for long." Skip gingerly touched his cast. "Dr. Snyder said me and Cale might have the same physical therapist."

"Physical therapy? That's wonderful news! Starting when?"

"Dunno. Soon, I think."

"Then you'll be able to get Mr. Tanner's autograph yourself."

"Randy says Caleb's got the bucks to go to a private sports-medicine clinic for therapy. Maybe I won't see him. Please, Crystal." He extended the ball.

Crystal ruffled the boy's sandy red hair. His mischievous green eyes and freckled cheeks went with his missing front tooth. "Oh, all right. Give me that thing. If he's trussed up like you, the guy can't very well tackle me and toss me out."

The boys' glee chased her to the nursing desk, where Pam Mason, an overworked floor nurse, rummaged through her desk for a pen. "Follow this hall. At the end, turn left and go to room 306. Good luck, Crystal. I heard Tanner's on a rampage. Hope you get Skip's ball autographed." She dropped her voice. "Skip's operation today didn't go as well as we'd hoped. His spinal ganglion didn't regenerate the way his doctors had expected."

"No!" Crystal said in a stricken voice. "But I thought Skip was going to be starting physical therapy...."

The nurse nodded. "They can't allow his muscles to atrophy, even if he's confined to a wheelchair. It's past time we weaned him off pain meds, too."

A light on the board flashed. "Omigosh! I left Eddie Trumble on the bedpan. Maybe we can chat before you leave. Will you be playing some tunes for the kids?"

Crystal barely managed an affirmative response. Clasping the football tight against her shaky middle, she fled down the hall so Pam wouldn't see her tears. What would Skip's fate be if he never walked again? Could his foster family manage that?

IN ROOM 306, Caleb Tanner, Cale to football buddies and fans, reeled from the latest shock. A set of X rays revealed that a compound break at the intertrochanteric line of his left thigh bone hadn't knit, despite weeks of traction. Worse, ligaments ripped from his left kneecap hadn't healed, either.

Dr. Forsythe, chief of Caleb's surgical team, tucked the film back into its envelope. "So that's why you're still in pain, even with strong medication," he said matter-of-factly.

Caleb gripped his agent's arm. "Dammit, Leland! I want a second opinion."

Two other surgeons standing at the foot of Tanner's bed exchanged glances. Forsythe pursed his lips. "We'll talk again, Caleb." He motioned to his colleagues. "He needs time to get used to the fact that his football career is over."

The veins in Caleb's neck bulged. His mind went on fast forward. Just like it did when he zinged a football through the air to a player who hadn't even appeared yet in the spot he'd selected.

My career is not over.

Then why was his stomach pitching worse than when a defensive lineman twice his size sacked him? He had to think. *I will get well.* Unfortunately Leland was in the middle of negotiating a new contract. If the press got wind of this...

"Everyone but Leland, *out!*" he demanded. "And don't forget I'm protected under patient-doctor privilege until I consult someone else."

"See here, Tanner. I stand on our collective credentials," Forsythe gestured to his pals.

Caleb wished they'd all shut up. He needed a plan. With rent on his posh apartment due, his sister Patsy getting married soon and Jenny's last-semester college fees fast approaching—to say nothing of having moved his oldest sister, Gracie, into an Austin apartment—he couldn't afford to take a season off. Truth be known, he was damned near broke. Again. Rationally he knew no amount of the material things he provided for the girls made up for the loss of their parents. But it eased his guilt about not being home for them more.

He wanted them to have the best—not to scrimp or do without. But the expenses just kept mounting. Weddings, college fees, allowances and rent.

Gracie, at twenty-two, had graduated from the University of Texas and had an offer of a good entry-level job, but that meant she needed a nice wardrobe. She wouldn't be paying her own bills for a while. Caleb was suddenly forced to admit that monthly expenses for keeping the Tanner clan solvent took every penny he made. And according to the team manager, Caleb made a pretty penny, indeed. That was why negotiations had hit a snag.

Hell. Money always slipped through his hands like water through a sieve. Sure, he wore tailormade threads. Sure, he owned a collection of gas hogs and was guilty of giving his dates expensive trinkets. He was a high-profile quarterback. That kind of thing went with the territory. But he should have saved a *few* bucks. No one knew better than a farmer about saving for droughts or rainy days.

The whole sports world was aware that he'd emerged from dirt-poor farming roots to end up a star in the NFL. "A melon jockey with magic hands," was how rural Texas reporters had described his feats with a football at the consolidated high school he'd gone to. There was enough truth to it that his dad had gone out on a limb and mortgaged the farm to ensure his son got a chance to play college ball at A & M. The old man enjoyed a one-year return on his sacrifice. Hell of a note.

After college, the Dallas Cowboys had snapped Cale up as relief quarterback. He sent half of his generous salary home. Then, at the peak of his second season, his folks died when their farm truck rolled. That same week, the coach tapped him to lead the team into the playoffs, replacing the regular quarterback, who'd suffered a minor injury. It was a hollow victory, but he'd buried his grief and gotten the job done.

He sat now, twisting the winner's ring that proved it. He twisted the ring around and around on his finger as he sank under morose memories.

It wasn't until after the final playoff game—nine years ago now—that he learned county social workers intended to split up his kid sisters and ship them to foster homes. The powers-that-be made it plain they didn't consider him an appropriate guardian. The court claimed the right to decide, because his parents hadn't left a will. He damned sure wasn't going to let strangers take his sisters. He did what had to be done, which included forking over every penny he had to wage a legal battle to keep his family together. It took ten months, but the court finally let his mother's cousin and her husband move from Illinois to work the farm and raise the three Tanner girls, ages twelve, eleven and ten. Of course he'd covered all the expenses incurred in the move from Illinois.

Settling his family problems cost him more than money. It cost him time. Too much time. Once their regular quarterback recovered, the Cowboys dumped him. After months of running the farm on promises, he finally signed with the New Orleans Sinners.

Until this accident, anyone who knew squat about football agreed that Caleb Tanner was at the top of his game. Sportscasters compared him to Montana and Elway. So no mealymouthed quacks were going to say his career was kaput.

"Just because you graduated from Harvard and Yale," he bellowed at the departing doctors, "doesn't make y'all God!" Fighting the fear that gnawed at his gut, Caleb grabbed an empty plastic water pitcher and heaved it across the room.

"Take it easy, Cale." His agent placed a restraining hand on Caleb's forearm while the last doctor ducked out.

Caleb shook Leland off. "And you…" He scowled at his agent. "What's the holdup on my contract? I started the season in good faith."

"Now, Cale. The money man's dragging his feet. He wants some kind of assurance he's not buying a pig in a poke."

"Then assure him. You tell him I'm starting physical therapy in a couple of days. I'll be stronger than moonshine before we play Detroit. Tell him that." Caleb poked a forefinger into the agent's skinny chest, forcing him to take flight, too.

His hand on the doorknob, Leland ran a skeptical eye

over Caleb's collection of wires and pulleys. "We've been associates a long time. I'm telling you, Cale, the chance of signing while you're in this shape…well, it stinks. I can't…won't lie to the man."

"I'm not asking you to." Cale's green eyes fired. "I'm gonna lick this thing."

"Yeah. For a minute there, I thought… Hell, Cale. A lot of guys retire at thirty-one. You must have a sizable nest egg by now."

Caleb clenched his hands. The thought of quitting the only work he knew set his heart beating so furiously he was afraid it'd fly clean out of his body. Football and farming were all he'd ever done. If he hadn't signed the farm over to his uncle and aunt last year…

But he had. He'd deeded them the land. They deserved more for putting their lives on hold to take care of the girls. Gritting his teeth, Cale forced a smile. "Emmitt Smith knows a doc who's first-rate at getting old bones shipshape. Have Medical Records overnight my X rays. I'm not washed up, Lee. That's God's honest truth."

"Sure, buddy. But I expect we'll have to wait for the new doc's report before we go back to the bargaining table. 'Cause the way it stands now, unless they see their money's buying a sound man, the bastards are saying *hasta la vista*."

Stunned by the finality of the notion, Caleb watched the door close. Despair warred with terror. Then a blinding rage welled up from his sandbagged toes. He swept a hand across the surface of his table. Paperbacks, a box of tissues, magazines and a water glass flew, hitting the floor with a satisfying crash.

He regarded the mess. It hadn't even begun to abolish his gut-deep panic.

Someone rapped on his door. Caleb chose to ignore the

intrusion. Leland had probably told a nurse he was in a foul mood. Well, he was. How in hell did they expect a man to feel when he'd just been told his career was over? Dammit, it wasn't over until *he* said it was over. And he didn't think it was asking too much to keep the news of his progress—or lack thereof—quiet. At least until he'd recovered enough to prove he was sound.

The knock sounded again. Louder.

"What do you want?" he thundered when the door opened slightly and a woman, a stranger with a pale face and huge blue eyes, peeked in. She was a bitty thing. If Caleb stood, the top of her shiny dark hair wouldn't hit him midchest. He ground his teeth. "You've landed in the wrong room, Pocahontas." As the woman eased through the opening, she flipped an ebony braid as thick as his wrist over a slim shoulder, facing him head-on, keeping both hands out of sight behind her back. *Hiding a needle, probably.* Forsythe must have ordered a shot to calm him.

"You can take that syringe and stab it into some other poor slob's backside."

As she noted the debris scattered on the floor, Crystal thought at least he hadn't disappointed *her* expectations. It was a shame Skipper couldn't see his idol in the throes of a tantrum.

"I'm not a nurse." She met the man's stormy eyes.

"No? Then who in hell are you?"

"I'm, ah, Crystal Jardin. From WDIX-TV," she said on a flash of brilliance. After all, what football jock didn't roll over and salivate at the prospect of gaining a little media attention? Crystal suspected he'd offer his autograph more readily if he figured he'd get something in return. Something he'd consider more substantial than the adulation of an ailing child. But if Tanner didn't act too arrogant, she might ask the WDIX sports director to send a reporter and a cameraman. That should make the man happy.

Busy congratulating herself on her cleverness, she was slow to realize Tanner wasn't reacting as she'd anticipated. Instead, his brows drew together over smoking eyes and he bellowed, "Vultures. Bloodsuckers! Do I have to climb off this bed and throw you out, too?"

Then he lunged. Pulleys spun wildly, unexpectedly snapping a cord. The flying hook knocked over an infusion stand that held an empty IV-drip container. The monitor mounted above his headboard flashed like a pinball machine. As he all but fell out of bed, a noisy alarm began to bleat in the entryway.

"Please stop!" she begged. "Lie still." Football forgotten, she charged forward. The sound of crunching glass—and the strangled epitaphs coming from the man who now dangled precariously—sent her into full retreat again. "Help!" she called, with her head stuck out into the corridor. "We need a nurse!"

Two nurses tore down the hall at a dead run. Crystal's last look at Skip's hero, after one nurse thrust her aside, was of a man writhing in pain.

Shaken, Crystal felt partially to blame, although she'd done nothing to warrant his outburst. He'd obviously been confused, thinking she was a nurse. Hurrying back to the children's ward, she caught a glimpse of herself in a window. He could have mistaken her summery white pants and loose-fitting blue tunic for a uniform.

Suddenly she smiled. So big tough Caleb Tanner was scared of a needle? He'd seen her white pants, thought nurse-with-a-needle and gone ballistic. It did make him more human, she decided, gazing at the football she still gripped.

The problem was, how did she tell the boys that she'd come back empty-handed? At least Tanner's fear of needles was safe with her. She'd never tarnish his image with boys who'd already been let down by too many male role models.

Or maybe she would. Boys Skipper and Randy's age ought to admire men who were sensitive and kind. Not ones spoiled by fame and fortune.

In the end, though, Crystal couldn't trample their rosy picture of Caleb Tanner. It was hard enough having to brave their crestfallen faces.

"Look, guys, I'm really, really sorry. You have my solemn word—" she placed a hand dramatically over her heart "—I will get Skip's ball signed. Even if they ship Tanner to a private facility, I'll track him down through his agent."

Skipper, ever the optimist, accepted Crystal's word. "It'd be neat if you could get the other guys some signed pictures of Cale in his uniform. Before he got hurt, he handed out a bunch of 'em at a new brew pub in the Quarter. We saw it on TV."

"Why, you little con artist. I failed my mission today, so I have to hit him up for photos, too? Can't you phone the Sinners' PR department?"

The boys exchanged worried looks. "Pablo's just back from therapy. He heard a tech say the Sinners won't renew Cale's contract because his knee ain't gonna heal. Would Nate Fraser know if that's true?"

Crystal glanced up from opening her instrument case. Nate Fraser, WDIX-TV's sports director, could find out if he didn't know. Even though Crystal passionately disliked Tanner's choice of career, she experienced an unexpected surge of compassion. She knew how she'd feel if she had to give up her music.

"I'll ask Nate tomorrow. If the story's true, maybe we should wait on that autograph. Tanner might be having a hard time dealing with the news."

"Yeah," Skipper said, suddenly empathetic. "But maybe hearing that some kids still think he's number one will cheer him up."

"It might at that, Skip. Hey, not to change the subject, but would you like me to play some tunes?"

"Yeah!" the boys exclaimed as one. Next to watching TV and talking endlessly about sports, they liked listening to Crystal belt out jazz.

She ran through a few warm-ups. Before long, nurses, residents and interns drifted in to listen. Patients on crutches and in wheelchairs lined the walls.

She didn't think any audience appreciated her more.

THE MUSIC, AS IT HAD on other nights, filtered into Cale's private room and shaved the edge off his pain. Closing his eyes, he tried to imagine the talent it took to make an instrument sob and wail like that. A seductive sound. His blood pulsed as the beat possessed him. N'Awlins blues certainly made a man feel…something. Any kind of feeling was preferable to the terrifying emptiness he'd plunged into earlier.

Why had he let the doc's words get to him? This wasn't his first injury. He'd always bounced back; he would this time, too. Yeah! He let those deep, shivery notes absorb his anger.

Ordinarily, when it came to music, Cale could take it or leave it. He knew when it was too loud at a party or too fast if he was trying to seduce a new lady with slow dancing. The music tonight lit a fire in his soul. But he couldn't put into words how it touched him, couldn't explain the way it made him feel. That was why he'd never asked the phantom soloist's name. Knowing the nurses, they'd parade the guy in here and expect Caleb to give him all kinds of flowery compliments.

Well, he couldn't. He could rattle off plays in a year's worth of football games, but he got tongue-tied trying to express the stuff he felt inside.

When fans waylaid him to praise a great pass, he loved it. He frowned as it occurred to him that musicians probably liked praise, too.

The distant beat slid like silk into a bossa nova, and Caleb felt a sudden urgency to connect with the artist whose music pounded through his veins. He fumbled to locate his call bell, then pushed it repeatedly. He'd just give the dude a locker-room clap on the back and tell him man-to-man that his playing had balls. Yeah. He drummed his hands on the bed covers. Where in hell were all the nurses? He pressed the button again.

A timid aide opened his door. "You rang, Mr. Tanner?"

Caleb had discovered that if you didn't speak with authority in this place, requests got ignored. "Tell that musician to stop by and see me. Tonight," he ordered.

"Is that it?" The aide sounded relieved and at his nod rushed out, leaving Cale to contemplate what an asshole he'd been the past few days. That was the word, all right. He'd heard it muttered by one of the nurses. Tomorrow he'd apologize. To the nurses, to Leland and maybe even to that pushy TV reporter.

The telephone beside his bed rang. "Hiya! Hey, Patsy...I'm doing great. Improving every day," he fibbed to his sister. One of the three girls called every night to check on his progress. No sense worrying them.

"The bridesmaids' dresses cost how much? Whatever

you decide, kitten. Sure. If you want buckets of mums at the church, fine. Have 'em send me the bill.''

Caleb tucked the phone into the hollow of his shoulder. ''Of course I'll walk you down the aisle. Who said I wouldn't? Gracie? She called Doc Forsythe?'' Caleb pinched the bridge of his nose. ''Quit crying, puddin'. Listen to me. You know doctors are full of double-talk. Have I ever lied to you girls? That's right. Never.''

Easing back, Caleb listened to additional plans for the late-October wedding and injected appropriate responses. It was now September 5. His head spun. A few minutes later, the excited twenty-one-year-old rang off. Cale gripped the receiver for a long time, attempting to add in his head the costs she'd listed. Patsy, his middle sister, a homebody who'd practically been their mother's shadow, had been the most affected by her death. Patsy did poorly in school. Having a husband and a house of her own was all she'd ever wanted. He wouldn't let his troubles affect her heart's desire.

It would be all right. By her wedding, he'd be good as new. Better than new. His contract would be signed and money wouldn't be an issue. Replacing the receiver, he lay down and let the throaty notes of the saxophone transport him to a zone free of stress.

CHAPTER TWO

THE NEXT MORNING, Crystal hopped off the streetcar at the end of its route, near the heart of the business district. Juggling her purse and saxophone case, she waved goodbye to the regulars and prepared to walk the two blocks to Lyon Broadcasting. She could have driven to work. For that matter, she had access to a chauffeur-driven limo. She happened to believe that one less car on the congested roads kept at least a trace of hydrocarbons out of the environment. Besides, she loved the eclectic group of people who used public transportation.

Margaret sometimes teased her saying she ought to write a book about the offbeat assortment of daily commuters. Crystal responded by suggesting Margaret do an exposé on the family. That reminded her—at their last meeting, Margaret had given her the key to a safe-deposit box. She said it contained her will and other documents important to the family. Her instructions were that André be given the key in the event of Margaret's death.

Crystal recalled thinking that Paul's death had sparked a morbid sense of urgency in Margie. She'd been adamant that the contents of the box be made public only if she, André and Gabrielle died simultaneously. A thought as gruesome as it was unlikely.

Crystal opened the wrought-iron gate that had guarded Lyon Broadcasting for fifty years. Darn, she wished Margaret would call home! Her continued absence was disturbing everyone.

Going directly to her office, Crystal breathed easier once she determined there'd been no further activity in the bank account. Then she set to work compiling reports for the end-of-the-month board meeting. Margaret would surely return for that.

As Crystal came to the figures from the sports department, she remembered the promise she'd made Skip—to call Nate Fraser and check on Tanner's retirement.

If she hadn't been so tired, she might have verified the rumor with Tanner last night. Certainly he'd provided an opportunity. At the end of visiting hours, a nurse's aide had flagged her down and said Tanner wanted—no, *demanded* she stop by his room.

Crystal had declined. She wasn't a masochist. But after she'd boarded the streetcar home, it struck her that maybe he wanted to break the news of his retirement. She'd told him she worked for WDIX, and maybe he wanted to arrange an interview to announce it. In that case, Nate would have her head for missing out on a real coup. Hmm. She'd better go see Nate right now and in person. She didn't stop to wonder how Tanner knew she'd remained in the hospital.

Entering the noisy newsroom, Crystal wove her way among the cubicles to Nate Fraser's domain. His four walls were weighted down by sports memorabilia. Crystal knew he'd once played for the Vikings and had won a Heisman trophy, which impressed most people. Crystal and Nate didn't have a lot in common, unless their endless arguments over his expense account could be considered common ground. Other than that, she liked his wife Jill, a lot. In fact, they'd become fast friends after Gabrielle had introduced them.

The man glanced up when she appeared in his door. "What's wrong now?" he barked, cracking his nut-brown knuckles one after the other.

"I thought you'd given up trying to intimidate me, Nathan."

"Can't help it if your mama didn't train you right, white girl."

Shaking her head, Crystal dropped into a chair. "Shall I phone Jill and tell her how you talk at work?" Nate's brilliant and beautiful Creole wife currently served on the U.S. president's council for the advancement of race relations. Nate doted on her.

He looked sheepish. "For a woman who detests sports, you play hardball, Miz Crystal. If you aren't here to hassle me about greenbacks, what *is* on your mind?"

"Verifying a rumor that Caleb Tanner's ending his football career."

Nate catapulted from his chair. "Not our prize quarterback?"

Crystal nodded.

Nate's eyes glittered with interest. Then he plopped back into the chair, crossed his arms and scowled. "You wouldn't be jivin' me, would you?"

"So you can't confirm it? Shoot. That means I'll have to brave Tanner's room again to get Skipper's football autographed." She stood up and moved toward the door.

"Wait." He rounded the desk fast for a big man. "This is no joke? You've been in Cale's hospital room?"

"Yes, and I don't relish going back. He's obnoxious and—"

Nate stopped her midsentence. "Every sportscaster in town's been trying to get past those battle-axes at the nurses' station. The docs, Cale's agent and the spokesperson for the Sinners all issued a standard no-comment."

Nate reached around her, shut the door and gently urged her back into her chair. "This is serious. Tell Papa Nate what gave you the wild idea Cale's cashing in his cleats."

She inspected her nails. "There's probably not a shred of truth to the rumor."

"Let me be the judge." He listened intently as Crystal explained how she came to be at the hospital and ultimately in Tanner's room.

"The skinny dude you saw Cale throw out on his ear sounds like Leland Bergman, his agent. So Cale's in mega-pain? This kid—he's sure the tech said Cale's career is in the toilet?"

"Not quite in those delicate words," Crystal drawled. "But that was the gist."

"Well, well, well, well." He rocked forward and back, singsonging the word. After a stretch during which neither of them spoke, Nate grabbed his phone. He made several calls, presumably to sources, all the while indicating Crystal should stay seated.

"What did you find out?" she asked when at last he hung up and rubbed his palms together excitedly.

"My source believes the Sinners are quietly casting the waters in hopes of landing a new quarterback."

"Then I guess that's that." Crystal got to her feet. "Don't you feel the slightest bit of compassion for Mr. Tanner? After all, an injury forced *you* out of pro sports."

"Of course I sympathize with his situation."

"Could've fooled me. You look delighted."

"I am that. My top sportscaster, Jerry Davis, took a job in L.A. If we work fast, we might entice Cale to replace him."

Crystal, who'd again started for the door, glanced over her shoulder. "An announcer? The man's like a buffalo in a china shop. You can't polish his rough edges enough to put him on camera. He wears a gold stud in one ear, for Pete's sake.''

"The guy's got a great voice.''

"He bellows.''

"He can charm the frogs off their lily pads.''

Crystal tapped her toe impatiently. "He has the manners of an orangutan.''

Nate smirked. "Yeah. He'll fit right in. And since you, lovely lady, have access to the man, you're going to hire him for us before a competitor hears he's on the loose.''

"Me?'' She tried to bolt, but Nate beat her to the door and held it shut with a ham-size palm. "Do your own dirty work,'' she snapped. "I've got other shrimp to peel.''

"No one else in the media can get near the man,'' he said, trying to wheedle.

"Yeah, well, he tossed me out and probably ruptured something doing it.''

"Didn't you say that later on, he wanted you to stop by his room? I bet he intends to apologize. Cale's got a rep for being real nice to the ladies. Tell you what. Give me an hour to put together an employment offer and get André's okay. I'll have to talk to Michael McKay in Human Resources, too.'' He stroked his chin. "Ought to have it ready for you to run over to Tanner by eleven or so.''

"Only if André says I have to,'' she said reluctantly. "But I'll go after work. I'm summarizing a report for the board. Besides, I promised Skipper I'd visit him this evening. I'm not making two trips to the hospital in one day.''

Nate straightened away from the door. "I hate to drag our heels in case somebody else gets wind of this. Let's see what André and Mike want to do.''

"Deal." She stuck out her hand and they shook. "It'll frost in the French Quarter before André gives sports precedence over company finances."

CRYSTAL HAD A PENCIL stuck in her hair, one between her teeth, and reports strewn all over her desk when her door swung open. Looking up, she saw Nate, André and his son-in-law, Michael, bearing purposefully down on her. "Hey, you guys are causing a draft," she shrieked, grabbing for a couple of pages that had skittered to the floor.

"Sorry." Nate closed the door while André and Michael collected the spreadsheets that had landed beside her desk.

"Nate brought us up to snuff on the Tanner deal. Thanks for calling this to Nate's attention, Crystal." André tucked the loose papers under her elbow. "Did Cale indicate what salary he'd accept? Can he be had for eighty-five thou?"

Crystal's chin almost hit the desk. "Eighty-five thousand, as in *dollars?*"

André tugged at his lower lip. "Probably peanuts to him, all right. But he must have a fortune socked away. We'll go with eighty-five. If he scoffs or claims to have another deal pending, angle for his bottom line. We'll try to match it."

"Why?"

"Why what?" André pursed his lips; Michael merely shook his head.

Nate grinned at Crystal. "I think it just frosted in the French Quarter, kid."

She stuck out her tongue at Nate, but appealed to André and Mike. "Tanner has no experience. That salary puts him on a par with our managers."

"We can afford it, can't we?" Michael asked.

"Yes, but—"

"His name alone will raise our ratings. That's our offer." André dug a sealed envelope from his suit jacket and pressed it into Crystal's hand. "The three of us are going to K-Paul's for lunch and to organize some plans. Michael has an idea for sending Tanner into the community—charity stuff, you know, to enhance the station's image. I'm taking my cellular. Phone us with his answer."

Crystal watched them walk out, talking animatedly. It was Caleb this and Caleb that. She felt like throwing up. André used to be so levelheaded. Having a son late in life must have affected his brain. Andy-Paul was barely six, but Crystal should have remembered seeing André racing around the yard at Lyoncrest, tossing various balls to the kid. Footballs. Soccer. Softballs. And where was Gaby during all this? Right out there with them, Crystal recalled. Gaby claimed Andy-Paul, a change-of-life child, was a miracle that had given her a new lease on life. That new lease on life had turned André and Gabrielle into sports nuts.

Crystal glared at the envelope. Why should she recruit a person whose profession she didn't respect for a television station she loved? *Because André asked you to.*

Well, maybe Caleb Tanner had other plans. She could always hope.

Sticking the envelope in her purse, Crystal retrieved her sax. She left the stack of reports on her desk. "After this, I deserve the rest of the day off," she muttered.

"I'm running an errand for André," she announced to the bookkeepers working in the next room. "Field my calls, please, April. If Margaret phones, tell her to use my cellular number. It's listed in the office directory in case she doesn't have it with her."

Ray Lyon burst out of his office across the hall. "What

errand are you running for André?'' He appeared agitated, more agitated than usual. "Did you mention something about a call from Aunt Margaret? André hasn't heard from her, has he?''

"If you spent as much time phoning clients with delinquent accounts as you do with your ear glued to the door, profits would double.'' Crystal wasn't in any mood for Ray's habit of butting into conversations that didn't concern him. Nor did she care to discuss André.

"Don't take my head off. Everybody's talking about the old lady's disappearance. If you ask me, it just proves she's short a few dots on her dominoes.''

"Oh, right. Like you came from the deep end of the gene pool. Get a life, Raymond.''

He hitched up his pants. His too-pointed incisors were all that showed when he smiled. "You've grown awful big for your britches, missy. I'm gonna love watching the seams split when the balance of power shifts our way.''

Crystal honed in on his size-fifty-two waist. She did nothing more than arch one brow to send him skulking back into his office.

April left her desk and came to the door. "He's worse than swamp crud, boss. But everyone's worried about Margaret. Especially the old-timers.''

"Has anyone suggested where she might have gone?''

"No. All the guessing is what's keeping the pot stirred.''

"I see." But she didn't really. She'd been telling herself that Margaret's jaunt to…wherever was nothing to worry about. That it was her prerogative as a woman of stature and means. Crystal gnawed her lower lip. It just wasn't like Margaret to worry her family—even if she'd been feeling smothered by their concern. "Has André or

Gaby said anything in particular to put employees on edge?''

"Only that if Margaret calls, to let them know at once. You've got to admit it's odd. People who've known her a long time say she dotes on André and his kids. Why would she go off without telling him?''

"She may dote on her son and grandkids, but Paul was the other half of her. Losing him dealt her a real blow. She said it was like having her heart torn in two.''

"I can't imagine loving any man that much, can you, Crystal?''

"It's possible. For instance—André and Gaby, Leslie and Michael, Nate and Jill, Sharlee and Dev. They're all crazy in love.'' She got a distant look in her eyes.

April screwed up her face. "Well, maybe *they've* found true love. My family, on the other hand, believes in supporting their local divorce courts.''

Crystal thought of her father and her ex-fiancé. They'd left footprints on her heart, her dad's departure leaving the deepest depressions. "I'm not looking for love, April.''

"I hear that love strikes when you're not looking. Hey, boss, weren't you going somewhere?'' April checked her watch. "We've been gabbing for ten minutes. I don't know where you're headed, but unless it's a command performance with the IRS, I could be keeping you from meeting the love of your life.''

Crystal remembered her destination. Caleb Tanner. "I have a greater chance of being abducted by aliens,'' she replied.

"Hey, if your love life sucks as much as mine does, I wouldn't be so hasty to write those guys off. The little suckers are kinda cute, with their big eyes and all.''

Crystal walked away laughing. If April only knew how

far off target Tanner was from her ideal lover. *No one* could be farther from it.

THE WEATHER HAD deteriorated. The sky was dark and with clouds. The monsoons were late, but it looked as if they'd finally struck. Crystal opened her umbrella at the first rumble of thunder. Sure enough, rain began to spatter from those ominous clouds. She debated returning to the office and charging a cab to André's expense account. But before she could retrace her route, a streetcar arrived.

Laughter spewed from the car as the slanting rain chased her inside. Crystal vaulted aboard quickly and wedged herself in beside a group of German-speaking tourists. They also spoke French, so Crystal pointed out sights until it was time to disembark.

She waved goodbye. If she could have, she would have joined their tour of the Beauregard-Keyes House. Not that she hadn't visited the historic cottage with its captivating gardens many times. It was more that she wanted to delay the inevitable.

"We'll come hear you play at the jazz pub on Bourbon Street," one of her new acquaintances promised just before she hopped out. "Friday night!"

Crystal waggled her saxophone case to let them know she'd heard. It doubled as a shield against the rain, which was falling in earnest now. Her red twill suit was wet through by the time she reached the lobby. She felt the soggy flop of her braid with every step she took. Outside Tanner's room, Crystal spared the time to unbind the heavy strands. She almost never wore her hair loose. But she wasn't here to impress Tanner. If André and Nate had hoped to do that, they should have come, instead.

She did, however, run a comb through her frizzy locks. Otherwise he'd take one look and head for the hills from whence he'd come. *Are there hills in Texas?* Skipper said Tanner had come to the Sinners from Dallas. That accounted for the difference in his drawl. His voice was rich and rough and slightly twangy.

Taking a deep breath, Crystal unearthed the envelope with the station's offer. Then before she lost her nerve, she knocked.

"Stay out," called the voice she'd been analyzing. It soared above a background murmur of several people talking.

Now what? Crystal weighed the order. If he had family visiting, she'd return another time. But if he was talking to his agent, she might slip inside and leave André and Nate's offer with them.

The door gave easily under her hand. As she'd done yesterday, she tried to peer through the crack. No luck. She leaned around the door to see more clearly. Her hair slithered forward, obscuring her face.

"Well, hel-lo." Cale clicked the remote and switched off the TV, which accounted for the voices Crystal had heard.

Perfect. He was alone. No lights flashed wildly on his monitor today. Likewise, the ropes and pulleys that held him immobile looked solidly hooked. One thing *was* different, though—a smile that spread crookedly from ear to ear. The smile made him look like a totally different man and gave Crystal pause.

"You're obviously new on the ward, sweetheart. In spite of what you've probably been told, I don't bite."

"Your alter ego snarled *Stay out?*" Crystal couldn't rein in a laugh.

"That's before I saw you were prettier than a bushel of roses. Where'd you come from? The morning nursing shift reminds me of a Packer defense line.'' He pretended to shudder. "Come talk to me. I'm really a likable guy."

Crystal snorted. "Modest, too," she said, using her instrument case to shove her way into the room. "Let's get a few things straight. I'm not a nurse and I am not your sweetheart. We met briefly yesterday, Mr. Tanner. My name is Crystal Jardin."

"We met?" His gaze shifted from her hair to the worn instrument case. Almost immediately his eyes lit up. "You must be the musician who shakes down the rafters. I did ask an aide to have you stop by last night. Guess you didn't have a chance."

"You heard my music all the way here? Sorry. Next time I'll shut the door and mute the sound."

His smile slipped. "You've got it wrong. I'm not complaining. Quite the opposite. That Latin tune you played was incredible."

She blushed. "You know about music? Jazz?" That threw her. She'd have to revise her first assessment of Cale Tanner. "I guess you mean Cannonball Adderly's 'Jive Samba.' He's the master. I was spang-a-langing his piece, is all."

"Spang-a-who-ing? You lost me."

Ah. So he didn't know the language of jazz. "Spang-a-lang is the rhythmic feel of a sound. Like, messing around trying to hit a certain groove." Grasping for ways to explain, she said, "It's the process of finding the ultimate groove."

"Yeah. Gotcha. You know when what you've done gels. It's the same in football. A lot of times there're too many men between me and the goal line to see the play I made. But when I've connected with a receiver, I know in my gut."

Crystal's brow puckered. She didn't think football compared to music and was on the verge of saying so when his face broke out in a lopsided grin. "Grab a chair and knock back a few songs, why don't you?"

"Now?"

"Sure. Why not?"

"It's lunchtime. And it's not visiting hours." She almost said she was here for another purpose entirely, but Crystal held off on that. Maybe it had to do with the light she'd seen burning deep in his eyes when he got the drift of spang-a-langing. Whatever else Tanner was, he felt strongly attuned to his sport. She sensed he was a long way from severing that bond. Maybe the rumors of his retirement were way off base.

"For what my insurance company's paying for this private room, I ought to be able to have an orgy in here twenty-four hours a day if I choose."

That comment was exactly what Crystal would expect of a football player. She didn't realize her face showed her distaste so plainly until Tanner narrowed his eyes.

"We *have* met. I've seen that look. Where?" He scrutinized her from beneath indecently thick eyelashes for so long that Crystal felt uncomfortable. So uncomfortable she jumped when he snapped his fingers.

"Yesterday! The reporter." He scowled at her saxophone. "Do you really play that thing? Or is this another trick to get an interview? If it is, you have ten seconds to vamoose, babe."

He looked so menacing when he frowned Crystal didn't know where to begin or what would buy her time. She set her instrument case on his bedside table and opened it to give him a clear view of the gleaming brass alto sax.

"I'm not a reporter," she said quietly.

He crossed his arms across a muscular chest. "They fired you since yesterday?"

"My purpose for being here yesterday was to get your autograph on a football for a young friend of mine. He's down the hall in the children's long-term orthopedic ward." She plunged a hand into her large jute handbag and produced the ball. "Darn, I returned the permanent marker to the nursing station. You don't happen to have a pen suitable for autographing leather, do you?"

"You mean I almost killed myself over an autograph?"

"Well, yes, and I'm sorry about that, Mr. Tanner."

"Caleb. Salesmen call me Mr. Tanner. You wouldn't be trying to sell me a bill of goods, would you, babe?"

Crystal dealt him a withering look. The kind she reserved for the Ray Lyons of the world. "No one calls me babe. You may call me Ms. Jardin."

Caleb sidestepped her remark as neatly as he avoided a pileup of defensive linemen. "Uh-huh. Give me the damned football." Leaning over, he yanked open the center drawer of his nightstand and pawed around until he found a marking pen. "I should've guessed you don't play that horn," he muttered. "A woman doesn't have the lungs to make a saxophone whisper one minute, then hold the note so long it spits fire."

Crystal rammed Skipper's football into Cale Tanner's diaphragm with enough force to make him blow out an *oof* but not hard enough to add to his injuries. "Trumpets, tubas and trombones are horns, Tanner. Saxophones are wind instruments. I play all four. Women have plenty of wind."

Caleb's right eyebrow disappeared beneath a shock of wheat-gold hair. "They do at that, Jardin. I stand corrected." As he lowered his laughing gaze, Caleb scrawled his name across the ball. "Does the kid have a handle?" he asked.

"Skipper West. Uh…Skip. Just make it 'to Skip,'"

Crystal said, giving Tanner points for not taking his irritation at her out on the boy.

Tanner handed her the signed ball. His eyes returned to the saxophone as he capped his pen.

"Thanks. Skip will be in seventh heaven."

"You're welcome. If you're really a musician who wanted me to sign a kid's football, why barge in here claiming to work for WDIX-TV?"

"I do. I'm their business manager."

The same eyebrow shot up again. "Busy lady. Business manager. Ace musician. Messenger for sick kids. Does that about cover your titles? Or is there a main man in the wings waiting to make you a missus something or other?" Cale wasn't very discreet in grabbing her left hand to check for a ring.

Crystal laughed as she pulled away and stowed the football. "In addition to my work, I play at the Jazz Pub in the Quarter a couple of weekends a month. And I'm more than a messenger for sick kids, as you put it. I entertain in children's wards around the city when I can, Mr. Tanner. There's no time in my life for a man."

"I thought we agreed. It's Caleb. And you're Crystal. Pretty name. Pretty lady. So you've sworn off guys. Pity."

The rough singsongy caress of Tanner's voice spiked a shiver of caution in Crystal's stomach. Caution—or longing. She shook off the feeling. "I haven't sworn off guys. There are six of 'em in Skipper's ward. The oldest is twelve. They all got hurt playing ball. You don't happen to have five autographed photos hiding in that drawer, do you? I promised I'd ask." She paused for a couple of seconds. "These boys aren't as lucky as you, Tanner. Pablo lost a leg dashing off the field after a wildly kicked soccer ball. He collided with a delivery truck. Skipper slipped and fell on a wet football field. Then four kids—

who didn't know he'd twisted his spine—piled on top of him. His injury may be permanent. Randy went for a basketball layup and slammed into a wall, resulting in major nerve damage that affects his whole left side." Crystal stopped because all color had leached from Tanner's face. "Sorry. I guess you understand what they're going through."

"Yeah, and I'm real lucky, too." He slapped the mess of ropes and pulleys. "It's been six weeks since I took the hit, and I still can't bear weight on my right leg. In case you were fishing, Ms. Jardin, that's not for publication. I *will* heal."

"I told you I'm not a reporter."

"I know what you said. I also know what can happen if information like that gets to the media. I'll be out of a job. I don't think you want that on your conscience, Ms. Bleeding Heart."

"Rumors are already floating around. Pablo heard the techs in physical therapy talking. Will you play for the Sinners this season?"

"Hell, yes!" He tried to sit forward.

"Stop." Crystal held him against the pillows. "I don't want a repeat of yesterday."

"Who's saying I'm washed up?" Caleb demanded, every muscle in his long body tensing.

"Are you?" Crystal gave him a penetrating look.

Cale shut his eyes and massaged the bridge of his nose with a thumb and forefinger. "I'm lively as an electric fence. Give me one good reason I should discuss any of this with you."

She let several silent seconds tick by, then reached for her handbag and pulled out the envelope. Since Cale paid no attention to the rustle of paper, she cleared her throat.

He threw her a wary glance. Crystal saw more than she

wanted to see. More than *he* wanted her to see. The man was hurting, and not just on the outside. She doubted it had anything to do with his physical condition.

"What's that?" Cale shifted his gaze to the neatly typed page she'd unfurled.

"An offer of employment from Lyon Broadcasting. One of our sportscasters took a job in L.A. Nate Fraser, the sports director at WDIX-TV, wants you to replace him. So does André Lyon, and Michael McKay, head of personnel. It's all in this letter of intent."

"I'm not some over-the-hill quarterback you can dress in a monkey suit and slap behind a desk to talk about the game. I'm a *player*. A damn good one. I've got six more years in me if I've got a day." He plucked the letter out of her hand and ripped it in two. As the pieces settled, he said venomously, "Tell Fraser to get the hell out of my face. Goes double for you, lady."

Once again Crystal changed her opinion of the great Caleb Tanner. He was a spoiled brat. An egomaniac, too. She slammed the lid on her sax case as the outer door opened. In whisked the wiry man she'd seen leaving Tanner's room yesterday.

"Cale? I heard you shouting all the way down the hall." The newcomer trained his eyes on Crystal. "I don't know the problem, so I can't apologize for my client. I'm Cale's agent, Leland Bergman."

"It's a case of killing the messenger. I could have brought Nate back a simple no just as easily."

"Nate?" Leland rested his briefcase on Caleb's bed.

Crystal hefted her sax and her handbag and started for the door, never glancing at Tanner. "I had the dubious honor of delivering Nate Fraser's offer to hire Mr. Tanner as a WDIX-TV sportscaster." She inclined her head toward the two halves of the letter. "I'm on my way now to relay Tanner's refusal."

"Hold on." Leland loped across the floor. He tugged Crystal back into the room. After releasing her, he fitted the letter pieces together and read them.

Caleb sat through the whole ordeal without moving, as if carved from rock.

When Leland finished, he dropped the pieces into Cale's lap and waited until he had his client's attention. "It's a good offer," Leland said with a catch in his voice. "I don't mind saying, Cale, it'll make my news a little easier to take. The Sinners won't wait on another doctor's opinion. They've given you the final sack, old buddy."

Crystal had to turn away and blink her eyes. The last time she'd seen a man look so utterly devastated, she'd been eight. The news had been as bluntly delivered. A doctor had stridden into a waiting room where Crystal sat with her father and announced that her mother had died in recovery after a simple tonsillectomy. She'd hemorrhaged, and no one had been able to stop the bleeding. Crystal's world—and her father's—had shifted on its axis. Tanner's had clearly just done the same.

Bergman was talking about a career change, not death. Still, Tanner obviously wasn't going to do it. In her opinion, WDIX would be better off without him, although Nate and the others would be disappointed. She'd better go call them. Except that she still hadn't fulfilled her promise to Skip's friends.

"Mr. Bergman, there are five kids in a ward down the hall who'd love a signed photo of your client. They will always be his fans."

Caleb rallied, emerging from his misery. "I forgot. Leland, are there any promo shots left in the bottom dresser drawer?"

Leland found them and shoved a stack at Crystal. "You want the little lady to hold off telling Fraser no—don't you, Cale?"

"I want to play, Lee. Call Miami. They were sniffing around in the spring."

"As soon as they hear the Sinners wire-brushed you due to injuries, nobody'll be interested anymore. At least consider Fraser's offer."

Cale looked stubborn. "The money's pocket change, Leland."

Crystal almost swallowed her teeth.

The agent slicked a hand through thinning hair. "So ask for a hundred grand."

"They'll never pay it," Crystal sputtered, fearing in her heart that they would.

Leland hustled her to the door. "Ask them, darlin',"' he whispered loudly. "Come back later with a counter. I'll keep the Sinners from releasing a statement until Cale hammers out this deal."

Crystal found herself outside in the hall staring at the closed door. A hundred thousand dollars to comment on a few games a year? They were out of their ever-loving gourds.

CHAPTER THREE

CRYSTAL DECIDED to grab some lunch and call André before going to see Skip and the other boys to give them their keepsakes. The crowded cafeteria pulsed with noisy chatter. Doctors and nurses who ordinarily ate in one of the hospital's three open courtyards had been driven inside by the storm.

She chose a shrimp salad and a cup of coffee and settled into a corner table by a window. Fat raindrops beat steadily against the glass. Warming her hands on the cup, Crystal dreaded calling André. It was hard to gauge how he'd react. Probably he'd be upset. She ought to have explained to Tanner how generous the offer really was. But no, he wanted more. He wouldn't have listened to reason. To top it off, he'd acted as if eighty-five thousand was a paltry amount.

Thank goodness it wasn't *her* problem. She coordinated all department budgets and gave input into spending patterns. The decision to spend an obscene amount of money to hire a name—and to Crystal Caleb Tanner's name was the only thing he had of any worth—belonged to the company principals, mainly André and Gaby. Margaret always backed them. Charles had almost ceased participating, and as for his sons…well, Alain and Raymond opposed everything André put on the table. Jason rarely attended meetings. Scott avoided all family politics. But spending money always caused major bickering.

Still, she couldn't sit here procrastinating forever. Swallowing a bite of salad, Crystal took her cell phone out of her handbag and quickly punched in André's number. "Hi, it's me," she said inanely in response to his greeting. "Tanner tore up our offer, André. I hope you don't fall off your chair, but get this. His bottom line is one hundred thousand. Plus benefits, I'm sure. I let him know the figure was preposterous."

She held the phone away from her ear as André responded.

"You're telling me to go for it? Do you know how much of a slice that takes out of the sports budget? We paid Jerry Davis half that and he came to WDIX an experienced broadcaster. For all you know, Tanner might freeze in front of the camera."

Crystal cradled the phone on her shoulder while she poked at the shrimp among her salad greens. The more determination she heard in André's voice, the less hungry she became. "Okay," she said. "I'll concede that might be far-fetched. I realize you've seen him field sports interviews. Of course Lyon Broadcasting is solvent. Yes, we have money in the discretionary fund. André, maybe it'd be better if you and Nate came and talked to Tanner. I'll go back to the office and adjust the short- and long-term planning figures to reflect your decision."

She shoved her salad away. "I know you want him. It just seemed such an absurd request I didn't seriously imagine you'd go that high."

Sighing, Crystal massaged her forehead. "Okay. Will you print another letter of intent with the new dollar amounts and run it over here? Two copies. You sign both and I'll have Tanner do the same—maybe. If he goes for it. You might want to include a list of benefits. I have a feeling he'll ask what all we're offering. Buzz me when you're a couple of blocks from the hospital. I'll come out to the curb and collect the envelope so you don't have to fight for parking.''

After she hung up, she drank her cold coffee and contemplated what quirk in male brains made them elevate sports figures to the top of the salary pyramid. Well, top salary for an independent TV station, anyway. And from Tanner's remarks it wasn't even close to what he made throwing a stupid ball around a cow pasture. But then, rock stars pulled down indecent money compared to most jazz musicians she knew. More of life's unfairness, she supposed.

The cafeteria had begun to empty. Rather than visit the boys while she waited for André's call, Crystal refilled her coffee cup. Better to sew up this deal with Tanner and get it out of her system. Kids were so perceptive. Skipper, especially, because of the stream of foster families he'd lived with could pick up moods easily. Crystal didn't want him worrying about her little snit.

Ultimately she downed three cups of coffee before André called. Her teeth might be on edge from an overdose of caffeine, but at least the storm had blown over and the rain had stopped. The sun had popped out and steam rose off the sidewalks by the time Crystal jogged out to the street to meet André's car. He wasn't alone. Nate and Michael were with him.

''Sure you won't handle this, André?'' she pleaded again as he shoved the manila envelope into her hand. ''I'll smuggle you past the nurses' station.''

Nate leaned across André. ''Pro athletes can be superstitious as hell, Crystal. We don't know that Tanner is, but no sense rocking the canoe, if you know what I mean. He's talking to you, and that suits me fine. Say, André forgot to ask—did Cale mention how long it'd be before we can expect him to come on board?''

"We, uh, didn't get to the particulars. I doubt we'd have progressed beyond him ripping up our letter if his agent hadn't shown up.''

André frowned. "Is Bergman involved in our negotiations? If so, the tab may go even higher.''

Crystal flattened herself against the car as an SUV plowed through a puddle and water sprayed from beneath its big wheels. "Mr. Bergman's the one who urged Tanner to reconsider taking the job. I gathered he's only just found out for sure that the Sinners aren't going to renew Caleb's contract.''

"So it's official?'' Nate played drumbeats on André's dash. "I'm glad you beefed up the benefits, André. We'll hit him while he's still reeling. Stay with him until he signs, Crystal. And be nice. Tell him what he wants to hear. That he'll have a generous travel allowance and his own expense account.''

"What?'' Crystal bent down and thrust her head into the car. "Am I going to have to fight with him over road expenses the way I do with you, Nate? You can't give an employee an unlimited expense account. It's financial suicide. Tell him, Michael.''

André cleared his throat. "It's not open-ended, Crystal. But we'd rather wait to set the parameters after Caleb starts work and we have a better sense of what his duties will be. Can you avoid stating an exact amount? Just indicate it'll be generous.''

"I think you're all nuts,'' she muttered. "A monkey in silk is still a monkey.''

"Oh, that's something else,'' Nate said. "While Michael drew up the new offer, I did some digging into

Cale's background. He graduated from Texas A & M with a degree in communications.''

"I'll bet. Everybody knows college counselors give jocks do-nothing courses.''

Nate smiled. "Used to be true, thank heaven. Otherwise I'd have never made it through Georgia State. Now everybody has to pull his weight academically. Cale carried a 3.8 grade point. So give credit where credit's due.''

"Sure,'' she said sweetly. "I happen to know you graduated magna cum laude, Nathan. Jill showed me your college scrapbook.''

"Why'd she do a dumb thing like that?'' He frowned.

"Maybe she wanted people at work to know you were more than just a pretty face.''

That brought guffaws from the others. Nate Fraser's face could be called many things. Rugged. Lived-in. Maybe even kind. But pretty? Definitely not.

Nate slumped back into his seat. "Get on with you, white girl,'' he growled. "Quit stalling. André's blocked the passenger unloading zone long enough. And don't you be telling Cale I do okay in the brains department. As director, I get more respect pretending to be a dumb jock.''

Crystal couldn't help smiling as she trudged back to Tanner's room. It wasn't often she got one up on Nate. She wished she'd thought to use the information about his academic career before. Like when Nate claimed he messed up his expense account because he couldn't get the hang of debits and credits.

This time when she approached Tanner's door, she didn't hear any noise. On checking, she discovered the drapes had been pulled to darken the room. Tanner was alone, but not asleep. He worked with a set of hand weights while staring dejectedly at a blank TV screen. His lunch tray sat untouched.

The ravaged expression on his face walloped Crystal before she had a chance to erect defenses. "Hi. It's me again." Her voice squeaked as she stumbled over the banal greeting.

His eyes, jade-dark and overflowing with dashed hopes, studied her. "I'm rotten company, sugar. On the other hand, I'd just as soon not be alone right now."

Crystal stepped fully into the room. Nate's recent directive pounded through her head. *Be nice to him.* He did look as if he needed a friend. She glanced around and saw that the room had three chairs. Selecting one, she sat and placed her handbag in another, then propped her sax case against the third. "Will Mr. Bergman be back soon?"

"Agents can't afford to waste their time on cripples. He's probably glued to his cell phone, looking for new blood."

Crystal pulled her hair over one shoulder, separated it into three heavy strands and began braiding it automatically. "So you exploded like a volcano and threw him out, huh?"

He stopped lifting the weights. "If you're planning to add shrink to your list of accomplishments, you can take a hike, too. I'll have agents beating down my door once this leg heals." He slapped at the covers, accidentally throwing one of the small barbells he'd been lifting into his injured knee.

His grimace of pain told Crystal all she needed to know. She wrapped a scrunchie around the bottom end of her braid and flipped it behind her. "I don't want to play devil's advocate, Tanner, but it doesn't appear that'll happen anytime soon. You can't kick a football until you can walk."

"I don't kick the football," he said coldly. "I'm a quarterback. I throw the ball."

Her arched eyebrow implied it was all the same thing.

Caleb crossed his arms. "I can see you're dying to give me the perfect alternative. Well, since you're back, I assume Fraser came up with a counteroffer. Let's have it, then," he muttered. "Get this over with."

Crystal reached into her bag and removed the envelope. This time she handed him the whole thing, instead of taking out the letter as she had before. "There are two copies of the agreement and a list of benefits. Read it carefully, Mr. Tanner. To be offered more, you'd have to be willing to live in New York or L.A. This is on the high end for a station our size. André's been more than charitable."

He flung the envelope down, unopened. Lips thinned into a harsh line, he said, "I'm not a charity case yet. You tell that to whoever the hell André is."

"André Lyon. The Lyons own WDIX radio and TV. His parents were television pioneers. Our station has left its mark on this country."

"And you don't want me tarnishing its sterling image, isn't that right, sugar? I can tell you think I'm not fit to wipe the feet of those Lyon dudes."

Crystal gasped. As a rule she masked her feelings well. Unable to meet his challenging green eyes, she lowered her lashes. "What I think or don't think isn't the issue here, Mr. Tanner. The offer for employment is a good one, and it's legitimate."

"Caleb," he snarled, grabbing the envelope and ripping it open. "Have you got a beef with the name, sugar? Or with me? Was I rude to you at a game once when you tried to flirt? If so, you have my humblest apologies. So many women slink up and wind around players after a game it's hard to distinguish one from another."

This time not only did Crystal gasp, she shot right out of her chair, trembling with anger. "I have never been to a game," she said haughtily. "I realize this may shock your ego, Tanner, but I don't consider myself deprived. And if you don't want the other leg to wind up in a cast, I'd advise you to stop calling me sugar."

Caleb stared at her a moment, then laughed. "I thought it was unAmerican to dislike the national sport. Which is football, sug…uh, Crystal."

Suddenly glad for André and Nate's sake that she hadn't let her temper totally blow the deal with Tanner, Crystal sank into the chair again and smoothed down her skirt. "There're probably only a couple of us renegades in the entire U.S. of A.," she said with a deprecating shrug. I'm certainly not representative of the crew at WDIX. Nor of our viewers. Our sports programs have a huge following. And it goes without saying that sports generates sponsors."

Drawing the sheets from the envelope, Caleb read through the offer twice before he moved on to the page listing the benefits. His heart plunged as he compared what Crystal thought was a generous salary to what he'd been getting. At a hundred thou, with Uncle Sam's bite, he'd be lucky to pull off Patsy's wedding and pay Jenny's college fees. For sure he'd have to find new digs. The five thousand a month he paid in rent now represented a huge chunk of change.

Crystal cleared her throat. "Is there something about the offer you need clarified? Something that particularly bothers you?"

"Everything about it bothers me, sweetheart. How long does Fraser expect me to sign on for? I mean, does he understand I'll go back to playing when my leg gets to a hundred percent?"

She looked perplexed. "I'm not sure I know what you mean. A two-week notice is standard. Jerry Davis gave three, I think. It's his slot Nate hopes you'll fill. But he did wonder when you'd be available. If the doctors have given you a release date, that is."

"You mean I won't have to sign a contract for a set amount of time?"

Her lips quirked at the corners. "Ever heard of free enterprise, Tanner? Haven't you worked in the private sector?"

He gave that question consideration. At last he shook his head. "As a kid, I helped on the farm. You don't get paid for that. You're lucky to get three squares a day and a roof over your head. I signed with the Cowboys right out of college."

"The Cowboys?" She looked blank.

Cale snickered. "Are you for real? The Dallas Cowboys, darlin'. As in NFL champions. Emmitt Smith, Deion Sanders, Michael Irvin." When she continued to look blank, he quit laughing. "Nobody can be that out of touch with sports."

"I am. And I don't consider it a laughing matter. I hate team sports. They're dangerous and violent."

"Hell, darlin', driving a car is dangerous. TV movies are violent."

"Don't call me darlin'. We were discussing André's offer. Are you interested in working for Lyon Broadcasting or not?"

"Not. I'm interested in getting back on my feet and into the game again. But as Leland pointed out before he left, Lyon's offered me an ace in the hole. Give me a pen and I'll put my John Hancock on this form."

Feeling smug at her success, Crystal pawed through her bag. When she failed to turn up a pen, she stood and walked over to his nightstand. "You had pens in the middle drawer earlier."

"Yeah. Say, is the kid happy I signed his football?"

"I haven't been to the ward to give it to him yet. He'll be ecstatic. That's all he'll talk about for months."

Cale started to say something, but the phone on his nightstand rang. "Catch that for me, would you?" he asked, his eyes vaguely panicky. "If it's any of the guys from the team, tell them I'm being X-rayed or something."

Sympathy kicking in again, she handed him a pen and nodded. "Hello," she chirped into the phone, sounding a bit rushed and breathless.

"No, I'm not Caleb's nurse or therapist," Crystal said smoothly. She nonchalantly handed him the receiver. "I can safely say it's not one of your teammates," she whispered.

Eyes narrowed, he tucked the phone against his ear. "Well, hello, sugar pie. 'Course it's not inconvenient. You can call me anytime, Jenny." He signed the second copy of the intent letter, shoved both toward Crystal, then settled into the stack of pillows. From the smile that softened his face, Crystal decided the female caller was his special lady. She felt uncomfortable eavesdropping. He tacked endearments on the end of every sentence. Even when they were evidently discussing his caller's car.

"Sounds like a clogged fuel filter, hon. I wish I could be there to change it, too, sweet pea. You know I can't. Call Waylon Gill. Tell him what I think the trouble is. Don't you worry about a thing, darlin'. What's important is for you to be on wheels I can trust. Have Gill put it on my card."

Crystal felt a moment's envy for the woman on the other end of the phone line. Caleb Tanner dispensed love along with his handouts. Her father had lavished her with money, but she couldn't remember a time he'd offered loving advice. Or any advice. When she was little, Roger Jardin had expected his aunt Anita to handle any problems that arose. And from the time she turned twelve, he assumed Crystal was old enough and capable enough to work things out for herself. For the most part she had. Still, there'd been times during high school and college when she would have liked someone to rely on. At least someone to run decisions by, to discuss things with.

Now she had Margaret. Or maybe not. Crystal's fear that something might have happened to her favorite relative tied her stomach in knots. From the minute Crystal had applied for an accounting job at WDIX—really from the minute Margaret realized who she was—the kind nurturing woman had brought her into a family who'd welcomed her, who'd opened wide the doors of Lyoncrest. And she loved living in the historic old house.

Crystal paced to the window. She tugged the heavy drape aside and pressed her nose to the glass, hoping the return of sunshine would calm her unsettled feelings. Paul's death had cast a gloom over the family. And then, before anyone could finish grieving, Margaret had vanished without a word. Crystal returned repeatedly to one basic truth: it simply wasn't like Margie to do this. No one was more devoted to family than Margaret Lyon.

"Hey, what's so interesting outside?"

Crystal turned and blinked. The low light in the room made it seem dark. "Oh—I didn't hear you say goodbye and hang up."

"I'm not surprised. You looked a million miles away. Sorry for the interruption. Where were we?"

"Uh...you signed the agreement. I would've left, but I

didn't know where you wanted me to put your copy. Also, I thought maybe you might have questions.''

"Will I see you at work?" He grinned rakishly and winked.

Since Crystal had just heard him fawning over the woman on the phone, she thought he had some nerve. Not to mention he obviously paid the woman's bills, which relegated her to a status beyond that of casual acquaintance.

Crystal mustered the no-nonsense scowl she reserved for employees who'd overshot their budgets or overspent on their travel-expense accounts. "You'd better hope you don't have dealings with me at work. I manage the money and oversee all department budgets. When people have to see me, it usually means they're in financial trouble. Not a good place to be.''

For a moment he looked as guilty as a boy caught stealing a slice from a birthday cake. As quickly, his eyes turned serious. "Is it hard to learn how to set up a budget?''

His question took Crystal by surprise. She wondered if the woman's car problems were the catalyst. Why hadn't she realized it might be his wife? For all she knew, he could be married and have six kids. Not all men wore wedding rings. "I do more than set up budgets. I manage all financial transactions for the radio and television stations owned by the Lyon family. I have an undergraduate degree in accounting and business administration. I have a master's in finance, and I'm a CPA.''

"Wow.''

He appeared so frankly impressed that Crystal felt herself blush. "Forgive me for sounding like I was bragging. I'm sure your financial adviser has at least those qualifications. Anyway...you'll want to notify whoever it is about the change in your financial status. He or she will want to do a new profile and possibly rearrange your portfolio.''

"My portfolio." Cale couldn't bring himself to tell her that he'd somehow managed to fritter away ten years' worth of income. Tough tightfisted Crystal Jardin probably had the first dime she'd ever earned enshrined under glass. "My, uh, portfolio is in good hands.''

She smiled. "Well, we've taken care of everything I came to do. Nate and André's business cards are in the envelope if you think of any questions after I leave. You might tune in to the sports report at five. You'll be a hot topic, I'm sure.''

The green in his eyes changed so rapidly into muddied distress Crystal let her handbag fall on the chair again. "What's the matter? Your retirement and launch into sports media are bound to make headlines.''

"Leland said the Sinners won't make any announcement until they sign a new quarterback," he said bitterly. "Lee swore he'd give me ample warning. He thinks the coach may play the first two season games with his backup—as if he's waiting for my return.''

Observing Cale's rancor, Crystal felt a tug of sympathy again. "You haven't told anyone, have you. I'll bet not even your family.''

He shook his head.

"I see." She sat down again and fiddled with her purse. "So the exercise we just went through is really just insurance for you. Do you really think you'll be through physical therapy and ready by that third game? You're counting on the Sinners rehiring you?''

"They should never have let me go," he said coldly.

"Wouldn't it have been crueler to leave you dangling? Which is what you plan on doing to WDIX." Crystal said with equal coldness. Enough to bring color to Caleb's cheeks.

He picked up the paper he'd signed and shook it at her. "I read this thoroughly. You said yourself it's a letter of intent. They intend to hire me if and when I become available. You said it's not a contract."

"It's not. But with you signing it, André and Nate are declaring the job is yours. Nate's filling in until you start. You're on the payroll as of now, and they won't be looking for someone else. It's referred to as a gentlemen's agreement. Which is apparently beyond your comprehension, Mr. Tanner."

"It's Caleb. I thought we agreed."

"So sue me. You agreed to work for WDIX-TV as soon as the doctor signs your release."

He raised his hands. "Hold it. Arguing is getting us nowhere."

"At last. Something on which we see eye to eye." She crossed her legs at the knee and swung one foot back and forth. "Do you want to start unscrambling the mess?" she asked. "Or shall I?"

"You, by all means. Ladies first. You might start by telling me why you lied when I asked if I had to sign a contract for a certain number of years. You said no."

"That's right. I stand by that statement. But you did indicate you wanted to work for us."

"No. I definitely recall telling you I wanted to play football."

"Well, yes, but—"

"There's no 'but' to it. From the way you talked, I thought this letter simply meant your boss wanted to hire me."

"He did. Does," she stammered. "By signing it, what do you think you promised?"

"To take the job if I'm available after the doctor releases me. I figured it locked me into a salary and benefits and that if one of your competitors showed up and offered me a better deal, I'd have to turn them down."

Color streaked up Crystal's neck.

"Bingo! That's precisely the reason you muscled your way in here and bullied me into signing. I might have grown up on a melon farm, Crystal, but I did not leave my brains underneath a vine."

"I resent your insinuating I tricked you. I tried to talk Nate, André and Mike out of hiring you."

He stared at her for a lengthy minute with an odd twist to his mouth. "Do you mind telling me why? Since we've never met before…"

"Not until yesterday." The red extended to her ears now. "Look, negotiations won't improve if we get personal."

He crossed his arms and said provocatively, "See there? You've admitted to not knowing anything about me. I happen to think negotiations would improve a lot if we got personal. By the way," he added in a low voice, "you ought to wear your hair down, instead of braided. Men have an age-old fantasy about women with long hair."

Crystal jumped up, snatched her purse and her saxophone case. "Sexual innuendos aren't acceptable in the business world. You're crude. You probably belch, too, and pick your teeth in public. And now you have my objections to hiring you. Goodbye, Mr. Tanner. I've done what I was sent to do. If you get the urge to rip up your copy of the letter of intent, do call WDIX Human Resources. Otherwise, our attorney may be meeting with yours. If that happens, remember *they're* the ones who eat caviar and drive Lamborghinis."

His delighted laughter halted Crystal at the door. Before she could ask what he found so funny, the door opened and a burly male orderly blocked her way with a wheelchair.

"Caleb Tanner?" The man with his hand on the chair consulted a clipboard lying on the seat. "I'm a big fan of yours," the orderly said. And he was if his look of awe was a measure of the truth.

Cale's laughter died. "Thanks, man. What's this all about?" He indicated the wheelchair.

"Didn't Doc Forsythe tell you?"

Cale frowned. "Tell me what? He hasn't been in today."

"He signed an order for physical therapy." The other man eyed Cale's traction apparatus. "Maybe there's been a mistake. Although I only pick 'em up and transport 'em," he said. "Normally guys don't start therapy until they're unhitched from traction."

Caleb reached for the top pulley. "It's simple enough to unhook. I've been champing at the bit waiting to start therapy."

"Should you call someone?" Crystal asked the orderly.

He glanced at her as if seeing her for the first time. "Are you Tanner's wife? That'd be a good idea, ma'am. I'll phone the physical-therapy office right now." He crossed to the phone on Caleb's nightstand.

"I'm not Mrs. Tanner," Crystal declared at the same time as Caleb said loudly, "I'm not married."

He wasn't? Crystal's pulse gave a peculiar little hop and her breath caught in her throat. By the time she swallowed and managed to breathe, she realized the news that he was single had no bearing on anything. He'd honeyed, darlin'd and sweetied some woman with a sultry Southern drawl. Definitely someone who had the inside track to

Tanner's heart. That was supposing he *had* a heart and didn't have a woman in every city the Sinners played.

The rattle and clank of metal on metal dragged her attention from her thoughts. Because Cale had unsnapped and dropped all the ropes and crossbars to his traction setup, the orderly had detoured from his mission to call the physical therapy department.

It wasn't any of her business, but judging by the agony creasing Caleb's face as he attempted to swing his leg off the bed, somebody should intervene. Crystal set her things aside and rushed to the bed. She picked up the phone. "What's the extension for your department?" she asked the orderly. She definitely didn't like the fact that he was listening to Caleb. Rather than phone for clarification, he'd rolled the chair over to the bed.

"Uh…171. We're two floors down."

Not knowing what that had to do with anything, Crystal nodded and punched in the numbers. Caleb caught her eye and glared.

"You have a football to deliver to some kid down the hall, don't you?"

But she'd tuned him out, suddenly hearing a woman's voice saying urgently, "Hello. Hello? I'm trying to reach Caleb Tanner. Is this room 306?"

Crystal shushed the men in the room with a brisk wave of her hand. "This is Mr. Tanner's room. Is this the secretary in physical therapy? No? Oh, your name is Gracie. Ah…I understand. I must have picked up the phone to dial out just as the switchboard transferred your call in." Covering the mouthpiece, Crystal turned to Caleb, who, although he grimaced in pain, now sat in the wheelchair. "It's Gracie," she said.

She expected him not to take the call. To ask her to say he was indisposed. Instead, he spun the chair's wheels with his powerful arms, and before Crystal could let out her breath, he'd yanked the phone from her hand.

"Gracie, darlin'. This is a treat. Listen, shortcake, can I phone you back? What? Your watch quit and you found one at Nieman's you like better? It's yours, sweetheart. And a new suit? Gray pinstripe. A power suit, huh? I thought those were red. Why not red? I think you look pretty snazzy in red." Caleb glanced up. He sucked in his breath and gritted his teeth as Crystal edged past him, accidentally bumping his tender knee.

"Where in hell are you going?" He clapped a hand over the receiver, then moved it back to his mouth and slid his fingers away. "I didn't mean you, dumplin'. It's kind of nutty here, Gracie. Forgive my swearing, shortcake."

Crystal scooped up her things again and strode out the door with a quick backward glance. More of a glare, really. She hoped it conveyed how she felt about his laying it on so thick to the second woman in one day. How many others would there be? "You're a cockroach, Tanner," she said in a voice she hoped was loud enough for poor snookered Gracie to hear. "Slime. Please do rip up André's letter. If you're too weak after therapy, the nurses down the hall have a paper shredder."

She sped out the door too fast to see the baffled expression shared by the men.

"What? Yes, Gracie, the lady did call me names. I know it's hard to believe, darlin'. But not everybody thinks your brother hung the moon and stars."

"And you might not, either," he muttered glumly after they hung up. "If this leg doesn't heal, and if I can't bring myself to say no to you three girls, your stupendous fantastic brother may end up in debtor's prison."

The orderly chuckled. "I think those went out with the guillotine, man." His face was still wreathed in smiles as he phoned downstairs to verify that Tanner was indeed scheduled to begin physical therapy.

CHAPTER FOUR

CRYSTAL PUT TANNER and his collection of women out of her mind as she headed down the hall to the kids' ward. She saw Nurse Pam, who acknowledged her by waving a full oversize syringe. Crystal was awfully glad Pam sped past the boys' room on her mission of mercy.

"Knock, knock. Incoming adult," she warned before she invaded the boys' space. "Hide the stash of peanuts, candy and bubble gum, guys." All six occupants burst into giggles.

"You're early." Skipper punched the mute button on his TV remote control, which garnered loud complaints from his roommates.

"Early, *and* I come bearing gifts." Crystal produced the signed football from the depths of her handbag and handed it to Skipper with a brief "Ta-da!" Then she hauled out the signed action shots of Tanner. After counting out one for each child, she discovered she had two left. Maybe she'd give one to André's son, Andy-Paul. She didn't have a clue what she'd do with the other. Paste it on a dartboard, perhaps.

"This is so cool, Crystal," Skip said. "Look, Randy. Cale wrote, 'To Skip. Kick 'em high, throw 'em true. Caleb Tanner.'"

Crystal leaned over to look. "I thought he only wrote, 'To Skip from Caleb.' I can't figure out why he'd give such off-the-wall advice. I explained about your accident.''

"I'm gonna play football again, Crystal. Cale knows that.''

"Yeah," his friends chorused enthusiastically.

She gazed into uncompromising green eyes, realizing for the first time how closely Skipper's eye color resembled Caleb Tanner's. Both pairs were indecently dark-lashed, too. The resemblance ended there. Skip had sandy red hair, pale skin and freckles. Tanner's hair was hard to describe. Full and thick, it seemed to have variegated hues from light blond to toffee. His skin was evenly tanned. Today, she'd noticed his jaw was shadowed by a slight stubble. Based on her limited visits, she judged him to be a man who shaved regularly. Except for the earring, he seemed conventional. And even the earring was pedestrian compared to those worn by some of her jazz compatriots.

Gracious. Why had her mind wandered so far afield? Crystal had barely shaken herself out of her stupor than the orderly she'd encountered in Tanner's room strode through the door.

"You get around," he said, grinning at her.

She didn't respond to that, but asked, "You're here for Pablo?" Of the six in the room, he alone had progressed to the point of physical therapy.

The orderly, whose name tag read Gibson, checked the top sheet on his clipboard. "Nope. The patient I want is West. Skip West. Or if you want to get technical, Sinclair West.''

"Yuck!" Skip rolled his eyes as the other boys made rude gagging noises.

"There must be some mistake," Crystal said faintly.

"Nah," Skip said, ducking his head. "It's awful, but my mom named me Sinclair Malone West. After her daddy. I never met him or nothin'. He died when she was little.''

Before Crystal could explain that she hadn't been referring to his name, Randy broke in. "How come everybody calls you Skipper, then? Was that what your old man called you?"

Skip shook his head and thrust his jaw out pugnaciously. "I never had no old man. So what?"

"Everybody's got an old man," Randy scoffed with worldly knowledge. "My mom says they don't all stick around after they've had their fun bouncing between the sheets." Over Crystal's sharply indrawn breath, he added, "It's plain dumb, Skipper, saying you don't got an old man."

The boys paid no attention to the fact that Skip looked ready to explode. Pablo injected his two cents' worth from the other side of the room. "Yeah, dude. Even test-tube babies got a *padre*."

"Well, I don't!" Skipper shouted. He jabbed a thumb into his skinny chest. "My mom said there was just her and me and nobody else. After she got shot by the coke-head who robbed the store where she worked, there was only me." His face had turned a mottled red.

Crystal stepped between the beds, put two fingers in her mouth and whistled. Then she made a T with her hands. "Time-out, guys. Randy, you and Pablo read a comic book or watch TV. I want a word with Mr. Gibson."

Though sullen, the boys settled down. "Now," she said to the orderly, "could you check with your office? Skip had surgery yesterday. I find it hard to believe they'd start PT today. Have they even had you sit up yet?" she asked Skip.

"Yeah. 'Course they have."

"Are you some busybody patient liaison sent by administration to bug me?" Gibson sputtered. "I'm just following orders from my boss, lady."

Crystal spread her palms. "You questioned whether or not Tanner should have therapy because he was still in traction. I'm merely doing the same on Skip's behalf. I don't work for the hospital. I'm the business manager for Lyon Broadcasting, and Skipper's friend."

"Nurse Pam said Crystal is a financial wizard," Skip put in, his temper obviously cooled.

Though Gibson muttered to himself, he looked at Crystal with new respect as he slouched over to the wall phone. In the children's ward, patients didn't have telephones beside their beds. Administration was probably afraid they'd run up long-distance bills. The kids came to the ward from all over the state. Pablo, like Skip, was in local foster care. Randy's mother lived in Baton Rouge. Felipe reportedly had family in the Atchafalaya Swamp; he spoke only French, and Crystal had never seen anyone visit the boy. Barry Hodges needed more specialized care than was available in Vidalia; he had a cousin in town who visited occasionally. Moses Brown, the last of the six to be admitted, never mentioned family; he hardly said boo. Crystal knew he liked the picture of Caleb Tanner only because Moses had immediately tucked it into his pillowcase. Nurse Pam said that was where he squirreled away his few treats. Crystal had heard that Moses was Jamaican. One of a large family. He'd been injured playing street ball. Which specific sport, she didn't know. Surgery hadn't rescued his pitifully small body from pain—that she did know. It'd be a while before they scheduled him for physical therapy.

The orderly hung up the phone and turned. "Dr. Snyder ordered this young man to start upper-body exercise today. That way he'll be able to balance on the bars in two weeks when they cut off his cast."

Skipper's eyes glazed in sudden fear. He grasped Crystal's hand. "I'm scared it'll hurt. Will you come with me?"

She glanced at the orderly. "Is that permissible?"

Gibson hitched a shoulder. "It's a big area. If the PT who's scheduled to work with Skipper has any problem with you being there, he or she will ask you to wait outside. There's a nice waiting room. We do a lot of outpatient work, as well as inpatient care."

"Then I'll go." She smiled at Skip, who still had a stranglehold on her fingers. He didn't let go, either, which made it awkward when Gibson tried to transfer the boy to the wheelchair. The man worked around the inconvenience. He kept up a line of banter without making Skip feel like a baby for needing to hang on to someone. For all his size, the man was gentle.

"You've obviously been at this job awhile," Crystal said.

"Six years. I hope to be a physical therapist someday."

"It's a tough course, I understand," she murmured sympathetically.

The man rolled Skip's chair into the hall. "It's finding the time and money to take classes. I have a family to support."

"No wonder you're so patient with Skip. You have children."

"Yes. And I'm responsible for two sets of parents who are getting on in years."

"That's rough," Crystal said. "The broadcasting company I work for ran a series recently on what's being called the sandwich generation. I caught part of it. Mostly people talking about the difficulties involved in juggling care for both.''

He grinned at her. "I wish they'd talked to me. We bought a big house in town. All of us live together. My kids know their grandparents. They're learning early about love and compassion and helping out around the house. If you ask me, it beats the alternative of growing up in small isolated families.''

Skipper leaned back in the wheelchair so he could look up at the man who pushed him. "Your place sounds neat. I don't s'pose you have room for one more?'' The wistful tone of his voice caused Crystal to tighten her hold on his hand.

"I'm afraid all the beds are taken,'' Gibson said lightly. He raised a brow at Crystal as if wondering what he'd inadvertently stepped into.

"Skip is in foster care,'' she informed him. Then, speaking to the boy, she asked softly, "You like living at Sandy's, don't you?''

"She and Mark are okay,'' he said listlessly. "There's a lot of kids and the house isn't very big. And Mark doesn't like us to make noise. Sandy says he takes complaints from customers all day. When he gets home he wants peace and quiet.''

"But they treat you well?'' she pressed.

"Yeah. Mark don't hit any of us like Leroy did at my last house.''

"Good. Because if you were having problems, I'd call Rachel.''

His face brightened. "I forgot you know my caseworker real well. Ms. Fontaine is nice. Not grouchy like some of 'em are.''

"That's because she's walked the walk, kiddo. She was a foster child in the house where I live. André Lyon, my boss, would've adopted her, but her mom refused to sign the papers. Lucky for Rachel, her mother agreed to permanent foster care. Rachel said the move to Lyoncrest changed her life. She knows the system *can* work, Skipper. Promise me that if you ever have problems, you'll let her know at once.''

"Sure. Okay. Wow!" His voice rose excitedly and he tugged on Crystal's jacket sleeve. "Isn't that Cale over there?"

Gibson had wheeled Skipper's chair to the doorway of a huge room that reminded Crystal of a fancy gym. She couldn't begin to identify all the equipment, but Tanner worked at one machine that seemed designed to strengthen his upper body. Crystal didn't want to stare. However, she couldn't seem to help it. Caleb was bare to the waist. Ridges of muscle stood out across his shoulders as he hoisted himself from the seat of his wheelchair using nothing but his arms. Sweat glistened on his skin. A few drops pooled like tears in the rough hair that fanned his broad chest. The thatch of light brown narrowed before it met his navel. Beyond that, Crystal could only guess. And guessing made her uncomfortable.

"Well, isn't it him?" Skip hissed, his eyes huge and eager.

Crystal wet her lips and cleared her throat. "Y-yes, it certainly is."

"Wait'll I tell the guys! He looks terrific. He don't have a cast on or nothin'."

As if sensing he was under scrutiny, Caleb glanced toward the door. The minute his eyes met Crystal's he lost concentration and relaxed his grip on the rings.

Even across the room they heard the slap of his butt as it hit the vinyl seat of the wheelchair hard. Crystal flinched. Her teeth snapped shut and she closed her eyes, imagining the pain. Next the air curdled from his harsh expletive.

Skip's cheeks paled. "I think that hurt him bad, Crystal. I guess maybe he's not doin' as good as he looks."

"Healing bone and muscle takes time," she murmured.

The therapist assigned to Skip walked up just then and blocked Caleb from Crystal's view. But not before she saw him grit his teeth, tune her out and reach up to repeat the exercise. Logically Crystal knew that the other woman with a clipboard, the one who stood beside Caleb, must be *his* therapist. Crystal wanted to scold the woman for assigning Caleb tasks that obviously hurt him.

Crystal didn't know how long Skip's therapist had been talking to her when she realized they were both staring at her and that some response was required. "Excuse me," she said. "I must have zoned out for a moment."

The young woman grinned. "I understand completely. All the women who work here have been drooling ever since Gib brought Caleb in. All except me. I like nerds. One football jock is the same as the next. It's body by Mattel, brains by Brio."

The insult didn't go over Crystal's head, but neither did she crack a smile. And when the therapist shrugged and looked at her with pity, Crystal had to wonder why she felt like retaliating on Tanner's behalf.

"Gib said Skipper asked to have you stay for his therapy session," the PT said, getting down to business. "I don't mind. Gib's bringing you a chair. We're starting Skip with basic upper-body testing. This session is more or less to evaluate his muscular strengths and weaknesses. Boring stuff, really."

"Will I hafta do what Cale's doing, ma'am?" the boy asked apprehensively. "He's really hurting, don't you think?"

Crystal followed Skip's troubled gaze. Indeed, Tanner seemed to be struggling. Veins stood out in his forearms, as did the cords in his neck. His therapist chewed gum and looked on. "His PT will call a halt if Tanner tries to overdo it, won't she?" Crystal asked.

"Tanner's her patient. My worry is this young man." Skip's therapist knelt to his level. "Call me, Mindy, okay? We're going to be meeting like this two or three times a week over a long period. We'll get to be friends. After your cast comes off, I may ask you to stretch some muscles that will hurt a bit, but today we're doing easy stuff."

He nodded, although his gaze kept straying to Cale's corner. It was obvious from his straining that he wasn't having an easy time of it. "Isn't this Cale's first day of therapy, too?" the boy managed in a high threadlike voice. "I think he's in pain big time."

Mindy didn't seem to know how to answer. Crystal intervened. "Honey, I know for a fact that Tanner's been working out with hand weights in his room. Plus, his athletic training has been far more intense than yours. You concentrate on what Mindy tells you to do, okay?"

"Yes, Skip. Lynelle is taking care of your friend. He's fine. I promise."

"All r-right."

Skip still kept turning to watch Caleb. But how could Crystal blame him when she was sneaking looks, too? Tanner did possess an impressive physique. Broad shoulders, but not too bulky. Each of his hands would probably make two of hers. But they were well shaped and his nails were short and clean.

When Crystal started to imagine what it'd feel like having those hands roam over her breasts, she made herself turn her attention to Mindy and Skip again.

Why on earth do they keep it so warm in here? Crystal

stood and walked to the door. She just needed to find the courtyard and get some air. Her sitting here served no purpose; Skip was doing fine with Mindy.

Crystal remained oblivious to the fact that the sway of her hips stopped Tanner's therapy session cold. He had to lean around his therapist to gain the full effect of Crystal's sudden departure. Lynelle didn't like losing his attention. Clearly the therapist, in her spandex shorts and crop top, thought she was hot stuff. But Caleb had never been crazy about buxom blondes. Especially when they were closer to his kid sister's age than his. Cale had accepted long ago that he might be the only football player on the face of the earth who was that choosy.

As a rule he gravitated toward tall leggy redheads. This week he'd changed his preference to petite saxophone players who wore their long black hair in a single braid. And he didn't even know why, since he and Crystal Jardin hadn't gotten past arguing. Then again, maybe that was the reason. Generally, everywhere he went, women of all ages fawned over him. Crystal was definitely not in that category.

"Chill out," he warned Lynelle, who'd begun a strident lecture. "I trained with weights and healed bruised muscles while you were still in diapers. Not to put down your schooling, darlin'. But I know when these old bones have had enough. I say this session is over. Tell Gibson to give me fifteen minutes to shower and change back into my pj's, and I'll be ready to have him wheel me upstairs. Oh, and could you tell that lady over by the door that I've seen the light? If she doesn't understand, ask her to drop by my room later and I'll spell it out in contract terms."

Lynelle tossed him a towel. "I'm a therapist, not your personal gofer. Hit on the woman yourself, Jack." She flounced off toward the PT office at the opposite end of the room. Caleb supposed he deserved the putdown. He'd been hit on so many times himself, being rude had become second nature. She was a cute kid, and she had to be smart to pass the course and certification. After his shower, he'd find her and apologize.

The way Crystal's eyes had bored into him while he sweated like a green-broke horse getting the kinks knocked out had been plenty humiliating. Discovering he didn't have a prayer of being in any shape to play this fall season had laid him low. He was neither a fool nor a masochist. Caleb couldn't recall a single time in his thirty-one years of living, when his body had let him down this badly.

Crystal Jardin's job offer stood to buy him time to heal. He'd give her a season—provided she hadn't called Nate Fraser and told him to offer the job to someone else. As Caleb showered, seated in the wheelchair, and then struggled to dress himself, he wondered how in hell he'd manage. But he'd asked himself that when his folks died and left him with three small sisters to raise. He had survived.

There were days he'd been sure he wouldn't. But he'd made it. And by God, he'd conquer this annoying disability, too. Know-it-alls, like the moneyman who'd counted Caleb Tanner out, had damned well better take off their shoes and count again.

Tanner's freshly washed hair stood up in sweaty spikes again by the time Gibson poked his head inside the steamy cubicle. "Lynelle said you're ready to call it quits."

"Are you going to make something of it, too?"

"Not me, man." Gib helped roll Caleb's chair out where he had more room to maneuver. It was also cooler. "I wondered about taking a man out of traction to go to physical therapy. Talk to your doc. He should send a therapist to your room."

"I butted heads with Forsythe already and insisted I was ready for therapy. But I think he figured I'll end up one of those statistics doctors bury."

"Feeling that rocky?"

"Worse." Caleb heaved a sigh and rubbed a hand the length of his sore leg. "I feel like a sheepdog who's been dragged backward through a kitty door."

"Don't take this as anything against Lynelle, but why don't you go to the sports-medicine clinic? They have the latest techniques and equipment at their disposal."

Caleb couldn't very well tell a man who worked a low-paying, dead-end job that a pro ball player couldn't afford the prices they charged at the sports-medicine clinic. Leland had suggested the same thing yesterday. Caleb had never admitted the state of his finances to his agent, either. "You know how it is, Gib. The best has a waiting list longer than your arm. I'm in a hurry to get back on my feet."

"So, I heard the Sinners dumped you. How close to being flat broke are you?"

Cale stiffened automatically. Was he that transparent?

"I see panic in the eyes, man. I've been down that road. Heard it happens a lot to lottery winners and guys in pro sports, too. Guess I never believed it. All they publicize is that you make these humongous salaries."

"Yeah. When a man's playing well, the living is easy. Things can go to hell fast," Caleb said with a wry twist of his lips. "A pal in Dallas told me to get myself a financial guru. I told myself I'd do it next year. Then next year, and so on."

"Maybe it's not too late," Gibson said optimistically as he hung Cale's clipboard on the back of his chair and wheeled him through the gym.

"It is," Cale said with finality. He might have said

more, but was interrupted by a reedy voice that came from one of the apparatuses.

"You ain't givin' up, are you, Cale? I heard you say on TV once, 'You get hit. Sometimes it hurts bad. But you make yourself go on.'"

Gibson stopped wheeling and Caleb jerked around to see who'd fed his hype back at him. A skinny ashen-faced kid, that was who. The boy he'd seen clinging to Crystal. One of the cubs she'd spoken of with such passion, he supposed. The boy wore an uncomfortable-looking body cast that started in the middle of his chest. "It's this way, half-pint. When it comes to injuries, we don't play by just one set of rules."

"I've got a name," the boy said, his voice marginally stronger. "You know it. You signed my football 'To Skip.' Remember?"

"I do. Ms. Jardin brought it to me. She's very persuasive. I'd keep her on my team if I were you, kid."

A shaky giggle floated toward him. "I guess you two didn't talk football. Randy says when it comes to sports, Crystal's running five laps behind the field."

"Not a big sports fan, huh? Who's Randy?" Cale asked more sharply than he'd intended.

"A guy on my ward. He mostly plays basketball, but he's a football fan big time. Crystal just plays sax."

"Just? That takes a lot more talent than it does to heave a ball. Give her credit, okay?"

"I meant, you can't make bucks playing music like you can in football."

Caleb was hurting, sitting in the chair with his leg hanging down. And the conversation didn't seem to have much point. Besides, the kid's single-minded focus on football reminded Caleb of himself at that age. Right now he didn't care to be reminded. In fact, he wished he'd had a more open mind and pursued a few other hobbies. Then maybe he wouldn't feel so much as if his life was over. "Look, Skip, I'm tying up Gibson, here. I've gotta get on back to my room."

"Sure, Cale. Maybe I'll see you down here again," Skip said shyly.

Cale hoped not. How could he help a maimed kid? It wasn't as if he even had a handle on his own future at the moment.

Gibson broke into Tanner's morose self-analysis as he rolled his patient toward the elevator. "Like I was about to say before the kid interrupted, that woman ought to be able to help you solve your problems."

"What woman? Which problems?" Caleb asked.

"The woman I saw in your room. The same one who came in with the kid. She's left, but I imagine you know how to reach her."

"Either you're talking in circles or I've missed something. Are we discussing the job Crystal Jardin offered me with WDIX-TV? If so, news travels fast on the hospital grapevine. Especially since I've only just made up my mind to give it a shot."

Gibson shook his head. "I don't know about any job. I'm talking about her being that financial guru you said you needed. Financial wizard, I think the kid called her. Last year I paid somebody big bucks to draw me up a budget plan. Since you two are friends, maybe she'll give you a deal."

"Friends? You were there when she called me a cockroach and slime. Did that sound like we're bosom buddies?"

"I took it to mean she likes you. You were tied up on the phone with another babe. I'd bet dollars to crackers Ms. Jardin was jealous."

Caleb laughed even though it hurt his hip and knee. "No offense, man. But as a love psychic, you'd make a better ditch digger."

Gibson stopped outside Caleb's private room and turned the chair around so he could wheel him in backward. "Just tellin' you the way it looked from where I stood. How you deal with the information is entirely up to you. Let's get you back into bed and prop that leg up again."

Getting into bed proved to be harder than sliding out had been. Caleb couldn't bear any weight on his injured leg, and his good one seemed too shaky to support him. "Ow, ow, damn," he muttered after two futile tries to get into bed using his arms alone.

"Here, let me lower that bed," Gibson said.

"Dammit! I hate not being able to do for myself."

"It's a common affliction among men. Sort of spoils the tough-guy image."

"Has to do with more than image," Caleb growled. "I have three sisters who depend on me." He didn't mention that they were nearly grown or that he encouraged their dependence. Partly to maintain a link, but partly out of guilt because he couldn't stay home and be the parent they'd lost. "The girls live in Texas," he said. "But if I don't get out of here soon, they'll put their lives on hold to come here and fuss over me. I hate being fussed over."

Gibson helped Caleb reconnect the traction device. Then he wheeled the empty chair toward the door. "Women are funny that way."

"Any chance you can leave the wheelchair? If I could use it to go to the john or even to travel up and down the hall, it might restore some sense of control."

"Sure. Nobody told me to bring the chair back. Don't

be hot-rodding in the corridor or popping wheelies to impress the nurses, though, you hear?''

Caleb grinned. Already he felt better. ''Hey,'' he called to Gibson before he shut the door. ''If you run into Crystal Jardin, could you tell her I'd like a word with her?''

''Aha! Gonna take my advice, after all. Way I figure, how can you lose? Those money babes have a way of manipulating your assets to make 'em grow.''

Caleb wadded up the small pillow he used under his hip and threw it at the man framed in the door. ''I'm not showing her my ass-ets,'' he drawled. ''So watch what you say to her, all right?''

Smiling, Gibson tossed the pillow back on Tanner's bed. ''Are you sure they shouldn't be treating you for a head injury? I know a babe when I see one—and hey, I'm a happily married man.''

''I never said she wasn't easy on the eyes. But I only met the lady a couple of days ago. And not under the best of circumstances.''

''Good. For a minute there you had me worried that I couldn't believe all the juicy stuff they print about my favorite jocks. Married guys like me can't share your exploits. We can only dream when we read about yours. You single guys have a heavy obligation to your brothers.''

He'd disappeared and the door had swung closed by the time Caleb mustered a reply. This wasn't the first time he'd met someone who couldn't see through the hype. More to the point, most men were like Gibson. They didn't *want* to see that the jocks, as Gibson called them, were just ordinary guys who had a little talent for playing ball and a lot of luck. Luck because they were picked to play for the pros.

Sure, they had some good-looking women hanging

around. A lot of them bought into the hype and imagined sex with a jock would be better. Others were attracted by the money. And Caleb wasn't trying to fool himself into believing he hadn't taken advantage once or twice. But less and less in the past five years. The partying got boring, his body, less tolerant. Oddly enough, if a man only wanted a dinner companion, he was out of luck unless the word circulated that the rewards were worthwhile. Mostly it got so lonely on the road Caleb found himself passing out increasingly more expensive gifts for an evening of decent conversation.

That had only contributed to the financial fix he was in. To some, like Gibson, it'd probably appear he was stupid. Cale didn't see it that way. So what if it took a bracelet or two to avoid facing four walls in meaningless hotel rooms?

Of course not one of those fleeting companions had been on a par with Crystal Jardin. It figured. He finally met a woman with brains and wit and beauty, and she happened to consider ball players scum. If he closed his eyes, he could conjure up an image of a woman whose eyes sparkled when she talked about her music. A woman who traded barbs adroitly while dickering with him over a job.

He heard the door open. Caleb lifted one eyelid, expecting to see a nurse with his afternoon medication. He wasn't prepared for his visitor to be the person he'd been fantasizing about for the past half hour.

"I didn't mean to disturb your sleep," she said in a smoky voice that sent blood rushing from Cale's head to a part of his anatomy that would be hard to conceal in his present garb. He grabbed a pillow out from under his head and flopped it across his middle.

All he seemed able to do was grin like an idiot.

"Lynelle and Gibson both passed on word that you wanted to see me. I thought it must be important. I can come back later, though. I realize your workout in PT must have taken its toll. I planned to grab a bite in the cafeteria, then go back and play some tunes for the boys. I'll stop by later."

He bent an arm and tucked it behind his head, which tilted him far enough forward to gaze directly into her Texas-bluebonnet eyes. "That workout gave me a good kick in the butt." He tried to turn and elevate himself on one elbow. The pain hit him hard. Caleb sucked in a breath. For a minute he was afraid he'd black out.

Crystal rushed to his bedside. "Ouch. Talk without moving. I can hear you. Stop abusing yourself, Tanner."

"How long is your boss willing to give me to get back on my feet?" he said through lips stretched tight in pain.

"Pardon? You said you weren't interested."

"I wasn't," he growled. "Now I am." Sighing, he flopped flat on his back. "I'm ready to promise WDIX-TV a year. After that we'll have to see." She failed to smile smugly, the reaction Caleb had expected from her.

"That PT session must have been tougher on you than I thought," she said gravely. "It's a good thing Skip asked me to go with him to therapy. Otherwise I'd have called André already and told him you said to stuff the job."

Caleb winced. "I deserve to have you stick it to me. A warning, darlin'. Watching Cale Tanner grovel isn't a pretty sight."

"As groveling works better from the knees and that lets you out, how about if we call it a draw? The job is yours. I'll call André from the cafeteria. Although Nate Fraser will decide on the actual start date. Shall I have him phone you?"

Cale gazed at her for a lengthy moment. "I'd like you to get his answer and then come back and tell me." He paused, almost as long as he had before. "I hate to ask, but what'll it cost to have you play some tunes for me before you leave?"

"Cost? The hospital doesn't pay for my services," she said stiffly. "I'm sure I told you I volunteer."

"I've never met a woman yet, sweetheart, who didn't have her price."

"You're absolutely right," she said frostily as she crossed the room and yanked open the door. "Mine is for you to learn my name. Until then, get your concert through the vents."

"Oh, you can dish it out, but can't take it, huh? I'm positive the words 'cockroach' and 'slime' do not appear on my birth certificate."

Crystal paused half in, half out of his room. Turning back, she gave a sexy, sultry laugh. "Guilty as charged. All right. The slate is clean. From now on I'll call you Tanner and you call me Jardin. And...I suppose I can swing by later and kick out a little improv."

His lips curved up on one side. "You drive a hard bargain, Jardin. But it's a deal." Caleb discovered he was still smiling several minutes after the door had closed.

CHAPTER FIVE

EVENING SHADOWS strafed the corner window in Caleb's room and sent leaf patterns skittering across the white walls. He studied their erratic flow, instead of eating, as he listened to the faint beginning strains of an Ellington tune he recognized. He'd had a college roommate for two years whose pile of cassettes consisted of the re-recorded music of Duke Ellington, John Coltrane and Charlie "Bird" Parker. At the time Caleb would've said he hadn't paid attention to those tunes. In fact, he was sure his focus had been on football, girls and maintaining his GPA. Who'd have thought he'd absorb so much background during his requisite study sessions?

Back then, the sounds had eased his youthful restlessness and allowed him to study; now he felt jumpy and impatient to see the music maker.

She promised me a private concert, dammit.

She took her own sweet time, too. He'd unhooked his leg from traction and was flailing around, trying to get from the bed into the wheelchair about the time Crystal sauntered in.

"What are you doing?" she gasped. "Have you rung for a nurse?" She dropped her sax case and oversize handbag on a chair and rushed to his side.

He clamped his teeth on his lower lip and said nothing.

Crystal slid an arm around his waist. She burrowed her shoulder under his arm and braced herself to take his weight. He was solidly built, outweighing her by a hundred pounds. "In or out?" she asked.

Cale teetered on his good leg. All that registered was how soft and fragile she felt and how good she smelled. For weeks he'd washed with medicinal soap. Even though he'd progressed to wearing his own pajamas, they'd taken on the antiseptic smell of his sheets. "I like your perfume," he said, throwing more of his weight on her as he bent to bury his nose in the back of her braid. "Mmm. Beats mine. What is it?"

"Tanner, I'm going to drop you. This is no time to explore fragrance, mine or yours."

He immediately straightened and scowled. "Mine? Football players may pose for cologne ads, but it doesn't mean we smell pretty. I'll have you know, men from Texas smell like men, Jardin."

Crystal studied the indignant slant of his stubbled jaw, the attractive tumble of his hair as it fell over his forehead. Suddenly she was very aware that he wore nothing but a thin pair of cotton pajama bottoms. Beneath her hands, holding his arm and torso tight, his skin emitted about a thousand BTUs. She felt the sizzle all the way to her toes.

Her fingers tightened on the solid ripple of muscle. Crystal steeled herself to counter the effect that touching him had on her equilibrium. "Tanner," she muttered, "at the risk of being repetitive, were you heading in or out of bed?"

"I risked life and limb to try and go down the hall to watch you play, darli—uh, lady."

"Why would you do that when you knew I was coming by?"

"I thought you might forget."

"I keep my promises, Tanner. I also said I'd phone André and I did. He put me through to Nate Fraser, who'll

be your boss. Nate says to take the time you need to get
well. If you want to come to work before the doctor says
you can drive, the station will provide a limo door to door.
Plus, Nate said to tell you our building's wheelchair-
friendly.''

Caleb pulled away from her at that and tried to hop
back up on the bed. "I'll get to work under my own
steam. This wheelchair is temporary. Very temporary. Tell
Fraser I'll be doing handsprings in two weeks.''

"Here's his business card. Tell him yourself.'' Crystal
tossed it on the nightstand. "Forgive my skepticism, but
I have a hard time believing you'll be agile enough to do
fancy moves when you can't get in and out of bed by
yourself.''

"Gibson lowered the damned thing earlier.''

"How?''

"I don't know, but it moved up and down like a fork-
lift.''

"Do you know the extension for your nurses' station?
I'll phone down there and ask.'' She leaned across the
bed to grab his phone. It rang, startling her so much she
dropped it. The receiver bounced against the tile as Crystal scrambled after it.

"Hello?'' She'd thrown herself on the bed, hanging
over both sides, her rump in the air. Her hello sounded
scratchy and breathless.

"Who is this?'' demanded a feminine voice. A voice
with a more Southern drawl than the woman who'd called
Caleb earlier. "Do I have Caleb Tanner's room?''

"Yes, indeedy, you have the great man's current
abode.'' Propelling herself off the bed, Crystal shoved the
phone into Tanner's free hand. "For you!''

Surprised by her changed attitude, Caleb issued a wary,
"Hello?'' He couldn't imagine what anyone who'd call

him might say to spark such annoyance in Crystal. And she was clearly annoyed. However, thank goodness she'd discovered the release button that raised and lowered his bed. As his bed sank to a level where he could sit on it, he heard his sister Patsy ask frostily who had answered his phone.

"Patsy, sugar, I've got company. Will you be home later? I'll call you back."

Crystal fingered the snaps on her saxophone case, revulsion coiling in the pit of her stomach at his syrupy greeting to yet another woman caller. She thought about collecting her things and walking out. But since he'd told the caller he had a visitor, good manners dictated she stay. And why should it matter to her how many girlfriends Tanner strung along? The obvious answer—it didn't— didn't seem to set well. Did he have any clue how silly he sounded? And where did he find so many women willing to be degraded and patronized?

Cale shifted on the bed, trying to give his injured knee some relief. He could make no sense at all of his normally sweet-tempered sister's grilling. Suddenly it dawned on him. Gracie and Jenny had evidently compared notes and felt it significant that a woman—not a nurse—had answered his phone on two separate occasions. Three, counting this one. It was precisely the kind of situation his sisters would jump on and blow out of proportion. They were always trying to read something into his relationship with whatever woman the press happened to snap pictures of him squiring about town. All three thought it was past time he picked one woman and settled down.

Maybe it was. But he damned well didn't need any help choosing. And he sure didn't want them meddling now. Not when Crystal Jardin had actually decided to unbend a little.

"I'm always happy to talk to you, shortcake. Something happened today that's gonna have some impact on me. On us. Yes, it's real important, but I can't talk now. Honey…" Caleb used the pad of his thumb to rub away creases that had formed between his brows. He glanced up in time to see Crystal pick up her saxophone and sling her jute bag over her shoulder. "Wait!" he yelped. "Don't go yet."

"No, not you, Patsy. Look, I've gotta hang up. This is business, sweetie. I promise I'll call you later. Yes, after *that* woman leaves. Her name is Crystal, by the way. But it's nothing like you're thinking. Bye. Love you, too," he mumbled, feeling heat steal up his neck and into his face.

"My sister," he said, shrugging awkwardly as Crystal continued to regard him coolly from the door.

Crystal shifted her sax case to the other hand. Who was he kidding? Did she look like she'd just fallen off a watermelon truck? "It's late, Tanner. Visiting hours are almost over. I gave you Nate's card. Our business is complete. I'm sure you want to tell your…sister the exciting news about your new job."

Alarm crossed his face. It darkened his eyes for a moment until he drove away the cloud with a wheedling smile. "I'll tell her soon. You have time for a few licks, don't you?"

That took Crystal aback. "You've talked to someone about jazz," she said, sounding faintly pleased.

He eased into the pillows, lips curved in a superior manner. "I have to confess. One of the morning nurses, Donna Jones, says she belts out a few Ella Fitzgerald songs on weekends down in the Quarter. Her husband, Jackson, plays keyboard for her."

"I know Jackson. He's got a mean style."

"Schizophrenic is how his wife describes it."

Crystal laughed. "That's what a lot of music lovers think about jazz, as well as zydeco. Jazz bands rarely practice together. We jam a little and play for our own enjoyment. So, frankly, we don't care." She removed her sax from its case and tested a couple of reeds before she felt satisfied enough to snap the mouthpiece into place. She ran a few experimental notes, then pulled up a chair and sat.

She opened with "Maiden Voyage," giving it a calypso twist. From there she shifted into a couple of classical Blue Note pieces.

Crystal glanced up once. Caleb was staring at her so intensely that had she been less seasoned, she would have faltered. According to the wall clock, it was almost 9 p.m. That explained her churning stomach and jittery nerves. She'd been at the hospital for eleven hours. She ended the tune abruptly and took a deep breath. "Why are you watching me like that? Close your eyes. You should be sleeping."

He'd laced his hands behind his head and looked awfully relaxed for a man who claimed to be in pain. "You have amazing hands, Jardin." The dark green of his gaze never left her fingers. "And your playing's incredible."

"Stop. You're embarrassing me." She wrenched the mouthpiece out and wiped it down before placing it in her case.

"I didn't mean to. People must tell you that all the time."

"In the town that birthed the sound of jazz? Hardly." She shook her head. "I'm adequate. When you get full use of your leg again, you'll have to visit the club where I play. Our group fills in between the big names. It's wonderful. Occasionally I get to be sideman for some of the legends."

"Not sidewoman?" His lips twitched in the barest smile.

Crystal slid her saxophone into its case. Her brow lifted only slightly. "Sidemen got the handle because they back up the chief soloist. I imagine if you ask around in the business, you'll frequently hear that women can't play jazz. Oh, they can be great singers, people will say, but if there's a woman among the all-time great instrumentalists, I have yet to hear her name spoken in elite circles."

"Ain't that a crock? I think you're great."

It was on the tip of Crystal's tongue to point out that a football player wasn't exactly qualified to be a music critic. She swallowed the retort and said, "That's a nice compliment, Tanner. Music seems to mellow you. Have you ever thought about learning to play an instrument?"

"Me? No way. Too complicated."

"Don't be silly. I imagine you have to learn a lot of intricate plays for football. The new methods of teaching music with color-coded note cards and practice videos make it simple, really. I had an instructor for the sax. I taught myself to play clarinet, trumpet and keyboard."

He removed his hands from behind his head and wiggled them in front of his face. "I've looked at those detached keyboards in stores. Nah. Teaching me would be like trying to put socks on a rooster."

Crystal heard his doubt snuff out the underlying eagerness. She gnawed on her bottom lip. Her business with Caleb Tanner had ended the minute she fulfilled Nate's request. She hadn't planned on visiting Tanner again. Now she found herself waffling.

"I have an extra keyboard I'm not using. Let me lend it to you. Your TV's set up for video, I see. I'll throw in a beginner's tape and a basic instruction book."

"I hate to put you out. And what if I break it or something?"

She watched the tug-of-war going on between his words and what glowed in his eyes. He was dying to try, yet afraid to fail. "You won't break it. André's son, Andy-Paul, is only six. I let him bang on it sometimes when I practice."

"If you bring it to me, what'll he use?"

"Believe me, that child does not lack for things to keep him entertained. When the kid was born, André practically bought out FAO Schwarz."

"So André's a young guy? I don't know why, but I thought he'd headed up WDIX-TV for a long time."

"He has daughters old enough to be mothers, as a matter of fact."

"Ah. The boy, Andy-Paul, is from a second marriage?"

"No." Crystal lifted her case. "His oldest, Rachel, is a foster child. Leslie's his stepdaughter. Charlotte, who turned twenty-four in January, is his biologically. I guess you could say Andrew Paul is a…gift."

"Like my kid sisters, I guess," Cale murmured. "Midlife gifts."

Crystal paused at the door. "You really have a sister?"

"Three." He waggled three fingers at her, his eyes sparking with wry humor. "You spoke to all of them at one time or another today. The last was Patsy. She's in the middle, which may account for her having the tenacity of a pit bull." Cale checked his watch. "I can almost guarantee she's pacing the floor and gnashing her teeth, waiting impatiently for me to call and explain who you are."

"Me?" Crystal fumbled the doorknob and almost dropped her shoulder bag. Guiltily she remembered thinking Caleb was leading the women on and handing them a line. She hadn't believed him, even after he'd claimed the last caller was his sister.

"It's my fault they're all in a dither wondering about you. Over the years they've gotten adept at reading what I *don't* say on the phone. And right now, they sense something's wrong, even though I didn't mention the job offer you brought. They wouldn't understand. Playing ball is what I've always done."

"But it's not who you are, Tanner. Surely they realize that."

He rubbed his bad leg, kneading the muscles along his thigh. "Isn't your music who you are?"

"Not at all. Who I am is the sum of a lot of parts."

"That's right. The kid you had me sign the football for told Gibson you're a financial whiz."

"My career is one layer of me, yes. I do other things, too. I'm an advocate for human and animal rights. I'm a collector of local art. And so forth and so on. I sincerely doubt playing football is all you do."

"It's the only thing that counts." He scowled. "Unless you want to throw in being head of the household since my folks died ten years back. If you ask my sisters, I think they'd say football is pretty damned important in their lives."

Crystal shrugged. "Those sounded like grown women I spoke with on the phone, Tanner. You won't convince me they're delighted that someone they care about is risking serious injury every day of every week. If it's loss of prestige that worries you, television personalities are pretty high up the ladder."

Caleb almost told her it all boiled down to money. In Texas there were three standards to gauge wealth. Land and cattle, oil, pro football. Somehow he didn't think Crystal Jardin would understand what it meant to a man's ego to know he'd have to stop running with the big dogs. How could he explain that he'd lavished his sisters with material things—probably more than André Lyon had bought to indulge his only son and for a lot longer? He didn't do it because they asked, but because it gave him pleasure to hear their excited squeals. His way of showing long-distance love. Before he managed to put it into words, a nurse strolled through the door bearing his night medication.

"Crystal, hi," she said. "I told Darla Mae you were playing on our ward for a change. She said I needed my hearing checked, that you only ever entertained in the kids' wing."

"As a rule that's true." Crystal tossed a lazy smile toward the man on the bed. "The boys on the orthopedic ward are big fans of Mr. Tanner's. It turns out he likes jazz. We did a little trade. He signed photos for the boys, and I...well, I promised to teach this man a few scores other than those he puts on the big board. You will keep it under your cap, I hope, Trudy. If a hint of this reached the press, they'd crucify a football star for dabbling in music."

"My lips are sealed," the nurse said. "I remember the flak the media gave that nice Rosey Grier when it got out that he did needlepoint to relax."

"It's hardly the same," snorted Caleb.

Crystal noted the sharp V of his brows and determined that he had his nose out of joint. "Writing poetry has calming tendencies, too," she said mischievously. "When you phone your sister back, ask her which of those hobbies she thinks you should take up." She felt irritation building in him even as she ducked out the door.

"Serves the macho jock right," she grumbled softly as she ran to catch her streetcar. If she hadn't seen the dreamy expression on his face when she coaxed the bluesy notes from her saxophone, she might think football was all he cared about. She'd also picked up on the marshmallow-soft spot he had for his sisters. Whether or not he wanted anyone to see, there were many dimensions to Caleb Tanner. For that reason and that reason alone, Crystal would go back and provide him with instruction on the keyboard.

LYONCREST BLAZED with lights from the first-floor beveled-glass windows, Crystal saw as she turned the corner a block from the streetcar stop. The mansions along Prytania, Lyoncrest included, had been built in the mid-1800s. With porticos, turrets and leaded-glass galore, they had the most elegant architecture in New Orleans. The Garden District had long been considered one of the city's stateliest thoroughfares, which was how the streetcar she rode to and from town came to be named the "silk stocking line."

During the day, tourists jammed the cars as they took self-guided tours designed by the historical society. When she met those visitors on her way to or from work, Crystal often advised them to make a swing through the area after dark, as well. She'd long thought the carriage lamps and indoor chandeliers lent a magical quality to the homes.

Crystal had all but wept over her good fortune the day Margaret invited her to live at Lyoncrest—even though by then she'd come into a trust fund established by her grandmother and enriched by her father's guilt. Had she been inclined to tap that money, money to which she felt no real right or connection, she could have leased a terraced apartment in the French Quarter or one of the many refurbished Creole cottages along Esplanade. But Margie had offered her far more than a roof over her head. Margaret offered roots, a family history, family ties worth more than gold. Lyoncrest pulsed with the love and laughter that had been absent throughout her life. Already Crystal missed Paul's sage advice. And things wouldn't get back to normal until Margaret returned.

Tonight, as Crystal entered the walled complex through the front gate, she realized someone at the house had visitors. A dark-green sedan sat in the circular drive. She didn't recognize the vehicle. Leslie's car and her husband, Michael's, were both parked in the garage. They, and Michael's daughter, Cory, lived at Lyoncrest; a second child was due in February.

As she drew closer to the house, she saw Rachel's car parked beneath a mimosa tree. For no reason Crystal's heart skipped in a butterfly flutter. The big sedan out front looked more in keeping with cars driven by Paul and Margaret's friends. Had someone brought news of Margaret? Perhaps she'd gone with a friend and now they'd returned. Crystal could think of no other reason for such a late gathering of the clan. Due to her workload, Gabrielle had missed so much of her older daughter's childhood that she'd cut back at WDIX and set most evenings aside for Andy-Paul.

Crystal jogged quickly up the twenty concrete steps that led to the veranda. She burst into the house and skidded across the marbled entry, instantly disappointed not to hear Margie's low contralto among the voices drifting from what had once been Paul's private study.

Crystal teetered a moment on the balls of her feet. The meeting obviously included only immediate family. Though everyone had always treated her as if she were a Lyon, technically she was a Jardin.

After debating whether or not to knock, she elected to

skip it and go on up to her room. As she reached the stairs, the study door swung open and Gaby peered out.

"Crystal!" she exclaimed. "What a relief. André's been trying to get you on your cell phone for the last three hours. I don't mind telling you we've all been extremely worried."

Crystal pawed through her bag. Coming up with her phone, she struck her palm to her forehead. "What a dunce. I shut the darned thing off after I spoke to Nate earlier. What's up? It's about Margaret, isn't it?" Her voice quavered.

"Indirectly, yes." Gaby motioned her toward the room. "André decided to call in a private investigator for our own peace of mind. We want input from the family. Sharlee couldn't come from California. She confided today that she's pregnant, which surprised us all. But her pregnancy's off to a rocky start. Come on, everyone else is inside."

"I hope Charlotte's going to be okay. Pregnant. Wow! But…has someone heard from Margaret?" Crystal's heart tripped in fear. Her hands felt clammy.

"No. That's why André enlisted the services of the private investigator." Gaby linked arms with Crystal and walked her into the study.

André stopped talking to a gray-haired man when they entered. His eyes signaled relief. "Crystal. We were concerned. I feared another disappearance."

Crystal wedged herself next to Leslie on a flowered tapestry settee. Leslie's husband, Michael, perched in a nearby chair. "I apologize," Crystal murmured. "Modern conveniences only work if you follow proper procedures. I unintentionally turned off my cell phone."

"I'm glad that's all it was. Crystal, this is David Patton." André touched the older man's sleeve. "Dave,

Crystal Jardin. As I explained, she's quite close to Mama. As well as being my second cousin, Crystal is the station's business manager and Mama's personal financial adviser.''

David studied the new arrival with interest. "I've told everyone else that I'll be conducting individual interviews with Margie's family and friends. This is a brainstorming session. I've asked the others to relay what happened during their last contact with Margaret. So far, everyone's cooperated and allowed me to tape our conversations. Do you have any objection to being taped, Ms. Jardin?"

"Uh, no." Now Crystal wished she'd informed André about the two withdrawals from Margaret's account. She certainly didn't want it to appear as if she'd withheld pertinent information.

"You seem hesitant…may I call you Crystal?"

"Yes, please do. If I'm hesitant, Mr. Patton, it's because Margaret is a very private person. Especially when it comes to money. She began an investment portfolio before it was fashionable for women to involve themselves in finance. I want her home as much as anyone here, but I have reservations about invading her privacy."

The investigator deferred to André, who looked at Crystal from troubled eyes. "It's all right, Crystal, I understand," he said. "That's the main reason I've held off notifying the police. I explained to David earlier that, on the one hand, Mama's independent and self-reliant. On the other hand, she is committed to the family. Gabrielle and I agree it isn't like her to be gone so long without contact. I've hired Dave to do some discreet checking. I can't sit idly by and do nothing." He rubbed both hands down his cheeks and over his jaw—a clear sign of his frustration.

Crystal inclined her head. "As you wish, André."

Beside Crystal, thirty-year-old Leslie Lyon McKay stirred. "I still think we should notify the police. Grand-mère has a standing weekly appointment at her hair salon. She's missed two. The owner called again yesterday to see if she was sick. He said she always remembers to cancel if she can't make it."

"What about other appointments?" Patton asked.

Rachel Fontaine, André and Gaby's foster daughter, rose and poured herself another glass of water from the Waterford pitcher on a tray. "We hadn't set a firm date, but Margaret planned to go with me this week to pick out wallpaper for my new home office." Rachel turned toward Mr. Patton. "I know it sounds vague. But if you knew her...well, a promise is sacred."

Gabrielle clasped André's hand while nodding vigorously. "I've known Margaret longer than I've known André. We've worked together and lived in the same house for over thirty years. Margie places a high priority on keeping her word."

The investigator pressed a button on the recorder and stopped the tape. Popping it out, he turned it over. "I don't think there's any doubt that you all agree this is unusual behavior for Margaret Lyon. Since there's been no request for a ransom and the inquiries I've made through a contact at the police department haven't turned up any elderly Jane Does, I believe it's safe to assume she hasn't been a victim of foul play. Grief over the recent loss of her husband could well be a factor in her disappearance. She may have gone alone. Or she may have enlisted the aid of a single confidant." As he hit the play button to roll the tape again, he zeroed in on Crystal. "Where were you all afternoon and evening?" he asked with seeming casualness. "Not at work, which I gather is irregular."

Crystal clasped her hands in her lap and leaned forward. "I was on a mission for André. Michael knew about it, too."

Michael frowned, then concurred. "Through her volunteer work at the hospital, Crystal met Caleb Tanner. Nate Fraser wants to hire him as a sportscaster."

André hurriedly cautioned, "That information doesn't leave this room, understand? The Sinners have cut Tanner from the roster, but they haven't made an official announcement. Negotiations are dicey. Crystal's acting as our spokesperson."

"And these negotiations took you all day and all evening?" David Patton asked.

Crystal shrugged. "Not really. I explained that to André earlier. A child I visit at the hospital asked me to go with him to his first physical-therapy session."

André let go of Gaby's hand and unbuttoned his suit jacket. "I phoned Skipper's ward when you didn't show up for dinner, Crystal. He said you'd left some time before I called. We got worried when you didn't come home. David's suspicious by nature. Just tell him where you were."

Crystal shied from the curious stares. "Tanner likes jazz," she explained grudgingly. "You'll have to take my word for it that I spent the evening playing the sax for him. His phone calls are screened by the switchboard. If you're not on his list, they won't put you through to him."

Rachel tossed an ice cube in Crystal's lap. "A private audience? Since I started working with Skipper West, I've often heard your views on contact sports. What gives? Is Caleb Tanner as great-looking as he is on TV?"

Crystal glared at her friend. Rachel knew about her ill-fated engagement and didn't usually tease her about men.

David Patton cleared his throat, prompting André to

restore order. "We're straying off the subject. I don't know what you want from Crystal, Dave, but I assure you that no one in the family is hiding Mama. The last anyone knows, her driver left her at the cemetery. She said she needed time alone. When he went back at the appointed hour, she was gone. If that's all the questions you have for us, it is getting late," he said, pulling back a sleeve to check his watch.

Patton capped his pen. "The others can go, but if it's okay, André, I'd like a word with Ms. Jardin. And I'd appreciate your staying."

André and Gabrielle exchanged glances. "I have no objection," he said. "Is that all right with you, Crystal?"

"Yes." She rose and bade goodbye to Rachel, who said she had to get home. Leslie and Mike hugged everyone before retiring to their suite. The goodbyes only took a moment. When Dave Patton crossed the room and closed the door behind the last person out, André again joined Crystal.

"It's obvious you think Crystal knows something, David. I thought we agreed to keep this investigation low-key. I won't have you harassing relatives or employees. Crystal's both."

"This isn't harassment, André," the P.I. said. "Just part of a thorough investigation." He paused. "It's virtually impossible to disappear without leaving any trail. André, you said you'd checked your mother's credit-card companies and there's been no use reported. That leaves the possibility of a money trail, but you claim not to have access to her bank records. I'd just like to ask Ms. Jardin to take a look at them."

André loosened his tie and placed his hands on his hips. He was still lean and trim for a man nearing sixty. He'd been silver at the temples for some time. Crystal thought that since his father's death and now his mother's disappearance, he'd developed deeper creases around his mouth. No one could say of André Lyon that he didn't bend over backward trying to be fair. Crystal could tell he was reluctant to force her into a discussion of Margaret's financial affairs.

"It's all right, André," she said softly. "Since Monday I've been in a quandary about whether or not to override Margaret's insistence on privacy and bring this to your attention."

"What?" André gripped her arms. "Do you know where Mama is?"

"No. Oh, no. If I knew that, I'd have said so. This has to do with two withdrawals from her bank account. Not large. Three thousand last week and again this week. André, I'm sorry, but she's drilled into me that what she has and spends is no one's business but hers."

The investigator rubbed his palms together expectantly. "I guessed you knew something, Crystal. Don't ever play poker, my dear. Now we're getting someplace. We only need to backtrack on the transaction to find out where Margaret withdrew the money. That should lead us straight to her."

"It's not that easy, Mr. Patton," Crystal snapped. "Do you think I didn't already run a trace? I know how to follow a money trail. Margaret, or someone acting on her behalf, wiped the transaction trail clean."

"What?" Patton and André said together.

"My sentiments exactly." Crystal laced her hands together and began to pace the room. "Sharp as she is, Margaret isn't a computer hacker. She must have someone at the bank helping her. John, the bank president, was one of Paul's best friends. She might have persuaded him to help her hide away for a time."

"Why would she need to hide?" André asked.

"She felt smothered by all our concern," Crystal told him. "I know that for a fact."

"Didn't it occur to you that someone might be bleeding her?" Patton interjected.

Crystal was beginning to feel really irritated with the man. "Most embezzlers or con men strip a large account and run. They don't stick around and tap it for piddling amounts over time."

"Three thousand is piddling?"

"To Margaret, yes. I've gone over it and over it in my head." Crystal turned to André again. "She's occasionally talked about chronicling the progress of Lyon Broadcasting. Maybe she's decided she needs solitude to work on it."

André seemed to brighten. "She could be doing that, David."

"Then you want to call off my investigation?"

"Maybe we should put it on hold."

Crystal took André's arm. "I'm not willing to risk a wrong guess. Now that you know about the money takes a load off me. What'll it hurt to let Mr. Patton investigate? If he finds her and Margie wants to be left alone, at least we'll be able to stop worrying."

André nodded. "You're right, Crystal. David, you're back on the case. But no badgering family. We're all in my mother's corner." The men walked out chatting amiably.

Crystal climbed the winding stairs that led to her suite, feeling freer than she'd felt since Margaret had vanished. Finally they were taking action—doing something constructive.

Surely Margaret would be found soon.

CHAPTER SIX

THE OFFICE DOOR opened and Crystal spun away from her computerized spreadsheet to see who'd walked in without knocking.

Nate Fraser stood just inside the door, a big grin on his face, a vase of roses in his hands. "You did it, Crystal. Cale called me at home last night and we firmed up the details of his work agreement."

"If it's as good for WDIX-TV as you, André and Michael seem to think, then I'm happy to have helped." The vase of flowers he put on her desk made her feel awkward. Roses were at a premium this time of year; not only that, it just wasn't necessary to give her a gift.

"They're beautiful, Nate," she said, cupping one of the deep-pink buds. "But you shouldn't have strained your budget this way."

"They're not from me."

"André, then? I should have guessed. He's forever buying Gabrielle flowers. He really is thoughtful. I'll call and thank him." She reached for the phone.

Nate stopped her hand with his. "They're from Cale. He asked me to deliver them to you."

"Tanner? Wh-why?" That threw a whole different slant on the gift.

Nate pushed a chair close to her desk and sat, tilting back on two legs. "I won't say it's to butter you up. I did tell him, though, that I'd have to ask you to find extra money in the budget to cover his insurance.''

"But André included the standard insurance package in his letter of intent. The same amount you budgeted for Jerry Davis.''

"Tanner needs more.''

"Our plan is generous. Why would he need more?''

"To pay premiums on three whole-life policies he already has. He's been paying on them for ten years. It's a fair request, Crystal.''

"Three?'' She pulled a calculator toward her. "How much are we talking?''

Nate lowered his chair to the floor, leaned his arms on his knees and mumbled a figure into the rose leaves. "That's annually,'' he added.

The silence in the room stretched like a rubber band. Then Crystal began drumming her fingers on her desk. "Tell me you're joking. We have clerks here who don't make that much. Why does he need all that insurance?''

"Cale has kid sisters. He's their guardian. With the Sinners, his agent arranged to have the club pay the yearly premium off the top of his salary.''

"Well, we aren't the Sinners. Ten years ago his agent should have recommended Tanner buy the policies outright. They'd have cost a heck of a lot less.''

"That's irrelevant, Crystal, because it's not what he did. So I want you to find the money. This morning the Sinners' owner called a press conference to announce they've hired Steve Young's backup to replace Cale. I saw a gleam in the eye of my counterpart at WEZY-TV. We already outshine them in the sports ratings. I know the sneaky bastard's going to make Tanner an offer.''

"Hmm. Since WEZY sold to a conglomerate, they have

money to burn. Of course an ethical man wouldn't look at their offer.''

''You insinuating Caleb isn't ethical?''

She wound the end of her braid around one finger. ''I shouldn't jump to conclusions based on how I feel about what the man does—did for a living.''

''Damn!'' Nate said, rearing out of his chair. ''Pro ball players get a bad rap because of a few. I resent your accusation, not just for myself but for every guy who plays because he loves the game.''

Crystal let him finish his tirade. He hadn't changed her mind. Pro players had a lot of influence with kids, and a large percentage weren't fit role models. To say nothing of the maiming and mutilating that occurred. ''I'll reserve judgment on Tanner until I see how he works out here.''

''That's *my* job. I evaluate his performance.''

''How he handles his expense account falls under my jurisdiction.''

''Dammit, Crystal. If you nickel and dime the guy to death, he'll quit before he even starts.'' Nate pounded a fist on her desk.

''Then keep him in line, Nate.''

''I will.'' He stood, hitched up his pants and stalked to the door. ''So you'll transfer money into my budget to cover Tanner's insurance?''

Crystal tucked a pencil through her braid. ''If that's what André wants to do. He's the one who'll have to explain the allotment in the upcoming board meeting.''

''Will you let Cale know it's all arranged when you see him today?''

''Today?'' Crystal glanced up in surprise.

''I forgot to ask him to put me on his authorized telephone list. But he said you promised to take him a keyboard. At least, I think that's what he said." Nate scratched his chin. "Maybe I misunderstood."

"No, you're right. I'll go by the house after work and grab the extra one I have. I think Tanner's bored with nothing to do except read and watch TV. It's odd, but he doesn't have a lot of visitors."

"Not so odd. Ball players are funny that way. When someone gets axed, it's hard to know what to say to the dude. Remember I told you a lot of players are superstitious? They're afraid if they hang out with a has-been it'll rub off."

"If that isn't the stupidest thing I've ever heard! These are grown men you're talking about, Nate."

He shrugged. "It's how things are. Listen, Crystal. We can't afford to let Tanner get so bored he decides to hightail it back to his family in Texas. You're at the hospital a lot. Can you swing by every so often and cheer him up?"

"Do I look like a cheerleader?" Even as she denied wanting to visit Tanner, she fussed with the flowers.

"Caleb's got a soft spot for you, Crystal. Why else would he buy you roses?"

"As a bribe, Nathan," she shot back. "For extra insurance premiums. Are you sure you want me going by to see him? I may suggest overhauling his finances."

Nate winked. "My wife did that when I quit the pros. Since Tanner doesn't have a wife, you might be the next best thing."

"Get out of here," she said, but the door was already closing on Nate's heels.

For the next two hours she juggled figures, nipped and tucked various floating funds, always with an eye to protecting André in the board meeting. André's uncle Charles had sent his son Raymond to college to be an accountant for the sole purpose of heckling Paul, Margaret and André in budgetary matters.

Crystal had learned after a few such meetings that Charles's branch of the family questioned every identifiable increase in department budgets. At approximately the same time, she'd discovered that Ray goofed up every project he got his hands on, whether accidentally or on purpose. It became a challenge to find him safe projects— which was how he'd ended up taking care of delinquent accounts. After André made her the business manager, it became her mission to outwit Ray and keep the people she loved off the hot seat.

Crystal thought she'd managed quite well. These days, Charles sat idly by and let Ray fuel the cannons with which to blast André at every meeting of the principals. But because Ray was lax about keeping up with new software, she'd been able to dazzle him with graphs, pie and flow charts. Rather than admit he didn't understand, he always latched on to the bottom-line figures.

Profit was really all that interested Charles and his clan. They wanted more to line their pockets and less put back into the running of Lyon Broadcasting. Crystal often wondered if her great-grandfather would have made his will so ironclad if he'd been given a glimpse into the future. Then again, maybe he wouldn't have changed a word. The will tying the business to the Lyon brothers and their offspring in perpetuity seemed to be the only thread that kept the family together. Fighting and arguing, but together. Most other family-owned broadcasting companies had sold out to conglomerates. Over the years doomsayers had predicted that Lyon Broadcasting wouldn't survive. But it had, despite some lean years in the seventies and eighties. Few disputed that the main reason for the company's success was the sheer determination of Margaret Lyon.

Crystal hoped Margaret was writing her memoirs. So many dark shadows obscured the family history. There were a number of situations and innuendos Crystal would love to have explained. Or maybe she simply had an overactive imagination; she was prone to do that when it came to puzzles or mysteries, especially those concerning family. Call it the only-child syndrome. Lonely kids tended to believe they'd sprung from mysterious backgrounds.

Crystal propped her chin in her hand and stared dreamily at the vase of roses. How many times had she caught herself smiling at them, touching them? She wasn't a woman who, as a rule, inspired flower-giving in men. Once, in high school, a date had brought her a corsage. It had wilted before the end of the dance, as had the budding romance. The story of her life, she mused, standing to sniff the nearest bud.

A light knock sounded on her door. April burst into the room carrying a stack of invoices. Close behind her waltzed a smirking Ray Lyon. Both ground to a halt, their attention on the massive bouquet.

"Awe-some," drawled April. "Is it your birthday?"

Embarrassed to be caught with her nose buried in the flowers, Crystal sat back and shook her head.

Ray strode straight to the desk and rooted around in the foliage, apparently looking for a card. "She must have bought them herself. In the five years she's worked here, she's never been on a date. How about it, cousin? Did these come from a man?"

"Yes, as a matter of fact." Crystal said it more for shock value than anything else. She had no intention of expanding. "I'm working on a report for next week's board meeting. Could we get to the reason for your visit, please?"

April set the pile of invoices in the center of Crystal's

desk. "Raymond asked me to cut checks for these. They're for contract labor. I need authorization."

"I authorized the work," he said, his face twisted in anger. "I got tired of waiting for maintenance to build bookshelves in my office. One of my mother's relatives is a carpenter. He's between jobs, so I had him do the work."

Crystal thumbed through the bills. Ray had had more than bookcases built. There were charges for countertops, a sink and cabinetry. Unless she missed her guess, Ray had ordered himself a wet bar. Well-stocked bars could be found in many of the executive offices in New Orleans. Southern gentlemen had been raised to believe business could only be properly transacted over a glass or two of bourbon. That Ray was neither a gentleman nor an executive wasn't the point. He thought the trappings made him equal to André. A delusion, to be sure.

"Pay them," Crystal told April. "Code it capital outlay." She hated seeing April's crestfallen expression and hated even more watching Ray puff up like a rooster about to crow. But it was exactly the kind of leverage André would find useful at the board meeting if Charles balked at what it cost to acquire Caleb Tanner. She doubted Raymond's daddy knew his son was taking advantage of the situation quite so blatantly. Just to ensure that he wouldn't leave feeling too cocky, Crystal stopped him before he reached the door. "April, you can go. Ray, stay a minute, please." When April shut the door, Crystal said, "As you know, Raymond, capital outlay requires preapproval by the board. If you have other carpentry projects in mind, you'll need to take that route."

The man deflated instantly. "Will anyone ask about this expenditure at Monday's meeting?"

Crystal rocked back in her chair. "I suppose that depends on how closely your father dissects this report. It's a simple matter for the principals to read and approve the entire budgetary package. Margaret's never been the one who asks to go over the financial report line by line."

"And she won't even be there this time." Ray's lungs filled again.

Crystal snapped forward in her chair. "What did you say?"

Ray fingered the knot in his tie. "Well, she, ah, Aunt Margaret hasn't shown up yet, has she? And this is Thursday. I just figured… Oh, hell, I don't have to explain anything to you. The only stock André has legally is the shares Margaret's dad gave Grandpa to hold in trust. If anything happens to the old girl, Paul's stock will go to the rightful heirs. And we all know that's my daddy." With that, Ray departed and slammed the door.

Crystal hadn't realized she'd been holding her breath until it escaped her lungs in a whoosh. She gripped the edges of her desk to keep her hands from trembling, then shoved back from it with a sigh. Why did she let Ray's convoluted accusations get to her? André had the look of a Lyon about him far more than Ray did.

Shaking off the pall that dealing with Raymond always left, Crystal finished rechecking the remaining departmental expenditures. Before she turned off her computer for the day, she printed out the forms April needed to make the quarterly IRS payments. Crystal took the forms next door, only to discover that everyone in the bookkeeping department had gone. She left the stack on April's desk with a note, then decided she'd better leave, too, if she hoped to run by the house and get to the hospital at a decent hour. Tomorrow night and the next, she played with the band. So she had to drop off the keyboard tonight, or Tanner wouldn't get it until next week.

She wanted to look in on Skipper, anyway. He'd worked hard in therapy yesterday. Someone should check to be sure he hadn't suffered any ill effects. With his foster mother, Sandy, so busy at home, that meant her, Crystal.

Back in her office Crystal considered whether or not to take the roses home. Leaving them here meant her co-workers would probe into who'd sent them. But if she took them home, Gaby would give her the third degree. And when Gaby sank her teeth into something, she didn't let go until she had answers. Hauling in one last lungful of the sweet fragrance, Crystal walked out of the office and closed and locked her door.

SKIP AND HIS FRIENDS were eating when Crystal popped into their room. Or rather, not eating, but complaining about what they'd been served.

"What is that?" Crystal asked, bending over Skip's tray.

"Hash," Randy said glumly.

"I don't know why they don't ever have tacos," Pablo said.

"Or hot dogs," Barry groused.

"*Grillades.*" Felipe said softly, referring to the roux-based beef-and-tomato mixture.

Crystal grinned at him. She and Felipe shared a love of native Louisiana grub. Almost every parish had a favorite recipe for roux, the gravy base for which Louisiana cooks were famous. She asked Felipe in French if he didn't like hot dogs.

"*Mais oui!*" He grinned, a smile that lit up his thin face.

"Tell you what, guys. Monday, I'll bring you dinner. Foot-long hot dogs. Red beans and rice, and potato chips.

Sodas, too, so give me a list of what you like.'' She repeated this in French for Felipe, then pulled a pad and pencil from her purse. It pleased her that even Moses Brown gave his request.

''Hey, why don't you guys teach Felipe English? It wouldn't hurt you to learn French, either. It could come in handy out in the workplace when you grow up and get jobs. I'm sure your tutor will agree''

Skip screwed up his face. He turned to Randy in the next bed. ''I haven't heard any football players speaking French. Have you, Randy?''

''Nope. Some of the baseball players talk funny, but I don't think it's French.''

Crystal threw up her hands. ''You might want to prepare for something other than playing ball. As a backup,'' she said, because she saw they didn't get it. ''Even your friend Tanner had the foresight to get a college degree in communications.''

''What for?'' Skip asked.

Feeling her frustration mount, Crystal stowed the boys' soda requests in her bag. ''Did you hear them announce on TV that Tanner's going to be doing sportscasts at WDIX?'' When it was obvious she had their attention, Crystal added, ''His college background gave him experience in public speaking and talking in front of a camera—things that are important for his new job.''

''I don't see why he needs to work,'' Randy said in a puzzled tone. ''Like, the guy has to have the bucks to take it easy for the rest of his life.''

As if he'd turned that statement over in his head, Skipper piped up. ''Doing nothing gets awful boring. Maybe I'll think about learning something else, too.''

Yes! Crystal thought if she talked long enough she might get through to them. Eventually. Reminding herself not to belabor her point, she changed the subject. "You guys eat. I brought a keyboard with me tonight." She pulled it out of its case, plugged it in and played a few chords. As she let a little jazz-rock unfold, she wondered if Tanner could hear her in his room.

After the last note had died away, Skipper said, "That's cool! I wish I could play an instrument. I think I'd like guitar, though."

"Naw, man. Drums," exclaimed Randy. As if to illustrate his desire, he beat the tips of his fingers on his table, first shoving aside his plate of food.

"Very good, Randy." Crystal gave him a thumbs-up. "You've got the rhythm. All great drummers hear the beat in their heads. Maybe when you get home, your mom will buy you a starter set of drums."

He clammed up.

"What is it, Randy?" Crystal returned the keyboard to its zippered pouch.

"My mom says if we can't eat it or wear it, we got no use for it."

Skipper pushed his own plate aside. "Yeah. I'll never have a guitar, either. That's not something they budget for foster kids. We're lucky to get shoes and socks."

Crystal never ceased to be amazed at the lessons she learned from these kids. Her life might have lacked love, but she had the best food, clothing and other material goods that money could buy. These boys humbled her.

"If you guys want to fool around with some instruments while you're stuck here, I'll see what I can do about collecting some things. I won't promise drums, Randy, but maybe a drum pad where you could learn the sticks."

"Cool," the boys chorused.

She made mental note to call a man she knew who owned a pawnshop. Musicians frequently blew into town wanting to play with the big names who drifted through the New Orleans nightclubs. Many had to hock their instruments to get back home to Cedar Flats or wherever they lived.

"Are you leaving so soon?" Skip asked her.

"I have another stop to make before I go home. I really dropped by to see how you were after your hour in PT yesterday."

"I'm okay. I'll be better when I can start working my legs, too."

Crystal straightened his covers. "I know you're in a rush, kiddo. But getting your muscles back isn't something you can hurry."

His eyes filled with tears. Determinedly he brushed them away. "Ms. Fontaine came by today. I heard her tell Nurse Pam I had to be walking or I couldn't go back to Sandy's. Her house ain't set up for wheelchairs."

"They're not releasing you right away, are they?" Crystal's heart beat hard as she asked the question.

"I dunno. What happens if they do, Crystal? I don't wanna go someplace new."

Crystal patted his bony knee. "Relax, Skip. Worry never helped anyone get well faster."

"Yeah." He struggled with a smile. "Will you call Ms. Fontaine and find out what she meant?"

"I'll call, but I doubt she'll tell me anything. I'm not connected to you except by friendship, Skipper. Where were they talking that you could hear, anyway? Maybe you only heard part of their conversation."

"They were outside the door. Yeah, maybe I missed something..."

She gathered up her gear. "I play with the band tomorrow night and Saturday. I'll try to come by on Sunday. You relax, okay?"

He nodded, but without his usual enthusiasm.

Crystal stopped at the nurses' station, hoping to get a word with Pam, only to be told she'd gone off shift and wouldn't be on again until Monday.

As she trudged down the hall toward Tanner's room, Skip's plight weighed heavy on her mind. She'd grown up without hugs and without much positive reinforcement. Her guardian had been a stern undemonstrative woman. But Crystal hadn't been shuffled from stranger to stranger. When she went home from her skateboarding accident, she'd returned to her own room filled with her own stuff. She hadn't been in a wheelchair, but she'd had to deal with crutches. True, Aunt Anita had left her to her own devices. Still, nobody had been threatening to turn her out. Poor Skipper. Darn. She'd talk to Rachel—see what, if anything, could be done.

Crystal reached Caleb's room and knocked. This time he called out immediately. "Come in."

"Hi." She marched right up to his bed. "Those were beautiful roses you had Nate deliver. Of course I recognized it as a bribe," she teased.

"They weren't a bribe," he murmured. "More like an apology." Cale hastily folded the newspaper he'd been poring over. He set it and his pencil aside. "I owe a lot of apologies. For being such an SOB lately."

"Whatever they're for, they're nice. Doing the crossword puzzle?" she asked.

He shook his head. "Huh-uh. Circling possible apartments. The place I have costs an arm and a leg. Mostly team members live there. It'll work out better for everyone if I move." He shrugged. "I'd like to be in a new place by the beginning of October."

"No problem breaking your lease?" Crystal asked.

"Lease? I don't know. Leland set it up."

"You might want to call the landlord. Sometimes it's cheaper to stay until the lease runs out. Especially since you'll have to pay for first and last months' rent when you move into a new place. Many require a cleaning deposit, too."

"They do?" He frowned as if she'd told him the world wasn't round. "Leland took care of stuff like that."

Crystal laughed. "You've never handled a rental agreement yourself? I guess you own a house in Texas, huh?"

"Yes. No." At her arched eyebrow, he shifted uncomfortably. "I inherited my parents' farm. My aunt and uncle worked it for nine years and made it a home for my sisters. Last year things were great for me, so I signed the homeplace over to them. I've got my apartment in town, but like I said, Leland took care of things. Besides, I haven't spent much time there. And when I traveled with the team, the manager booked us into hotels. I guess I'm pretty green at this."

"At least there's no rush." She patted the end of his bed. "I see the good news is that you got rid of all that traction equipment. Congratulations, Tanner."

He rubbed idly at his injured leg. "That's the good news and the bad. My doctor is releasing me Monday. He said I can do my therapy on an outpatient basis. If you ask me, I think he's afraid the team will jerk my medical insurance."

"That's crazy. You can't even bear weight on that leg. How does the doctor expect you to get back and forth to therapy?"

"Does he care?"

Crystal was still thinking about his finding a place to live. "Monday, wow! You'll have to rent a place right away, since you want to move so soon. They'll need time to check your references and run a credit check. Feel free to give them Nate's name and number. He'll vouch for you.''

''References? Credit check? To *rent?* I'm not buying a damned apartment building!''

''Renting's more difficult because so many landlords get stiffed. A lot of people drift into port towns. They rent a place, then can't find jobs. Plus, some of them walk off with everything but the kitchen sink. Sometimes even that. City housing authorities instituted tougher standards a few years ago.'' She saw Tanner looking distressed and she conjured up a reassuring smile. ''None of this affects you. Your accountant will give a prospective landlord your net worth, and they'll roll out the red carpet.''

He wore such a dismayed expression Crystal's words tapered off. ''What's the matter, Tanner?''

''You just gave me a peek at what my life might've been like if the folks hadn't owned the farm. Except for once a year when they sold the melon crop, they hardly had two dimes to rub together. But they were respected in town. No one had to vouch for them. Banks, stores, they all extended credit on the basis of a few hundred acres of soil that my great-great-great-granddaddy probably stole from the Indians.''

''Well, cash rules. As I said, you're sitting pretty, Tanner.''

''Yeah. Sure.'' He was oh-so-tempted to tell her the truth about his mounting bills and ailing bank account. However, he didn't want his sisters finding out until after Patsy's wedding. By next season he'd be back on top of his game and this temporary cash-flow problem would be history, anyway.

Lost in thought, Caleb didn't realize for a minute that Crystal had skipped to a new subject.

''I brought you a keyboard and the teaching manuals

and videos, like we discussed. You probably won't want this now that you're going home.''

"Nate gave me two weeks to get myself mobile. Until I start work, I'll be rattling around an apartment when I'm not in therapy. Assuming I *find* an apartment. Maybe you don't want to trust an expensive instrument to a guy whose life is kind of iffy.''

What surprised Crystal was that Tanner hadn't mentioned any desire to get back to the high life. Dates. Rounds of parties. "I explained yesterday that this keyboard mostly gathers dust,'' she said. "Since you'll be working at the station, I'll know where to find you if I need it back. The question is, do you want to have to deal with taking it home from the hospital and then having to pack it up again to move?''

He ran a hand over the vinyl case she'd parked next to him on the bed. "All I have is a duffel bag with an extra pair of sweats and my shaving gear, and this. A cabdriver ought to be able to handle that, don't you think? And my wheelchair of course.''

"You're leaving here by cab?''

"Sure. It's a cinch I won't be driving for a while. Especially not a stick shift.''

Crystal blinked as she absorbed the latest information. "What about family or friends coming to pick you up?'' She didn't specify women friends, but she thought it.

Caleb seemed slightly abashed. "I don't have family here.'' He rasped the knuckle of his thumb over a lightly stubbled jaw. "There are a couple of guys on the team who'll help me move if the team's not out of town. Or Leland. 'Cept he's got other responsibilities now.''

Crystal shifted from foot to foot. Nate had more or less charged her with taking care of Tanner. The immediate future he'd just outlined sure made it sound as if he needed looking after. She swallowed to alleviate a dry throat, then plunged in. "Look, Tanner, I usually ride the streetcar, but I have access to cars. Do you know what time Monday they're springing you? Well, whatever time—it won't be a problem. I'll park in the loading zone and wait for an orderly to bring you out, then give you a lift home."

"I couldn't put you out like that."

She waved off his objections. "Really, it's no trouble. You're on the WDIX team now. We look after our own."

"I'll only be on the team a year," he reminded her gently, his gaze roaming over her face, looking for... Caleb wasn't sure exactly what. Resentment? Regrets? Seeing nothing but a friendly offer, he couldn't explain a sudden compelling urge to let his thanks take the form of a kiss.

Which was downright dumb. She'd probably deck him, and rightfully so. He wasn't a guy who hugged and kissed people randomly or on a whim. Yet Caleb's hands found Crystal's face and bracketed her soft cheeks, seemingly of their own accord. He snatched them back the second she shied away. "Thanks," he muttered gruffly. "You ever need a favor after I get on my feet, I'm your man." He clenched his hands on the spread covering his legs.

Crystal's hand flew to her cheek. For a minute there she'd been sure he was going to do more than touch her face. His eyes had gone from the color of grass to dark moss, and he'd leaned forward with his lips parted—as if he intended to kiss her. *Why would he? It hadn't been that big a favor.* Caleb Tanner was probably a demonstrative person. Just because she thought she still felt the shiver of his fingers on her skin didn't mean a thing. His touch had taken her by surprise, that was all.

If she commented on it, however, he'd think she was

some kind of sexually deprived nutcase. So Crystal did what she always did when she felt out of her depth; she submerged herself in music. "I'll just show you the particulars of the electronic keyboard before I go." She zipped open the case and took out the thin keyboard. Standing well back from the bed, she showed him how to connect the cord. "Where do you plug in your razor?" She bent to check the railing along the bed where she thought she'd remembered seeing an electrical socket.

"Other side," he growled after her thick braid slid over her shoulder and tickled his bare chest.

She glanced up and saw where he pointed. He'd have to do contortions to reach it. Either that or she had to lean across him or balance the keyboard and trek awkwardly around the foot of his bed. Her mouth went dry at the eye-level expanse of tanned flesh between her and the outlet. Crystal had never considered herself a prude when it came to men and sex. After she'd become engaged to Ben Parker—and until she learned how easily he'd cheated on her—they had enjoyed a full normal relationship.

Ignoring the bronzed muscles and her cottony mouth, Crystal extended her arm across Cale's prone body and jabbed repeatedly in the vicinity he'd indicated. She hadn't taken into consideration that the angle would force her bare arm into contact with the dusting of hair on his chest. Goose bumps peppered her arm from her wrist all the way to her sleeveless top. She only bungled her mission further. "I'm sorry," she croaked.

But if she thought she was alone in her discomfort, she was mistaken. Caleb tried to suck in his stomach to avoid contact. The casual touch of her arm against his belly sent a river of blood racing to his groin. The result made it damned difficult to think, let alone send messages to specific parts of his anatomy. And if feeling the brush of her underarm on his midsection wasn't torture enough, the sweet scent of her perfume curling into his face nearly did him in.

Teeth clamped tight to hold in both his stomach and a curse, Caleb grabbed the cord in one hand and half turned to shove it into the outlet, grunting at a twinge of pain. With the other hand, he gripped Crystal's elbow and stood her upright again. "There," he announced, releasing his breath. "Electricity."

Crystal hauled in an unsteady lungful of air. Tanner had that right. More than the requisite hundred and ten volts, she'd say. It was totally absurd that she'd get so sweaty-palmed over a football jock. Though she shouldn't be surprised by Tanner's reaction to a woman's touch. He probably thought she should be flattered.

Fortunately for both of them, Crystal had as many years' experience hiding her feelings and reactions as Tanner did perfecting his machismo.

Calmly, and as controlled as if she was conducting a seminar in accounting, she popped in the training video and proceeded to cover the essential functions of the keyboard. Then she stood and headed for the door. "The way that's plugged in is awkward. Next time I come, I'll bring an extension cord."

He gave her a wave indicating he'd heard, even though she was already out the door.

Minutes later as she waited outside the hospital for the streetcar, her speeding heart and shaking knees presented a different, softer side of Crystal Jardin.

As for Caleb, he didn't resume breathing until she'd left the room. Nor did he learn one damned thing about operating the keyboard. All he could say was that it was just as well she'd been immune—even though it had pricked his ego. "Shape up and fly right, Tanner," he muttered. "You need a friend a whole lot more than you need a romantic entanglement."

CHAPTER SEVEN

FIRST THING EVERY DAY Crystal checked Margaret's private bank account. The tightness in her chest eased the minute she saw the status hadn't changed. She reported her findings to André, even though he'd said she needn't unless there was another deduction.

By Friday noon Crystal had her portion of the board packet copied and ready to distribute to board members. She'd optimistically made one for Margaret and stacked it with André and Gaby's printouts.

Crystal's first stop was Ray's office across the hall. She tapped on his door and went in before he responded. It didn't come as any surprise to see him hurriedly pressing computer keys to back out of whatever program he was in. When she neared his desk, it looked to her as if Ray had been working on a legitimate spreadsheet rather than reading one of his reputed porno sites. Perhaps he was making headway on past-due accounts. Would wonders never cease?

"Last time I checked, the sign on my door was clearly marked private," Ray snarled as he struck a series of keys to blank his screen.

"According to the handbook, Lyon promotes an open-door policy."

"Really? Then why has yours been shut tight the last few days?"

"So I could prepare the board report with fewer interruptions. Here's your copy. I'm on my way to lunch, but I'll be back in an hour to deal with any questions or changes." She dropped the pages on his desk and started to walk away.

"Aren't you leaving copies for my father and Alain?"

"I'm having lunch at Chez Charles. I'll deliver theirs."

Ray half rose from his desk. "You never go to Chez Charles. What gives?"

"It's none of your business, but I'm meeting Rachel. She chose the spot, not I."

"Aunt Margaret poisoned your mind against our branch of the family tree. It's a miracle she missed tainting Rachel." He settled back and thumbed quickly through the report. "This is a welcome surprise," he said abruptly. "Profits are up by a bunch."

"Twenty-seven percent. Expansion of the TV and recording studios played a part. Changes your family bitterly opposed, if you'll recall. Adding a popular late-night talk show and winning most of the Louisiana Associated Press programming awards hasn't hurt our drive for sponsors, either."

"We should've taken first place in the Best Sportscast category. Maybe we will now that Nate's had the good sense to snap up Cale Tanner."

Crystal barely hid her surprise. "I'm glad you feel like that. I guess you won't argue about the money we had to pay to bring him on board."

Ray flipped to the page where Crystal had listed the budget for the sports department. "A hundred G-notes. That's not bad. Did you expect a superstar like Tanner to work for peanuts? Sports reporting is what draws in the really big bucks, you know. Alain says hiring Tanner is the first smart move André's made since he weaseled his way into the company."

Crystal rolled her eyes in exasperation as she yanked open the door.

"I forgot about your anti-sports bias. Didn't you picket against adding lighted soccer fields to one of the parish parks last year? Something about how many of our poor little kiddies get hurt," he trilled snidely. "André should have chewed your butt for that. Alain said it was damn lucky you didn't lose us big-money sports-equipment sponsors over it."

"It's a free country, Ray. Radio and TV broadcasters have an obligation to present all sides of a controversial issue. I'm entitled to express my opinion. If you'd actually listened to the interview, you'd know I said at least three times that my views were not those of my employer."

Ray brushed imaginary specks from his silk Armani tie. Crystal thought it a shame no one had ever informed him that clothes didn't make the man.

"Stay away from Tanner with your quirky views. We don't want him quitting. Jason hopes Cale will grease the skids so we can get exclusive rights to televise the Sinners' road games. They've been with WEZY for too long."

She wasn't about to tell Ray that she'd handled hiring Tanner. But darn, if she'd known how happy hiring him would make the dissident side of the family, she wouldn't have worked so hard to disguise the money transfers. She almost laughed, though, wondering what Ray's reaction would be if she casually mentioned she'd be chauffeuring their newest employee home from the hospital. "Rachel's on a tight schedule, so I'll let you get back to your spreadsheet."

"What spreadsheet?" His head jerked up.

"The one you had on your computer when I walked in. I'm really glad to see you attending to our delinquent accounts, Raymond." At least, she *assumed* that was what he'd been doing. "It's not an easy assignment, but Margaret's reasons for wanting family to handle the job makes sense. We can't afford to alienate community businesses even if they've fallen on hard times. They deserve the personal touch." As Crystal swiveled to keep eye contact with Ray over her shoulder, she caught what appeared to be a flash of guilt in his eyes. Still, it might have been no more than the play of sunlight and shadow streaming in his window. He probably hated ruining his bad-boy image by being caught working.

He didn't refute her right to comment on his work or lack thereof, as he usually did. Odd, she mused, leaving his office. She might hold the title of business manager, but Ray Lyon had let it be known he didn't answer to her. They'd worked side by side as accountants for several years. Then, when the former business manager had left and recommended Crystal for the job, Ray had been furious. That weekend, he'd cleaned out a room used for storage and moved his things in. Ray pretty much did nothing. A few months ago Margaret had a long talk with Charles, and as a result, Ray had been given uncollected accounts. Unless he really was working on them now, Crystal had reason to believe he hadn't touched even one.

So if he wasn't doing his job, what spreadsheet *had* he been studying? His own personal investments? She'd seen enough of the screen to know he hadn't been on-line betting. That was another vice he indulged in on company time.

"Oh, well," she muttered, dumping three reports in André's empty office. "Maybe it's better if I don't know what Ray's up to."

CHEZ CHARLES had regained its original elegance since Alain replaced his father as manager in 1975. The restaurant had been built by Alain's grandfather Benoit. It was a lovely place, but if you added up all the money Margaret and Paul had advanced Charles over the years to keep the restaurant afloat, it ought to be a palace. For all Charles's whining, Crystal knew that Margaret and Paul had never drawn profit from the TV station without scrupulously giving Charles an equal amount. If you stopped to consider the salaries that went to his kids and the contract labor jobs the company gave Catherine's extended family, Charles had actually ended up with a disproportionately large share.

The one and only time Crystal had pointed it out to Margaret, she'd said money didn't matter. Family mattered.

"Crystal! Over here." The maître d' had gone to seat a party in a side dining area, so Rachel Fontaine collected her royal-blue napkin and slipped from a plush chair near the back of the main room. She discreetly beckoned her younger friend. The nine-year difference in their ages wouldn't be noticed by patrons who didn't know them. Rachel, at thirty-eight, looked slender and chic. College friends and co-workers found it difficult to believe this confident woman had ever needed rescuing by André Lyon from a mother who neglected her. Crystal could believe it though. She also knew the scars of neglect could be successfully overcome.

Both women appeared at ease in their business suits. Rachel's five-eight frame towered six inches over Crystal. Neither let the disparity in height stand in the way of a hug.

The two hadn't met until after Rachel had left Lyoncrest and begun her career as a state social worker. Past traumas, the Lyon family and a beautiful old house they both loved provided them with an instant bond.

"Let me look at you." Crystal stepped back and studied her friend. "You've cut your hair. I like it...."

"I'm on the go so much it's easier to take care of."

Crystal wagged her head, making her braid flop. "Maybe I'll cut mine."

"Don't you dare." Rachel hooked her arm through Crystal's and led her to the table. "I've never forgiven Gaby for taking two feet off her beautiful hair. Long hair becomes you, Crystal. Yours is so shiny and thick. You should wear it down more often."

"Someone else told me that recently," Crystal murmured, recalling how, at the time, Caleb Tanner had embarrassed her.

"A man?" Rachel handed Crystal a menu. "You've met someone special, haven't you. I wondered what this last-minute lunch was all about. I'd hoped you had some word from Margaret." Rachel's expression switched to a worried frown.

"We all hope that. Leslie's down in the dumps. Cory and Andy-Paul simply won't be appeased. There hasn't been a peep from her, Rachel."

"I feel terrible, but I'm glad André hired that detective. Shall we move on to something brighter? Tell me what's going on in your life."

"I haven't met anyone special," Crystal said, crimson creeping up her neck. "Well, a man did make that remark about my hair, but—"

"Who?"

"Caleb Tanner, but—"

"Oooh! That'll be convenient, working at the same place and all. Tell me more. At the house you never did say if he's as yummy out of uniform as he is on TV."

"Yes. No. I don't know. I've never seen him in a uniform. Except in a PR shot. Stop it, Rachel. There's nothing going on between Tanner and me. He's hospitalized on the same floor as Skip. To make a long story short, I only met the man because I asked him to sign Skip's football. I'm sure Skipper showed you his prize."

"Several times." Rachel might have said more, but a waiter arrived to take their orders.

After they'd both settled on shrimp Caesar salads, Crystal idly stirred the lemon slice in her water. "Skipper's the reason I asked you to meet me for lunch. He overheard you talking to Pam yesterday, Rach. He thinks he can't go back to Sandy's."

Rachel's demeanor instantly changed. She turned and stared out over the center tables. "I can't discuss a client's case with you, Crystal."

"Client? Case? Rachel, come on. Aren't I a friend to both Skip and Sandy?"

"You are. But that doesn't mean I can involve you in professional decisions I make concerning anyone in my caseload."

Shaken, Crystal gripped her napkin tightly. "So it's true. Otherwise you wouldn't be so touchy. Oh, Rachel! It's so unfair to uproot Skip again. Sandy's husband doesn't want him back—I bet that's it."

Rachel leaned across the table. "I made the decision, Crystal. Blame me. Or their house. The rooms are small, the doorways narrow. There are stairs to get in both front and back doors. Sandy's house isn't set up for physically challenged kids."

Crystal held her tongue until the waiter had delivered their salads. "I'm sorry I snapped at you, Rachel. If anyone knows how much you worry about the kids you serve, I should. There hasn't been a holiday at Lyoncrest that you haven't spent following up on a dozen problems or more. The difference is, I know and love Skip."

"So do I." Rachel stabbed a shrimp. "I had no idea he could hear me talking to Pam."

"You need to sit down and explain this to him, Rach. He suspects something isn't right. He asked me to talk to you."

"He did? Dammit, Crystal. His doctor intends to keep the full extent of Skip's disability from him until he completes physical therapy."

"Why?" Crystal's hold on her fork slipped.

"Skip needs to build his upper-body strength. Pam said kids frequently go into depression and give up on therapy once they're told they'll never walk again."

Crystal winced at the harshness of Rachel's words. She shoved her barely touched salad aside. "Will the state pay for a second opinion? *Never* sounds so…so final."

"Our state foster-care program provides better medical coverage than most. But it's still a no-frills system."

"I'll pay for a second opinion. I hear the specialists at the Sports Medicine Clinic are top-notch. Maybe Dr. Snyder missed something."

Rachel blew out a frustrated breath. "I have no authority to let you do that, Crystal. The rules don't allow individual benefactors."

"The rules stink." Crystal stood up angrily, leaving Rachel seated, and yanked up her attaché. "How do you manage to sleep at night?"

Rachel's dark eyes flared. "The rules are there for a reason, Crystal. For one thing, they keep rich people from buying kids under the guise of benevolence and then exploiting them. They also ensure equality of treatment and—"

"If André had played by all the rules, where would *you*

be? Margaret said he fought the social-services system when he was single to keep you at Lyoncrest. Think about *that*, Rachel.''

As she turned her back on Rachel and stomped off toward Alain Lyon's office at the rear of the restaurant, Crystal knew she'd dealt a low blow. Tough! Skip was a child who asked for nothing but a little stability in his life. In Crystal's estimation, the system had let him down.

Then a guilty conscience assailed her. In effect, she'd asked Rachel to risk losing a job in which she did a lot of good for a lot of kids. Crystal hesitated outside the door to Alain's office. Making up her mind, she whirled to go back to the table and apologize to Rachel for her outburst.

The table was empty. New crystal and silver had been set. It hit her then—not only had she been rude to someone she considered practically a sister, she'd stuck Rachel with the entire bill. Crystal slunk back toward Alain's office. She'd drop off the reports and then go find Rachel and make amends.

The plan sounded simple. Except that nothing involving Alain was ever simple. In keeping with the rest of Crystal's bad day, Charles was in Alain's office with him.

''Come in. Have a seat, Crystal.'' Alain leaped up and shoved a rolling chair against the backs of her legs, forcing her to sit whether she wanted to or not.

''I'm in a hurry. I have another errand to run on my lunch hour. Let me just say I know the report is late. Aunt Margaret generally comes in to troubleshoot while I run departmental budget figures.''

Charles lit a filtered cigar and blew smoke in her direction. ''I don't understand what Margie's trying to prove, taking off the way she did.''

Crystal noticed that the liver-spotted hand holding the

match shook with palsy. He looked far more than three years Margaret's senior. "Grief for a loved one hits some people hard," she murmured. She glanced pointedly at Alain, who'd attended Paul's funeral but hadn't returned to Lyoncrest with the other mourners.

Charles's gaze remained vacant. The match singed his fingertips. He swore ripely before dropping it into an ashtray. "If André believes Margie's holed up in grief somewhere, why's he hired that jerk to nose into family affairs?"

Alain, who'd been scanning the report, aimed a sharp look at his father. "Who did André hire?"

"David Patton, some P.I.," Charles mumbled. "Haven't you run afoul of him in court a time or two?"

"Yes. That sneaky son of a bitch! André hired him to do what?"

"Find Margaret."

Alain let the budget report flop closed. "When did this happen? Why haven't you said anything?"

Crystal's head bobbed between the two. Alain never liked surprises, but the way he snarled at his father seemed extreme even for him.

"I figured Patton had already visited you," Charles said haltingly. "He's talked to Jason and Scott."

Alain drummed the fingers of one hand on his desk. "Ray hasn't said anything. Has Patton seen him?"

"Don't know." Charles struggled to his feet and poured himself three fingers of bourbon. "Ray'd just tell him the same thing. Last time we saw Margie was at the funeral. Half of N'Awlins did. If Patton's thorough, sooner or later he'll talk to everyone who paid his or her respects to the family."

The fingers drummed faster. "Patton's thorough, all right. Man's like a damned mongoose."

Crystal rose and shouldered her purse. "Much as I'd like to stay and enjoy this family powwow, I've got other people to see. If you have questions about the report, I'll be in my office later." She glanced at her watch. "Say, after two."

Alain didn't even acknowledge her departure. Charles lifted his empty glass in a salute. By the time Crystal closed the door, he'd sloshed another generous serving into the squat glass. If that was his daily pattern, the family would be attending Uncle Charles's funeral next, Crystal thought sadly.

Clouds were building toward the usual afternoon thunderstorm by the time she emerged from Chez Charles. While the layers of cloud provided a respite from the blistering sun, they also held in the heat and increased humidity. Crystal hailed a cab to take her to Rachel's in Metairie. Rachel rented a two-level place in a complex of old redbrick townhouses that had been completely refurbished. She'd designated the lower floor as an office, where she hoped, now that she'd received her certification to work with private clients, to one day do family counseling. She lived upstairs, which had an elegant white iron grillwork balcony.

Rachel responded to the staccato ring of her ground-floor doorbell. When she saw who her caller was, she stood back and allowed Crystal room to enter. "Should I turn the other cheek?"

"I came to apologize and to pay for my lunch," Crystal admitted sheepishly.

Rachel's smile brought out a dimple in her cheek. "Good. I've already shot this month's food budget. However, I had the waiter box it up. I knew you'd stop by as soon as your temper cooled. I made iced tea to go with our salads. What took you so long?'' She closed the door and led the way to the stairs.

"Monday's the quarterly board meeting. I figured since we were lunching at Chez Charles, I'd hand-deliver Uncle Charles and Alain's reports.''

"Say no more. You're lucky to get here this soon.''

"Actually they didn't bend my ear about the report. They started talking about André hiring that investigator to find Margaret. Alain apparently didn't know. I got the impression the news irritated him.''

Rachel removed the containers from the fridge and carried them to the table. "He's probably wondering if André's going to charge it as a business expense,'' she said as she poured two frosted glasses of tea. "Alain's obsessed with power and money.''

"He and Ray are two of a kind.'' Crystal hooked her bag over the chair and sat. "You've refinished the kitchen cabinets since I was here last. I like the sand-washed look. The whole place is so homey.'' She glanced around. "I have no talent for decorating—that's why I stay at Lyoncrest. And I love the family atmosphere.''

"I did, too. But I also got tired of hearing about all the ups and downs of WDIX at every meal and throughout the evening. That's part of your life, Crystal. It was never part of mine.''

"I know, but even I can't live there forever.''

"Why not? Maybe Margaret or André'll leave the house to you. They both know you'll preserve its intrinsic historical value.''

"Andy-Paul will eventually inherit Lyoncrest, Rachel. As he should. I'll probably stick around for a few more years, though.''

They finished their lunch in silence. Then after Rachel took a drink of tea and set her glass aside, she said, "It's too bad you don't need an apartment right now. There's one going to be available in the building across the street. Ground floor. Has its own courtyard. It's really small but nice, I've heard."

"Costs a mint, too, I bet."

"Actually, not for the area. All the other apartments in that building are larger." She named a figure far below what Crystal would have guessed.

"Hmm. That *is* affordable. I do know someone who's looking, as a matter of fact." She walked through the door that led to the balcony, thinking of Caleb Tanner.

Rachel followed her. "They haven't posted a sign yet. It's the unit on the corner. If you'd like to see it I'll take you over and introduce you to the building manager. He and I chat in the checkout line at the grocery store. That's how I learned it's coming on the market."

Crystal leaned on the wrought-iron railing, debating whether or not to involve herself.

"Might as well look since you're here," Rachel advised. "If you don't like it, you can save your friend a needless trip once it's advertised in the paper."

Nodding her assent, Crystal pushed away from the rail. The building manager turned out to be a nice-looking man of about forty. He seemed surprised, then delighted, to find Rachel standing at his door.

Crystal noticed a blush on Rachel's cheeks as she quickly made the introductions. "Jacob, this is Crystal Jardin. She knows someone who may be interested in the corner apartment if you haven't leased it yet. Crystal, Jacob Harris is an architect, and he manages this building, as well."

They shook hands. He lifted a key ring from a hook beside the door. "It's still available. The cleaning crew just got finished. I expect the ad will hit tomorrow's paper.

Your friend will need to see it today. Our policy is to rent to the first person who clears our credit check." He disappeared a moment and came back carrying a sleepy-eyed little girl. Crystal guessed her to be three or four.

"Jacob!" Rachel exclaimed. "Why didn't you tell us Jordanna was napping? We could've come back later."

Crystal gave the man a second look. "You work at home, manage the complex *and* baby-sit? Are there more men like you out there or did they break the mold? I hope your wife knows how lucky she is."

"Jacob is a widower." Rachel jammed a warning elbow in Crystal's ribs.

"Uh...I'm sorry," Crystal stammered.

Jacob flashed her a smile that shaved five years off his age. "Thanks to Rachel for steering me to a widowers' support group, I no longer sink into a black mood when someone mentions my wife. I'm fortunate to have a job that allows me to be with Jordanna. Here we are," he said, unlocking a door that opened off the street.

The apartment was a beauty. It might be small in size, but hardwood floors and tall ceilings gave it a feeling of spaciousness. The bath off the master bedroom looked masculine with its oversize shower and cocoa-brown fixtures. A breakfast bar separated the kitchen from the living room. The doors were wide and all the rooms were on the same level. Crystal thought Tanner could manage here quite well during the time he still needed a wheelchair. The big problem, as she saw it, was that he wouldn't be released from the hospital until Monday, which would be too late. The price, the location—everything—guaranteed the place would be rented the minute it was listed.

"You're frowning, Crystal. I know it's small. But did you see the courtyard?"

"It's perfect, really. Everything about it is perfect."

"Then let's go back to my place and you can call your friend. Maybe she can swing by to check it out sometime this afternoon."

"It's a he, and he can't. Monday's the earliest he's available."

Rachel gaped but didn't say a word.

Jacob, who still held his daughter, joined the women in the living room. "I'm afraid it'll be gone by then. Tomorrow night I'll have ten credit checks in the works. If I give you an application, can your friend fax it to me from work?"

Crystal felt helpless. For this kind of money, he'd never find anything as nice. Yet she couldn't even call him—she wasn't on his authorized call-in list.

"You're looking at this for Caleb Tanner, aren't you?" Rachel burst out as if a lightbulb had suddenly flashed on.

"Yes," Crystal admitted. She saw no sense in denying it. "The doctor's releasing him to outpatient care on Monday."

"Are you talking Caleb Tanner, football star?" Jacob asked as if he couldn't believe his ears.

"He's Caleb Tanner, WDIX sportscaster now," Crystal said. "Or will be in two weeks after he finishes a round of therapy."

"Man, *nobody* can thread a football through a defense line like Cale Tanner. I'd rent him this place in a New York minute. I'll waive the credit report. If you want to give me a deposit—say, one month's rent—as a binder, I'll go ahead and pull the ad."

Crystal stared at Jacob as if he'd sprouted a second head. "You'd cancel a credit check based on how a guy throws a football?"

"You bet! The man's a household word."

Crystal figured she'd never understand the mystique professional sports figures had. She had nothing to lose, however, by accepting what Jacob Harris willingly offered. Nothing except a few hundred bucks, she amended a few minutes later as she wrote a check from her personal account. What if Tanner hated the place? What if he thought she'd been too presumptuous? Oh, why had she meddled in his affairs?

As the two women left the building after saying goodbye to Jacob and his daughter, Rachel turned to Crystal. "Tell me again there's nothing going on between you and Tanner." She crossed her arms. "I can't see you shelling out that kind of dough for a casual acquaintance."

"If you must know, Ms. Busybody, Nate Fraser has charged me with taking care of our Mr. Tanner. You heard Jacob say Tanner's a hot property. And speaking of Jacob..." she drawled. "Lonely widower. Helpless father to a motherless child. Where does Rachel Fontaine fit into this equation? *You're* qualified to counsel him, but you sent him elsewhere—because it's personal, right?"

"I, uh...I told you," she stammered, "We see each other occasionally at the market. He looked so lost. Then the market owner told me Jacob's wife died about a year ago. Anyway, Ms. Know-it-All, I *wasn't* certified for private counseling then. I gave him my card one day when he seemed to be at wit's end with Jordanna. I told him I had a list of resources if he needed help. He called the next day and asked for the list. Really," she protested, "that's the extent of our involvement."

"He looks at you like a man who'd prefer greater involvement—if you know what I mean."

"You think so?" Rachel gazed longingly at the building they'd just left.

"A man who spends that much time at a market probably cooks his own meals. I bet he'd like a break, Rach. I happen to know you throw together a mean court bouillon," she said, referring to a Louisiana fish stew.

"Shouldn't you be getting back to work?" Rachel asked, trying to hide the fact that she'd gone red again. "It's time I got back downtown to Social Services myself."

Crystal laughed. "Yes, you're right—I should go. But I have a telephone and a long memory. I'll call and bug you until you relent and invite that poor man over."

"I don't have time in my life for a man," Rachel protested.

"A lame excuse, Rach. I know, because I use it all the time."

"Don't psychoanalyze me, Crystal. I've read all the books on what it takes to make a relationship work. I really don't have the time or the energy."

"Hmm. Last time I told Gaby that, she said we all have the same number of hours in a day. I promise I won't nag, Rachel. I guess you could say I live in a glass house and therefore shouldn't throw stones. Anyway, I came over to apologize for one faux pas, not create another."

Rachel hugged her. "You have a good heart, Crystal. But sometimes you take on too much. I know you want to do more for Skipper. I wish I could wave a wand and make it happen. I can't. I have to find him a new foster home. He won't like me much when I do, so he needs a rock-steady friend, Crystal. One who'll see him through this latest ordeal."

Crystal's eyes watered. Pulling back, she clasped both of Rachel's hands. "I can be strong when I have to."

"I know. But you're risking more heartbreak."

"It mended before. I guess it'll mend again. I just hope

his heart's as resilient as mine. Now that you've effectively diverted me from discussing your handsome neighbor, I do have to run. I can't wait to field Ray Lyon's complaints on the board report!''

"Call me if Margaret shows up at the meeting, will you?''

"Definitely. Either way, let's get in touch again on Monday. I've promised to chauffeur Tanner home from the hospital. If this place meets with his approval, you can come over and I'll introduce you. Maybe Jacob will be there.''

"Crystal,'' Rachel remonstrated, "you're impossible. Give it up.''

Laughing impishly, Crystal crossed the street and hailed a cab. After directing the driver to Lyon Broadcasting, she was tempted to have him swing by the hospital, instead. She wanted to visit Skipper. And to tell Tanner she'd poked her nose in his business. She rode straight to her office, instead, and spent the remainder of the day waiting for Ray to pounce on behalf of Alain or Charles.

Five o'clock came and went. The building grew silent around her. Half an hour later Crystal locked up and left. She must have done a better job of juggling funds into Nate's budget than she'd given herself credit for. Over the weekend she'd show André what she'd done in case he had to defend the transfers at Monday's board meeting.

Though she was sorely tempted to go directly to Tanner's room, her first stop at the hospital was the children's ward.

"Hi, Crystal,'' one of the regular nurses sang out. "The kids are all crowded in the playroom watching a magic show. You're welcome to join them. It's pretty elementary, though.''

Crystal's pulse scrambled at the news. "That's okay.''

She offered a disarming smile. "I have another patient to visit. Tell Skipper I came by and I'll be back Sunday. He's expecting me then."

"I will. No music tonight?" She sounded disappointed.

"I'm going straight to the club. Another band member transports my instruments. It's difficult dragging them all here on the streetcar."

"Well, bring down the house, okay?"

Crystal waved. She sped down the hall and around the corner to Tanner's room. Her heart slammed so loudly she was surprised the aide who went whipping past didn't hear. The rapid heartbeats had everything to do with her gall at choosing Caleb Tanner a place to live, and nothing to do with any excitement about seeing him, she assured herself.

As she reached his room, she heard the stumbling strains of a fledgling piano tune. Easing open the door, Crystal watched the man on the bed, electronic keyboard across his lap, doing his best to follow the left-handed key pads highlighted in the silent video. Unexpectedly her heart swelled. "Keep this up, and before you know it, the world will be touting you as the new McCoy Tyner."

He lifted his gaze slowly, and a smile spread across his face. "Are you making fun of me? Who's McCoy Tyner?"

"He was a noted jazz pianist. He played rhythm backup with a wicked left hand."

"Loud, you mean?"

"Booming. He played ragtime like nobody plays ragtime anymore."

The smile stayed on Caleb's lips. "I didn't expect to see you tonight. Aren't you playing at the club?"

She pulled an extension cord from her bag. "I promised you this. I expect you'd like a bit more operating room."

"It's nice of you to worry about my comfort. And since we're on the subject of comfort, you know what I did in PT today?"

She shook her head as she handed him the extension cord. His smile was certainly infectious. "Do I have to guess or are you eventually going to clue me in?"

"I did a turn on crutches."

Crystal was silent as she wrestled with the news, wondering if he'd still need her help on Monday.

"That's a giant step, Jardin. One that warrants applause."

"I'm happy for you. I suppose that means you'll be running up and down stairs soon. So, I guess you'll want to keep your old apartment."

He shook his head. "I'm light-years from negotiating stairs."

"In that case I'd better confess. I signed a lease on a ground-floor apartment for you today. I know it was nervy, but here's the deal..." Her words tumbled over each other as she relayed the facts. Three times he tried to interrupt, but she only talked faster, even using her hands to describe the decor. "There, I think that's everything. Now you can yell at me and throw me out," she said with a small shrug.

"Yell? Throw you out? I can't recall anyone ever looking after me this way before. Other than someone I hired." He caught her chin between his hands and leaned toward her, his lips parted as if to kiss her.

Crystal would never know if that was what Caleb Tanner intended. For the keyboard slipped off his lap, bounced against the floor and was jerked by its short cord.

"Oh, damn. Did I break it?" He dived for the side of the bed.

Crystal threw her arms around him to stop him from

falling. They both breathed as though they'd run a five-minute mile, then sprang apart when a nurse suddenly burst into the room. She smiled and clucked, "Sorry for the interruption, but it's time for Mr. Tanner's nightly meds."

Embarrassed by how their clinch must look Crystal declared in a loud voice that she had to leave. Then, she tore out of the room in spite of Caleb's calling her to stop.

CHAPTER EIGHT

CALEB LET IMAGES of Crystal Jardin fill his mind as the pain medication took hold. The impressions swirled pleasantly, lightly fuzzed around the edges. Her eyes, still and watchful. Skin, the softest he'd ever touched. Lips, moist, parted and free of artificial color.

Every time their paths crossed—after their second meeting—he'd felt increasingly intrigued by her. Tonight he'd been seconds away from kissing her when his intentions had been thwarted by the night nurse.

Caleb thought it safe to say they wouldn't have stopped at one kiss.

At least *he* wouldn't have been inclined to let it end there.

And his experience with women had been substantial enough that he felt reasonably confident he hadn't misread her expression. Or her interest.

And maybe you're full of bull, said a little voice. *She ran away faster than a scalded chicken trying to escape the butcher's knife.*

"She did you a favor, lamebrain," he said aloud, pounding a fist on the bed. "Yeah, I know," he argued back. "I was trying to thank her. Not many women do a man a favor and then apologize for it. Most expect a payback."

What makes you think she's different? You don't know her that well, buddy.

The telephone rang, saving Caleb from continuing a fool's argument.

"'Lo," he mumbled, tucking the telephone in the crook between his shoulder and neck. His palms were sweating and he went dizzy for a moment thinking it might be Crystal calling to explain her hasty departure. It was Patsy, and her voice made him feel guilty. They'd had words last night. The girls wanted to know why, if he was quitting football like they'd heard on the national news, he wasn't coming home to Texas.

"Sugar, we'll have to talk fast. Those ol' painkillers kick the juice outta me." He laughed. "I may sound drunk, but I'm not. What's that, darlin'? Hollis says I can come work for him at the car dealership? Just so I don't get bored?" He grinned. "That's right nice of your fiancé, sweetheart. But I told you girls last night—I'm only leaving the Sinners for a season. I'm gonna stick around N'Awlins so the coach doesn't forget who I am."

"Now stop that cryin', honey. I'm not as stove up as the media made it sound. In fact, I walked with crutches today. Yeah, I swear on Mama's Bible. I'm getting out of here Monday. So quit worryin'. Everything's gonna be hunky-dory." He paused. "Know what? I'm gonna try my hand at sports announcing on WDIX-TV."

"Whazzat? Sorry, Patsy, I'm fading. Let's talk tomorrow or Sunday. Monday? Okay. I forgot you were going to Austin. Have fun at the shower. Nice of Hollis's sister to throw it. Call me from Gracie's apartment. On Monday? Dang, that won't work. I'm gonna be busy. I'm moving out of my old place and—"

He held the receiver away from his ear. "I haven't seen the new digs yet, babe. Crystal rented it today. Crystal Jardin… No, I'm not moving in with her. Look, after I get settled, you, Gracie and Jenny can fly in for a weekend and give it the Tanner stamp of approval. Yeah, I mean it. 'Course we'll paint the town red, hon. Next week I'll figure out a date and wire you tickets.''

In the midst of her effusive goodbye, Caleb endured a crushing weight against his chest. *His heart?* Nah! Forsythe said he had the heart of an ox. He dropped the receiver and heard it strike the floor.

He let it hang there. He didn't need any more calls tonight. Patsy would tell Gracie and Jenny about the trip, and they'd each get on the horn and put in requests for sightseeing sprees and shopping. Caleb saw dollar signs fluttering around him. The pressure on his chest increased. They were smart women. Why couldn't he bring himself to tell them the truth about his financial state? *Because then you'd have to admit that for all your high-and-mighty career, you couldn't fill Daddy's shoes.*

If his daddy had lived, he'd have seen to it that his girls lacked for nothing. His father had a knack for bartering, trading and making something out of nothing—a gene that had obviously bypassed Caleb. In the years since he'd taken on responsibility for his sisters, he'd seen shoes, dresses, even underwear triple—no, quintuple in price. Then there were the extras like stereos, TVs, computers, enlarging the house. The list went on to include class rings, graduation expenses, proms, college tuition, apartment rents and now weddings. Lordy, he had two more of those still to go.

He finally drifted into a troubled sleep. His last coherent thought was that he'd have to swallow his pride and ask Crystal Jardin to refer him to one of those financial consultants she seemed to think he already had. And what did *they* charge? It was a foregone conclusion they didn't work for free.

SATURDAY, CRYSTAL TOOK care of domestic chores. She cleaned her bedroom and bath, even though Margaret hired a cleaning service once a week for the rest of the house. Lyoncrest had a cook, a chauffeur, a gardener and a nanny. All were like family. It was a life-style many of Crystal's friends and even the members of her band couldn't imagine. They tended to be struggling musicians who juggled family with other jobs. And it was hard to explain to people who lived hand-to-mouth that no one at Lyoncrest felt special or pampered. They could all drive, cook, clean and baby-sit if they had to. In fact, they did fill in with those chores. André had taught his daughters to drive. Gaby insisted they learn to be self-sufficient. Andy-Paul was the most spoiled, although he had to pick up his toys and feed the cat.

The gray-and-white alley cat belonged to no one. There were even differing opinions as to how and when he came to make Lyoncrest his domicile. But there was no doubt he belonged. Someone, Gaby probably, had named him Mouser because he'd developed a disgusting habit of laying his catch of the day on the back porch, presumably so the occupants would be properly appreciative that he kept his home rodent-free. In exchange for this service, Mouser expected two squares a day and didn't care who fed him.

Crystal, who'd never had a pet in her life, loved every snooty thing about the cat. She'd long since decided she'd have one or two whenever she moved into a place of her own. Beyond that, and knowing she'd have a music room and walls filled with paintings by local artists, she hadn't given much thought to what she might want in an apartment or a house.

Today, as she vacuumed her bedroom and scrubbed out her shower, she started a plan in her head. She snipped

pieces from the three apartments with which she was most
familiar. Nate and Jill Fraser's, Rachel's and Caleb's new
place. Nate and Jill's condo boasted an Italian-marble fire-
place that Crystal loved. Rachel's rooms were large and
airy. And who wouldn't want Tanner's courtyard? Its pro-
fusion of wax myrtle and wisteria lined a brick patio with
an ornate fountain in the center.

Thinking of Tanner's apartment soon had Crystal thinking about the man. No sense lying to herself. Last night,
as she played with the band, she'd been distracted by
thoughts of Tanner. Very distracted. Not just because he'd
come so close to kissing her, either. By the time she
reached the club, she'd figured out that he'd actually
meant what he said about being grateful for her help in
renting him a new place. What had made it hard to keep
her mind on her music—something that'd never happened
before—was the realization that she'd *wanted* him to kiss
her. She'd left his room, embarrassed at their being
caught, but also vastly disappointed that they'd been
thwarted.

It was one thing for her to know how she'd felt, and
quite another for Tanner to know it. Crystal was afraid
her face had divulged everything. If she didn't have to
see him again until Monday… Unfortunately there were
things they needed to discuss, since he'd be moving into
his new home in a week and a half. Like did he have
furniture to move? Was someone taking care of his belongings or did he assume Nate would hire a moving company? It wasn't her concern, but she wondered whether
he'd broken his lease or perhaps manage to sublet his
previous place.

Crystal practically scrubbed the color off her bathroom
tile trying to avoid the unavoidable. She could always
advance her visit to Skipper. And then swing by Tanner's

room. She sighed. Time to shower and change and stop procrastinating.

"SKIPPER WENT to physical therapy, Crystal," Randy informed her the minute she walked into their room.

"When?" She slid her watch around for a better look.

"I dunno. Ten minutes, maybe. Skip hopes Cale's scheduled at the same time. Yesterday he tried crutches, Cale did. Skip wants Cale to give him pointers on how he can learn to walk quicker. Then he'll tell me. I get to start PT next week."

Crystal underwent a series of shocks. "You boys need to listen to your individual therapists. Tanner's not qualified to give you advice."

"Sure he is. Players get hurt all the time. They know more about what it takes to get muscles in shape than somebody who only learns from a book."

Crystal opened her mouth to refute Randy's logic. She closed it again, thinking the kids weren't the ones she should chastize. Tanner was the adult; surely he'd know better than to dole out guidance. "I'll just go down there and look in," she said.

Downstairs, when she glanced into the PT area, she saw the therapists seated on the floor in a semicircle. Caleb leaned on crutches. He seemed to be talking earnestly to them and Skip, as well as two girls about Skip's age. One sat in a wheelchair, the other supported herself on a walker.

Crystal slipped into the room. She trod softly, not wanting to draw attention to herself. No one paid any notice as she joined the circle. Everyone seemed mesmerized by Tanner's deep voice.

"You can sit back, take it easy and wait for nature to heal you," he said. "Or you can conjure up a picture in your mind of how you'll look, act and feel when you're functioning at one hundred percent. Don't ever underestimate the mind, kids. It's your most powerful tool. Guys and gals in pro sports learn to psych themselves up to perform at peak capacity. In other words, if you think you can do it, you will.''

He gave a convincing pep talk. But Crystal didn't fall under his spell. She had intended to keep silent. So much for intentions. ''That's bunk, Tanner. It's why so many athletes end up permanently damaged. There's such a thing as tricking your body into going beyond its endurance.''

Everyone gaped at her, including Caleb. Crystal expected his censure. She'd never imagined Skip or the team of professional healers would tell her she was full of baloney. But they did.

Skipper didn't give the slightest indication that he was happy to see her. ''You don't know what Cale's talking about, Crystal.'' The boy glanced around. ''She doesn't play sports,'' he announced. ''She doesn't even *watch* ball games.''

Skip's physical therapist tore her gaze away from Tanner and attacked Crystal in a low furious voice. ''Cale's right. Negativity has no place in the healing process. Please wait outside while we finish this session.''

Reacting as if she'd been slapped, Crystal bounded to her feet. ''Adults have the right to practice whatever nutty philosophies they wish. Children depend on us to be rational and make good choices.'' Quietly she told Skip she'd see him in his room and walked off.

It was Caleb who called out to her and awkwardly propelled himself forward to intercept her.

She fingered the strap of her purse. ''Are you aware

the doctor says Skip will never walk again?'' she hissed, well out of earshot of the others.

He sliced the air with his hand. ''Maybe that's true. But he sure won't get out of that chair if he gives up before he even tries.''

Her lips trembled and tears began to leak from her eyes.

Caleb disengaged his hand from one crutch long enough to scrape a thumb lightly over her cheeks. ''The therapists asked if I'd say a few words to motivate the kids. I said my piece. I told them what works for me. Beyond that, I'm not getting involved.'' His good leg slipped a bit and sent the crutch he'd released tumbling to the floor.

''I'm glad to hear it.'' Crystal knelt, picked up the crutch and handed it back. ''Skip and his friends take every word you say as gospel.''

''I would never deliberately hurt a kid, but I can't help it if he shadows me. What's he to you, anyway? Are you related?''

''I wish we were.'' She crossed her arms and rubbed her chilled skin. It was the air-conditioning, she decided. ''I told you Skip's in foster care. He has no family. I explained it when I brought you the football to sign.''

''That's tough. I guess I wasn't listening too well that day.''

His admission coaxed a tentative smile from her. ''An understatement if I've ever heard one. Look, your therapist is glaring at us. She evicted me, remember?''

''Evicted—that reminds me. I spoke with Leland today. A new halfback the Sinners picked up in third-round draft wants my old apartment, but he needs it right away. I told him I'm moving by the end of the month. Boy did I feel dumb when he asked where and I discovered I don't have an address.''

She reached into her bag. "Here's the lease I signed. I planned to drop it by your room. This place isn't furnished except for stove and refrigerator. Do you have furniture?"

"The basics. Bed, couch, stereo and TV."

"The apartment is vacant now. No reason you couldn't move in early next week. Monday?" At his nod she continued, "There's a bookkeeper at work whose husband rents out trucks. He could probably help me find people to move your stuff tomorrow, unless you've made other arrangements."

He gazed at her from steady grass-green eyes. "You've already gone to a lot of trouble for me."

Crystal had asked herself the same unspoken question. Why? Why, when she barely knew the man? "I told you before," she said huskily. "You've joined our communications family. You're not the first staff member I've helped move. I can introduce you to a few people I've packed boxes for. Don't make a federal case out of it, Tanner."

"Okay. And I accept your offer." He kept his disappointment at her answer to himself as he dug in his pocket and pulled out a ring of keys.

It was the first time Crystal had noticed he was wearing jeans today, instead of loose-fitting sweats. They were worn in spots, holey in others. Caleb Tanner did more for a pair of Wranglers than was respectable. She could barely tear her gaze away and take the key he'd finally removed from the ring. She missed the address of his old place when he rattled it off and had to ask for two repeats.

"Are you all right?" he asked, a faint frown marring his brow.

"Fine," she croaked. "Does this place need cleaning before I turn in the key?"

He suddenly thought about the extent of the favor she

was doing him. It entailed packing his clothes, including his underwear, and stripping the sheets off his bed. His mind balked when he envisioned her scrubbing out his shower, and a scowl settled over his face. Rubbing a hand briskly down his injured leg, he muttered, "Dammit. I should be doing my own dirty work. Hire a cleaning crew. Don't you scrub my toilet."

A lock of hair flopped over his left eye in an endearing way. Crystal grinned. "A real pigsty, huh?" She reached out and patted his arm. "Your secret is safe with me, Tanner. Quit worrying. We use a very discreet cleaning service at Lyoncrest. I'll give them a call."

"What's Lyoncrest?" He looked mystified.

"The Lyon family home. In the heart of the Garden District," she added. "Um, I guess you've never toured the Garden District or you'd remember it. Tourists always stick their noses through the grillwork in the iron gates. André said when he was a kid it bugged him a lot. He doesn't like it much now when he's out there trying to teach Andy-Paul how to ride his bicycle. They don't bother me, though. I wave if I'm sitting on the porch swing reading."

"You live with the head honcho of WDIX-TV?"

Her eyes narrowed to blue slits. "I don't think I like what I hear in your tone. It's insulting. You don't deserve an explanation."

"Explain, anyway," he said coolly.

She sighed. "My grandmother was the sister of André's father. Both are dead now. Lyoncrest is huge. Margaret Lyon occupies one master suite, André and Gabrielle another, Leslie and Michael a third. There's room for all the kids to visit at one time and still not displace me. If I've quite satisfied your nasty mind, I believe I'll go. I'll see if Nate can pick you up on Monday, instead."

"No," he said softly. "Listen, I'm sorry. You mentioned André's kids before. I don't recall hearing about a wife. I apologize for jumping to conclusions. My teammates have often accused me of letting my old-fashioned values show."

"A professional ball player with principals? There's a novelty."

"Now who's insulting?"

"Touché." Crystal dipped her chin. "I'll try to have better control of my manners by Monday."

Cale chuckled. "Don't change on my account. I like a woman who speaks her mind."

That flustered Crystal. Fortunately his physical therapist interrupted them. "If you're forfeiting the rest of your time, Cale, I'll send Gibson after another patient."

"I'm coming. I had some business to conclude with Ms. Jardin. Will you stop by here tomorrow after your movers finish?" he asked Crystal in an undertone.

"I hadn't planned to."

"Will you at least call?"

"I'm not on your preferred-customer list."

He looked puzzled, then realized she referred to the elaborate screening policy Leland had set up. "I'll take care of that. About Monday? The doctor said he'd set a time when he makes rounds tomorrow."

"Okay. But it may be late when I call you. You'd better go." She made shooing motions with her hands. "Lynelle will send Gibson after another patient." She tossed a last wave at Skipper and hurried through the double doors.

The room felt bigger, colder, emptier to Caleb after Crystal's departure, in spite of the noisy equipment and the chatter of patients. How could he miss her so much when all they ever seemed to do was argue?

CALEB WAS DESTINED to feel the loss through the next evening. His wall clock said eight. He'd checked it a thousand times and had just dragged out the copy of the lease agreement she'd signed, hoping to find her home number, when his phone rang. "About damned time you called," he said, snatching up the receiver.

"Hello to you, too, Tanner. Were you afraid I'd run off with your furniture?"

He heard the weariness in her voice and suffered a twinge of guilt because she'd been taking care of matters he should be handling. "How'd it go?"

"You said you didn't have much furniture. You should have warned me that what you did own was Texas-size."

He didn't respond.

"Tanner? Are you still with me?"

"I guess my bed is heavy."

"Weighed a ton. So did your leather couch and chair. Add to that a double dresser, solid-oak coffee table, end tables. Oh, and let's not forget the cast-iron bucking horses some fool made into lamps."

Caleb winced as she ran down an inventory of his belongings.

"The only thing you lack," she accused, "is china, silver and pots and pans. But there's a smoker and a barbecue. I found them stuffed in a back closet. What do you do? Eat only beef, and then off paper plates?"

"My sisters. They'd never seen my place, because I always flew home for any breaks in my schedule. Grace bought me the smoker for my birthday. The other two gave me the barbecue. I never had the heart to tell them my high-rise didn't have a balcony."

"That's another thing. Half your furniture wouldn't fit in the service elevator. I bet you didn't know there are 1,212 steps from the curb to your old apartment door."

"I did. Sort of. My teammates said that when they moved me in it took the place of a week's worth of calisthenics."

"And look at the size of those bruisers! Today, two anemic-looking men and one scrawny woman did the same job. Anyway, what time are they springing you tomorrow? I need to hurry and shower before I fall asleep on my feet."

"If you're trying to make me feel guilty, Jardin, you've succeeded. Would you rather I took a cab? I can, you know."

"Actually you can't. I have the keys to your apartment. I forgot to leave you the spare. Not only that, I have a couple of friends who are going to meet us there and help place the furniture where you want it. Right now it's all piled in the living room."

"My debt to you is mounting. Bring the bills when you come. The doc's releasing me at one."

"See you in the patient loading zone. And Tanner, wear sunglasses. I don't want to be mobbed when your fans see you."

He laughed at that and would have said more, but she'd already broken the connection. It wasn't until he'd fielded a late call from his sister Jenny that Caleb realized how lonely his life as a player had really been. He'd had adulation from fans, a working relationship with Leland and occasionally he did things with teammates. Those friendships were all superficial. It struck him how much he looked forward to Crystal Jardin's visits. He went to bed, anticipating her arrival the next day with the same eagerness he felt the night before a big game.

MONDAY MORNING, Crystal discovered aches in muscles she hadn't known existed. As she unlocked her office door and flipped on the lights, she wondered ruefully why she'd gone out of her way for Tanner.

She sank gingerly into her chair and booted up her computer, content to let the why of her actions hang in limbo for the time being.

"Oh, no!" she gasped. Her routine check of Margaret's account revealed another three-thousand-dollar withdrawal. Even as she went through all the steps, seeking the source of the withdrawal, codes began to disappear. She had an excellent memory for numbers, but good as it was, she only caught the first two digits of the ATM code, signifying where the money was withdrawn. Not local. She had all those codes in her head.

She grabbed the U.S. code book, which rivaled the New York City phone book in size. *Florida.* Margaret loved St. Petersburg. She and Paul used to go there often. After nearly an hour of poring over the tiny numbers, Crystal had to admit defeat. Now she wondered if she'd read the numbers correctly.

Upset and doubly distressed because she'd been so positive Margaret would show up for today's board meeting, Crystal backed out of the screen and went in search of André.

He turned to face her when she burst into his office. He'd been gathering the reports he'd need for the meeting. "Crystal? What is it? My stars! Have you heard from Mama?"

Catching her breath, Crystal shook her head. "Another three thousand was withdrawn from her account." She paced furiously in front of his desk. "If I'd pulled up her account five seconds earlier I'd have had the codes. They disappeared as I flipped from frame to frame. André, I'm worried sick. What's happening here is illegal. Whoever is doing this must be crazy, making spreadsheet adjustments during peak banking hours.''

André closed his briefcase. "We have to notify David Patton. He was going to talk to John Neville at the bank. Will you do that for me? Gaby's picking me up in ten minutes to go to the board meeting.''

"It's not here?''

"No. At Chez Charles. That was Mama's last concession to Charles, remember? Rotating meetings so that half of them are on his turf.''

"I guess that's why Ray's in early. His office lights were on when I arrived.''

"Maybe Ray's turning over a new leaf. You said he didn't hassle you about the board report. Maybe they're all mellowing.'' André smiled. "I know.'' He held up a hand. "I won't hold my breath. Darn, I wish Mama would show up. I'm like you, Crystal—I figured she'd roll in last night. Ask Dave to come to your office, okay? Show him exactly what's happening to her account.''

Crystal checked her watch. "I hope he can get here on short notice. I'm taking the afternoon off to settle Tanner into his apartment. I thought Nate would tell you.''

"Caleb's being released from the hospital?''

"At one.''

André looked relieved. "That, at least, is good news. If the cousins are as pleased as you say over his hiring, I'll be able to spend more time today talking about how we're going to use Tanner and less on what it cost to entice him here.''

"André, don't you ever get sick of fighting with Charles and his brood?''

"Things improved to a degree after Alain left WDIX in 1975. Or else I became inured. Mama and Gaby have already kept me on an even keel.''

"Now you have to think about Andy-Paul's future."

"At this point, who can say he'll want the job? If you're going to be successful in broadcasting now, you need to do more than provide news and up-to-the-minute programming. There's cable and HBO to worry about." He shook his head. "The workload, combined with the family squabbling, drove the girls away. Andrew isn't old enough to learn about the pitfalls yet."

"You're only discouraged because Margaret isn't here. As soon as she returns, you'll feel differently again."

"I hope you're right," he said, walking her to the door. "I do know I'd feel a whole lot better if she'd even phone. That's the part I can't understand, Crystal. Her silence. Plus those consistent withdrawals. I keep thinking that if she's hiding out somewhere, she wouldn't be so methodical. And the amounts never vary."

"I agree. Normally a person on vacation pulls fifty here, a couple of hundred there."

"You will point that out to David?"

Crystal assured him she would.

And she did. She spent all morning with the P.I. He might have kept her longer, but she told him she had to leave, to meet Tanner.

As it turned out, she was late. She didn't drive often and had forgotten how congested the downtown area could be. To make matters worse, she'd borrowed Paul's Cadillac. The old boat hadn't been driven much in recent years, although the family chauffeur saw to its servicing. Crystal much preferred borrowing Gabrielle's spiffy convertible. Gaby had offered to trade today, but Crystal thought that with his injury, Tanner needed the Cadillac's extra leg room.

He seemed happy that she'd arrived. His face switched

instantly from scowl to grin as she jockeyed the big car into a too-small space.

"It's about time," a pinch-faced nurse exclaimed. "You've left us waiting twenty minutes in this humidity, young woman."

Crystal plucked Caleb's sportsbag from the nurse's hand and tossed it into the cavernous trunk. "Sorry. Got tied up at the office. But I'm here now," she said brightly, collecting the keyboard and two bedraggled-looking potted plants. "I'll stow all this if you'll assist Tanner into the car. I thought he could ride in the back seat where he can spread out."

"You'll look like my chauffeur." Caleb peered over his dark glasses and winked.

Crystal slammed the trunk lid. "Freedom makes you awfully cocky, my friend."

He changed his tune as the nurse tossed his crutches into one side of the back seat and made Caleb hop on his good leg until she'd stuffed him in, too.

"Ouch," Crystal said for him the minute she took her place behind the wheel. "It hurt to fold that leg, didn't it? Would you like me to move those crutches so you can stretch your leg out fully?"

"Yes, please," Caleb said between his teeth.

The way he grimaced after she got on her knees and leaned into the back to offer assistance prompted her to ask, "Are you sure they aren't releasing you too soon, Tanner?"

"No," he snapped. "Just go. I prefer to suffer at home among my own things."

Crystal pulled into the traffic, then glanced at him in the rearview mirror. "How will you get your meals? How will you get to therapy every day? The distance from the bed to the shower in your apartment is farther than it was in your hospital room.''

"I talked to Nate Fraser this morning. I guess he didn't reach you. He promised you'd lend me a hand for a few weeks.''

"What?" Her gaze flew to the mirror again.

"Not with the shower part," he said around a toothy grin. "He said you'd arrange transportation to and from the clinic, and that you'd work out some arrangement for meals.''

Crystal's heart hammered in her chest. She didn't, however, want Caleb to know that the prospect of seeing him every day left her light-headed. She gripped the wheel and said calmly, "I'll type you a list of takeout places and pizza-delivery numbers.''

"Thanks," he drawled. "You're too kind.''

She allowed a small smile. "I know. Here we are," she announced twenty minutes later, drawing close to the curb. "The end unit is yours.''

"Who's the little girl with her nose pressed to the window?" he asked.

"The manager's daughter. He and a friend of mine who lives across the street are giving us a hand unpacking and moving the furniture around. Oh, here comes Rachel now.'' Crystal waved to the woman jogging across the street. "Rachel is André's foster daughter and Skipper's social worker. Between you and me, I twisted her arm to get her to help us today. I'm sure she has the hots for Jacob Harris—the building manager," she added. "That's why.''

"Matchmaking is alive and well," he grumbled softly. Too softly for her to hear as she vaulted from the car and ran to greet the woman.

Caleb forced down his dissatisfaction over not having

the afternoon to spend alone with Crystal. It amazed him how strongly he felt about it. As he struggled out of the car, he thought that maybe it was time he simply admitted that his situation wasn't so different from Rachel's. He had the hots for someone, too.

CHAPTER NINE

IT WAS NEARLY SEVEN in the evening by the time a weary Jacob scooped up his daughter and headed for Caleb's front door. "I have to get this kiddo bathed and fed. We've arranged all the heavy furniture. I'm sure the ladies can unpack the remaining boxes without me."

Caleb levered himself out of the chair. "I didn't see any *we* moving furniture, Jake. You did it alone. I owe you," he said with emotion. "These stilts make things damned inconvenient." He slapped an impatient hand down the side of his jeans.

Jacob tossed off a shrug. "It was a treat to talk football again, man. Since I've become a single work-at-home parent, I miss doing some of the guy things."

Crystal leaned across the bar from the kitchen where she was busy cutting and installing the shelf paper Rachel had thoughtfully provided. "I'd say you made up for lost time today. I'm greatly relieved to know Tanner can do sports speak, Jake. He's talked football nonstop for almost six hours. He shouldn't have any trouble going on air."

Caleb and Jacob exchanged guilty glances.

As Rachel made another trip from the living room to the kitchen, Jacob's daughter lunged toward her. "Rachel give me bath tonight. Peas, Daddy?"

"Sweetie, Rachel's busy." Over his daughter's head, Jacob telegraphed his chagrin.

Again Crystal climbed off her stool to address the others. "I can finish up here alone. There's not much left to do. Jordanna asked so nicely, how can you two refuse her?" She focused on Jacob. "It's late. Wouldn't it save time if you and Rach pooled resources for dinner?" Crystal's query sounded innocent enough.

Rachel gave her a mortified glance.

"Food!" Cale snapped his fingers. "You guys must think this injury affected my brain. The least I can do to show my thanks for all your help is to order in dinner for everyone. Crystal mentioned a good Chinese takeout nearby. Is that okay?"

"Jordanna hasn't developed a taste for Chinese," Jacob said. "But don't let us stop you all from ordering in."

Bolting out of the kitchen, Crystal sent Caleb a quelling look as she gently hustled Rachel toward the door. "What a coincidence. Rachel doesn't like Chinese, either. Maybe we can get together for pizza another time. Tanner's looking a little peaked, if you ask me. We've forgotten he's just out of the hospital and needs plenty of rest."

Though Caleb thought Crystal's tactics obvious, he let her take charge. He restated his appreciation to Jake and Rachel amid all the goodbyes.

"You weren't very subtle," he said to Crystal. Once the door had closed on her friends, she went to a window where she took pains not to be seen as she peeped out.

"Jordanna provided the perfect opportunity to get Rachel and Jake together. If we left it up to them, they'd still be making small talk at the corner grocer's a year from now."

"Before today, I wouldn't have figured you for a matchmaker." He swung back to his chair on his crutches.

"I've never done this before." She paused. "I doubt you noticed, because men usually don't, but all afternoon Jordanna didn't stray six inches from Rachel's side. The kid misses her mother terribly. When they were leaving, I...I felt so bad for her. She wanted Rachel to put her to bed.'' Crystal gazed directly at him as she made her case, but Caleb soon realized the lost expression in her eyes wasn't focused on him. Not only that, her expression mirrored one he'd observed too many times in his kid sisters' eyes.

"You've walked in Jordanna's shoes, haven't you?'' he asked quietly.

Her yes sounded high-pitched. A little breathless. Then she shook herself out of the mental stupor. "A long time ago. I...must be getting rummy. Probably from the contortions it's taken to measure and cut four rolls of shelf paper to fit all the nooks and crannies in your kitchen, Tanner. Thank goodness that part is finished.''

"Leave the rest,'' Caleb said, his voice taking on a sharp edge. "You've already accomplished more than I've had any right to expect. Since you picked me up at one, I'll bet you missed lunch on my account, too. Now it's suppertime.''

She opened her mouth, but he held up a hand. "Don't give me any more lip, Jardin.'' He grinned. "Help me locate the phone book. I'm having a meal delivered and that's final. I take it you have no objections to Chinese.'' He clamped both hands on the arms of his overstuffed chair and prepared to rise.

Crystal watched him heave himself up. "I love Chinese. But the boxes that are left won't take me half an hour to empty. Yesterday I picked up some inexpensive pans, dishes and flatware from a department store. While it's washing, I'd planned to run to the market and stock up on the usual milk and cereal and bread. Maybe enough deli stuff to get you by until you have time to prepare a full shopping list.''

"You shouldn't have gone to the trouble of buying me dishes, but I appreciate it. Let me show how much by buying you dinner."

"I wasn't kidding, Tanner. You ought to rest."

"You've given orders like a head coach all afternoon. Now it's my turn." Caleb spied the phone book sitting on the breakfast bar and changed course. "What's the name of that damned Chinese restaurant?"

"It's actually Thai." Crystal tilted her head to one side and smiled. "I know you're used to snapping your fingers and having people jump, Tanner. But this I've gotta see. How good are you at mental telepathy? Rachel tried using your phone to call her office. There's no dial tone."

He swung around so fast the rubber tips on his crutches slid on the gleaming hardwood. Reflexively Crystal threw an arm around his waist, catching him before he fell. Her heart skidded erratically. No telling what further damage he'd have done if she hadn't been handy.

"Will you *sit,* for crying out loud?" she said.

"Worried about me?" He dropped one crutch so he could lean on her to balance himself.

"I'm worried you'll kill yourself before WDIX realizes any revenue on the money they're advancing you."

The green eyes that studied Crystal exploded to life in a swirl of golden flecks. "I don't think that's the truth at all." Cale dropped his second crutch on top of the first and deliberately slid both palms up and down her arms. Inch by agonizing inch, he drew her steadily closer.

When he brushed the tip of her nose with his own, Crystal's heart hit a rocky stretch of road. *Caleb Tanner is going to kiss me.*

"You can say no," he rasped, his breath warming her lips. "But you ought to know I've been thinking about this all day."

Crystal savored the heat that slammed through her body as she placed her palms on his chest. Rising on tiptoe, she said softly, "Just do it, Tanner."

He didn't need a second invitation.

Street sounds faded. Where there had been a steady flow of traffic noise in the background before their lips met, now there seemed to be silence. Crystal didn't know what she'd expected. Up till now, one kiss had been pretty much the same as another. A few were pleasant. Most were tepid. Tanner's kiss carried punch enough to explode a fireball of heat to her stomach. Yet his lips were soft and cool. So how come her throat felt raw and her mouth scorched?

Caleb's head reeled. He'd kissed plenty of women. And even though Crystal Jardin had a tantalizing mouth, he'd imagined that when they finally got around to this, kissing her would be no big deal. Not so! The more she kissed back, the more he craved. When she whimpered and opened her mouth to receive his tongue, he felt the room tilt and the light recede.

His good leg trembled as she flowed against him. He dragged her so close he couldn't tell if it was her heart pounding or his. Or both. He loved the feel of her silky hair as his fingers tunneled through her loose braid, anchoring her head solidly so that his mouth could claim hers.

Bells clanged in Crystal's head. Starbursts erupted behind her eyes. Crazy thoughts cartwheeled through her brain when he rocked his pelvis against hers. Kissing Caleb Tanner was good. Very, very good.

But mere kissing wasn't enough. Not nearly enough. Crystal felt a feverish need for more. To get naked, explore all that heat and muscle held in check by the cloth she twisted feebly beneath her hands.

Cale hauled in a ragged breath. "Baby, baby, baby," he muttered, smoothing his thumbs over Crystal's delicate cheekbones. "Where have you been all my life?" Dipping his head, he captured her lips again, and Crystal experienced the sensation of a weightless free fall.

Nothing like this had ever happened to her before. She'd never lost her control around men. Never. Not even during her brief engagement. Panic reared suddenly, shutting off her intake of air. It made no sense. The faces of people she'd loved, people who'd left her, beat at the back of her eyelids. Women, as well as men. Her mother and Margaret Lyon. Her dad and her fiancé. Funny, Crystal couldn't recall his name.

Her lungs still refused to take in air. Words of warning shrieked in her ears. *Back off! Back off! You're nothing to Caleb Tanner. You're a fool to fall for him.*

Gaby insisted some men were different. She'd been through hell with her first husband, so she ought to know. Hadn't she found André? Gaby said he'd filled all the empty lonely places in her heart and soul. She'd fought her attraction to him at first, too.

Crystal willed the panic to subside until little by little reason returned.

For her.

Not for Caleb. He'd quit thinking about anything except how perfectly their mouths and bodies fit. Until, in spite of his fever, he felt the passion leave her. One-sided lovemaking had never appealed to him. Even a man who'd clearly drifted over the edge could only kiss for so long if he wasn't being kissed back. Filling his lungs with air scented by her perfume, he braced his forehead against hers. No sense letting her see how unsteady he was. But he should have been prepared. He hadn't met a woman yet who didn't know when it was time to lay out her bargaining chips. What made him think Crystal Jardin was different?

They each eased back a little. Crystal released his shirt-front, a bit mortified at how wrinkled she'd left it. She wished he'd say something. But why should he? He might have laid the fire, but she'd struck the match.

Crystal bent to retrieve his crutches. As she propped them beneath his arms, she noticed his eyes were tense and wary. "I think it's safe to say we had similar thoughts today, Tanner. There's obviously an...attraction." She stepped well back and linked her hands loosely, though she gazed fixedly at something beyond his shoulder. "Now that we've appeased the basic urge, we can put all the wondering behind us. Get the attraction under control. Which is good," she hastened to say, darting a cool glance his way. "Otherwise the sexual tension might have built and eventually spilled over into the workplace. Co-workers have to be so careful these days. But I'm sure you know that."

She was proud of how rational she sounded—and on such short notice, too. Shrugging lightly, she sidestepped him and returned to the kitchen. And was extremely grateful for the breakfast bar that hid her quaking knees and trembling hands as she unloaded the dishes and flatware and filled his dishwasher.

Caleb bounced back and forth between wanting to shake her and wanting to kiss her again. His "basic urge" wasn't in the least "appeased." Nor had he put anything behind him. He was frankly irked at how easily she skipped from passionate kisses to a trite unemotional speech. *Get the attraction under control.* As if what they'd just done was solely in the interest of workplace harmony.

"I'll take your word on the climate at WDIX," he said.

"I've got nothing to compare it to. I can't recall a single time I ever wanted to kiss another football player."

Crystal glanced up from her self-imposed chore. He looked so fiercely serious that she couldn't help laughing.

"What's so funny?"

"You are, Tanner. Care to explain all the hugging and butt-slapping that goes on during a football game? That's not acceptable behavior around *my* workplace."

"I thought you didn't watch football," he said, eyeing her suspiciously. "That's what your pal Skip said."

"It's hard not to see bits of it when you surf the TV channels. Not to mention the sports segment at the end of the nightly news. Football, soccer and hockey are so barbaric I'd never sit through an entire game."

Her attitude toward his profession grated. He'd do well to remember it the next time he got the urge to kiss her. "Don't knock it till you've tried it."

Crystal turned on the dishwasher, then rolled up the leftover shelf paper, thankful they'd hit on a subject that reminded her how foolish kissing him had been. "I admit I can't understand the appeal of rough-and-tumble games to fans or players. Fans, especially. The player at least earns big bucks."

"Earns and spends them," he lamented, bracing himself on his crutches. "Now that the subject's come up, I've been meaning to ask if you could recommend one of those financial counselors you keep talking about. What kind of cut do they take? Are they expensive?"

Turning from where she'd been opening yet another box, Crystal studied his earnest expression. Well, he'd certainly gotten over kissing her easily enough. Her heart still tripped a few speeds faster. "Who's been looking after your business affairs so far?" she asked, hoping to sound as casual as he.

"No one. Leland steered me to a guy who does my taxes. He puts sticky notes on the form telling me where to sign. Last year he included a letter saying I ought to shelter part of my earnings." One of Caleb's broad shoulders rose and fell in a gesture stating more clearly than words that he'd done nothing about the suggestion.

"I'm...dumbfounded. You've played professional ball for over ten years and no one brought up investment savings until last year?"

"Oh, they did. But I thought I had plenty of time. So it's too late to consult a moneyman, huh?"

"No, it's never too late. I set up initial investments for an older employee at WDIX. Would you like me to do a workup and financial profile for you? No charge," she said hastily into the silence.

Cale stared at her a moment, then swallowed the pride that urged him to refuse her generosity. "Sure. You bet." Even as he accepted, he knew this wasn't the type of relationship his body wanted to have with this woman.

"When?" Crystal felt guilty at the joy his agreement spurred. Their jobs at WDIX would rarely cross. Not at all, unless he mismanaged his expense account. Even then she'd work through Nate. Directing Tanner's financial plan ensured regular meetings.

"Whatever suits you," he finally said.

Afraid to show her pleasure, Crystal grabbed her purse and made for the door. "No sense letting moss grow under your feet. I'll run to the market and when I get back, we can sit down and get the process rolling. I have worksheets in my briefcase. I'll transfer everything to a computerized spreadsheet later. Then, if you want to switch to someone else, the file will be easy to transfer."

"You want to start tonight?"

Her smile slipped. "I'm sorry. I wasn't thinking. Of

course you're not up to it. I'll buy groceries, then we'll set an appointment for another day."

"No. Hey, I feel fine. Tell me what preliminary information you need. I'll dig stuff out while you're gone."

"Last year's tax form. Checking and savings balances. Plus you should make a list of assets and liabilities. I won't be gone long." She twisted the doorknob.

Caleb stayed her with a glance while he pulled out his wallet and removed a sheaf of bills. "Use what you need to stock my cupboards. Save enough to swing by the Thai place for takeout, okay?" He held out the wad to her. As if on cue, his stomach growled.

"A hundred ought to do it," she said dryly, plucking one from the thick stack. She shoved the remaining bills back into his hand. "If you're always this free with your cash, Tanner, it's a good thing you have plenty more where this came from."

Caleb said nothing. But his heart sank as he watched her flip her braid and disappear into the sultry night. He'd given Crystal the impression, as he had his sisters, that he had a limitless supply of cash. The truth was, until he earned his first paycheck from Lyon Broadcasting, paying for his next meal was iffy. Well, maybe not quite that bad. He had enough to arrange for a phone, utilities and to pay two months' rent. Plus a Visa payment. Provided Patsy didn't go overboard on her wedding.

As Crystal's car engine roared to life, Caleb slapped his forehead with a flat palm. Whatever had possessed him to invite Crystal Jardin to scrutinize the sorry state of his finances?

But he knew the answer. Crystal and her music enriched a portion of his life that had been growing steadily bleaker. So be it. If he had to accept her services as an accountant to ensure her continued visits, that was exactly what he'd do.

Tanner, you're a sorry son of a bitch!

What would the fans who considered him a star quarterback think of this latest development? A man reduced to plotting, to accepting a woman's generosity, just to keep her in his life. He'd be the laughingstock of the NFL.

Tough!

No one, not fans, media or teammates, knew the real man who resided beneath the cocky football player's persona. He'd been two people for so long he hardly knew who he was himself. An ordinary guy whose roots sprang from deep in the Texas hill country? Or the jock he'd learned to let people see because that was what they expected? He realized, although it'd been a realization slow in coming, he'd been wrong to fear that without football he'd be nothing. His life had simply taken a different direction. Thanks to Crystal Jardin. She'd helped him scale one hell of a hurdle. Now if she could only put his finances in some kind of order, he just might marry her and—

Whoa, dude! Gracie, Patsy and Jenny would nail his hide good for that kind of thoughtless notion. Cale grinned. Those three kept him grounded in reality, too. The girls had been suspicious of Crystal's bursting into his life. They'd probably all get along if they ever met. It shocked him to realize how much he wanted that.

He broke off musing and trolled the rooms in search of the box that contained his tax forms and financial records. He found what he was looking for in a corner of the bedroom closet. Carrying the heavy box into the living room on crutches proved impossible. These were the inadequacies Caleb hated. But he wouldn't knuckle under, dammit. Painstakingly, he removed a layer at a time from the box and made several trips into the outer room, where he stacked everything on the dining-room table. He'd just emptied the box when he heard the jingle of keys at the front door.

Caleb was exhausted. A triumphant kind of exhaustion, to be sure. He still had a smile on his face when Crystal staggered in, carrying a leather briefcase and an armload of sacks.

"Here, let me help." Swiveling, he navigated toward her.

"Don't be silly." She pushed his hand aside with her elbow. "You might fall. I can manage," she assured him, kicking the door closed.

"The more I do, the quicker I'll get better."

"If you don't kill yourself first," she grunted, hefting the bags onto the counter.

He studied her jerky movements before he said in a dangerously soft voice, "Are you moving in with me, Crystal?" She whirled, almost dropping a carton of eggs, before he added, "That's the only way to keep me safe from all of life's pitfalls." He locked on her stormy gaze a moment longer, then muttered, "Do you nurture everyone you know, or am I a special case?"

She yanked open the refrigerator door and put the eggs and a carton of milk inside. "Macho jerk. These floors are slick, and you did almost fall earlier."

"What makes you think that wasn't calculated to get you in my arms?" He sent her a pleased smile.

Crystal slammed a container of orange juice and several packs of cold cuts into the fridge. "Stop it. You'd change your tune if you lost your balance and couldn't even dial 911. Lord knows why I care, but I realized my cell phone was in the car. I'm leaving it with you until you get yours connected." She unsnapped her briefcase and tossed a small black phone onto the counter.

"Th-thanks," he stammered. "My cell phone is still packed in some box. So thanks for the loan...." He paused, then said in a low voice, "Forgive me for being sarcastic. I hate being disabled. It's been a long time since I depended on anybody but Caleb Tanner."

She took the last bag from the counter and carried it to the table. "Dinner," she announced. "Will it injure your ego if I set the table?"

A flush stole over his cheeks. "I'm afraid the extent of my talent in the kitchen stops at icing a six-pack of beer."

"At least you're honest. Sit," she directed, then returned to the kitchen where she grabbed two warm plates and a couple of forks from the still-hot dishwasher. Opening the fridge, she lifted two brown bottles from a carton. "You're in luck tonight, Tanner. I bought cold beer. If it's not your favorite brand, too bad." Back at the table, she smacked the two bottles down in front of him and then doled out the meager table service.

He eyed her speculatively as he twisted off the first cap. "I'm a one-beer man. I trust you're joining me?"

She nodded but continued to open several white cartons. Steam rose in a cloud, enveloping them in spicy aromas. Simultaneously they leaned into it, closed their eyes and sniffed. On discovering what they'd done, they both dissolved into laughter.

"I'm so hungry my tongue's hanging out," Caleb admitted.

Crystal pushed a carton and a set of chopsticks in his direction before she sat on a chair across from him. "Then dig in."

"Ladies first." He bracketed the array of boxes with his large hands and slid them toward her.

"I'm not bashful," she said, dipping out a dollop of rice. "I didn't ask what you liked, Tanner, so I bought my favorites. You may be sorry you let me help myself first."

He watched her make dainty piles around her plate. "If that's all you're taking, I don't think I have to worry." When she'd finished filling her plate, he generously heaped his own.

"It's your money." Setting her fork aside, Crystal extracted a five, two ones and some change from her pocket and laid it on the table. "I tried to spend carefully, but I don't have much left."

He swallowed the bite he'd taken before speaking again. "Looks to me like you got a lot of food for less than a hundred bucks. Not that I know what groceries cost. I always ate out."

"Really?" She paused, a forkful of peppery chicken halfway to her mouth.

Caleb nodded. "Except for the times married teammates took pity on a lonely bachelor and invited me to their homes."

"You had a kitchen in the apartment you just left that any woman I know would die for. If you don't cook, why on earth rent a place with a gourmet kitchen?"

His shoulder rose and fell. "All the single players lived in that building." He waved a stalk of broccoli. "Did you notice the view? 'Course, I wasn't home to enjoy it much."

She stared at him through a few more bites.

He finally stopped and blotted his lips with a napkin. "Don't ever play poker," he advised. "You can't hide your feelings worth shit. Spell it out, lady. You've got something on your mind, so let's hear it."

"I heard that the rent in that high-rise *starts* at three

thousand a month. Your place must have been closer to five. Why would you pay over fifty thousand a year for housing you weren't there to enjoy?''

''Because it's what NFL players do.'' Caleb shoved his empty plate away.

''Or maybe you did it because an upscale address impresses the women.'' Crystal pursed her lips as she resealed the cartons.

Leaning across the table, he grabbed her hand. ''For damn sure I wasn't trying to impress a woman with a calculator for a mind.''

Crystal rose stiffly. ''If that's the way you feel, Tanner, it's rather pointless for me to handle your financial planning. I believe in conservative spending and careful investment.''

She'd gathered the cartons, placed them in the fridge and returned for the plates before Caleb spoke again. ''I need your help, Crystal,'' he said in a husky voice. ''If I don't cut back, I'll never make it through this year.''

Crystal had seen bloodhounds with less-soulful eyes. ''All right,'' she said, glancing away. ''Let me rinse these dishes. Go ahead and spread your papers out on the table.''

By the time she came back, he had several neat stacks laid out in a row. He'd also set her briefcase on the table.

The first thing Crystal did was pull out several sharpened pencils, a calculator, a tablet of ledger sheets and a pair of half-glasses, which she perched on her nose. One pencil she stuck crosswise through the top of her braid. With another, she wrote neat headings across two of the sheets.

''How do you manage to write so straight?'' Caleb asked. ''Mine always goes uphill or down.'' He moved forward for a closer look.

Crystal chuckled. "I'm writing on lines, silly. That's the advantage of working with numbers. You get to use graph paper."

"My writing isn't the most legible," he acknowledged, cracking the knuckles on both hands.

She lifted her head. "Why do men always do that? Crack their knuckles," she clarified when he raised an eyebrow in question. "It's something they start in elementary school."

He turned the chair sideways and slouched so he could stretch out his bad leg. Linking his fingers, he placed both hands on his chest and tapped his thumbs together briskly. "I guess it's a nervous habit."

"Are you nervous?" Crystal peered at him over the top of her glasses.

He shifted uncomfortably. "Yes, I am."

"Why? You're under no obligation, Tanner."

He quickly loosened his hands and scraped back a lock of hair that had fallen into his eyes. "Maybe I'm nervous because women I kiss aren't in the habit of calling me Tanner. I have a perfectly good first name. Caleb." He tapped the sheet where she'd penciled "Tanner." He spelled it slowly, never releasing her eyes.

Though her heart leaped wildly and blood whooshed in her ears, Crystal gave no indication that his mention of the kiss they'd shared affected her in any way. She simply wrote "CALEB" above his last name. Lowering her gaze, she began asking questions. Halfway through the first sheet, she'd already broken the tips off all but one of her pencils. Rather than explode over his frivolous wasteful expenditures, Crystal methodically opened her briefcase and extracted a full box of sharp pencils. She held her tongue until she'd filled in all the blanks, run her calculations and double-underlined the final figure.

Frowning, she tapped the eraser on the number several times while she tried to assemble what she was going to say.

"That bad?" he murmured, squinting at her as he massaged a kink from his neck.

She sighed. "I guess it isn't *entirely* bad. At least, it's not a negative figure, Tanner, uh, Caleb."

He craned his neck to read what she'd written. "One thousand eighty-three dollars? Is that spendable money?"

Crystal looked up, aghast. "You frittered away a million bucks last year alone. In ten years, you haven't saved a dime. I ran the figures twice or I wouldn't have believed my eyes."

Caleb parked his elbows on the table and let his chin drop into his hands. "Anybody ever tell you you're cute when you get steamed?"

She sputtered ineffectually. "Quit trying to sidetrack me. This isn't funny, Tanner. You're flirting with financial disaster. Outside of utilities, you can't spend a nickel this month."

"No can do." He shook his head. "I've got Jenny's college tuition due, plus I owe for her car repairs. And a slew of bills are coming in for Patsy's wedding."

"But...but..." she stammered. "You have no money." Crystal tore off her glasses and stared at him, eye to eye.

"I've never had a loan. But I suppose I'll have to take one out."

"What will you use for collateral? You said you'd signed away your farm."

"Yep." His eyes turned a muddy green. "The cars are all mine, though. I house them in one of the barns."

"What cars?" Crystal felt the beginnings of a nagging headache.

"You mean I forgot to mention my cars? I sort of collect them."

"Vintage?" Crystal donned her glasses and pulled a new sheet of paper toward her. "How many?"

He bent his fingers one by one, then lost count and started over again. "They aren't all vintage. Some are high-performance cars. Maserati, Alpha Romeo, a Rolls and a Jaguar or two. I forget exactly how many there are."

She closed her eyes and counted to ten. "Can you estimate their worth in cold hard cash?"

"That's difficult. Hey, how'd you like to go take a look?" He named a date in late October. "That's my sister Patsy's wedding. Could we keep it to ourselves about you being my financial guru, though? Maybe we could pretend you're my date."

Crystal heard a crash. She thought in her shock that she'd fallen from her chair and blinked down in surprise to see that she'd knocked her briefcase off the table, instead.

"Terrible idea, huh?" Caleb said.

"Actually, I like the idea. Ever since Uncle Paul died, I've been under a lot of stress." She bundled up all the papers she'd been working on and crammed them into her briefcase, along with those that had scattered on the floor. "I have to go now. Tomorrow I'll ask André for the time off. When I pick you up to take you to therapy, I'll let you know what he says. Meanwhile, keep this ledger sheet and list any other assets you happen to remember."

She had the door open by the time he shook himself alert enough to ask, "Like what kind of assets?"

"Oh, gee, I don't know, Tanner. Yachts, diamond mines, champion Thoroughbreds. Any little ol' thing you have tucked away in Texas."

He gave a start as the door slammed behind her. "That's one touchy female," he muttered to the empty room. "I wonder if my four gold fillings count...."

CHAPTER TEN

AT BREAKFAST, André, Gabrielle, Leslie and Michael caught Crystal up on everything that had happened at the board meeting.

"Without Mama there and in the absence of her proxy, Charles, via Alain, forced us to table all our proposals," André complained.

"All expansion plans, including updating equipment," Gaby said. "They didn't fight us on monies allocated to hire Cale Tanner. Outside of that, it was a useless meeting."

Crystal waited to ask her question until the nanny, who'd come to collect Andy-Paul and Cory to take them to school, let the kids hug everyone at the table. When they'd gone and after André had poured fresh chicory coffee all around, Crystal folded her hands around the hot mug. "This morning I heard Andy-Paul crying and asking for his Grandmère. We've been so long without word from Margaret, I'm getting scared."

Gabrielle and André gripped each other's hands on top of the table. André was first to clear his throat and speak. "You're not alone, Crystal. The worry's beginning to interfere with my ability to concentrate at work. I've set a meeting with Dave Patton this morning. I don't want this to go any farther, but we feel Alain's agenda at the board meeting was too...pat."

"How?" Crystal stirred cream into her thick black coffee.

Gaby's gaze drifted to her pregnant daughter, Leslie, who concurred with a nod. "It's difficult to pin down precisely," Gaby told Crystal. "Everyone at the meeting knew Margaret's gone off somewhere. But our family really expected her to show up. Even Charles, I think. He wanted to delay the start of the meeting, although Margaret's never late."

"We're probably way off base, Crystal," André put in. "Alain didn't say anything overt. It's more that he had a ready rebuttal for every issue needing a vote."

"The four of us agree he could have spent a lot of time poring over the financial packet you prepared," Michael interjected. "But..." He glanced at the others and let his sentence trail off.

"But what?" Crystal pressed. "As staunchly as Margaret supports family, I've seen her go out of her way to avoid Alain. Still, he is a lawyer, don't forget."

Leslie spoke. "A shyster. Grandmère hated the way Alain treated his ex. I say it's too bad Yvette didn't kill him that time she shot him."

"Leslie!" Gaby sounded shocked. "Your grandmother would never approve."

Crystal defused the mother-daughter argument. "Gaby, surely you don't think Alain knows where Margaret is, do you?"

"We don't...really." André sighed. "I know he's an unfeeling bastard. But if you'd seen how fast Ray jumped in to second all of Alain's motions... It was as if they knew in advance we wouldn't have Mama's vote."

Crystal frowned. "Ray is such a jerk. He's putting the moves on April Stockton. Michael, you remember her? The accountant I hired?"

He opened his mouth, but André growled, "I hope you told her to report Ray to Michael or me if he persists in bothering her."

"April has his number. She's heard he hustles every new female employee under the age of thirty-five. I was sort of surprised he laid it on so thick while I was around. He gave her the old song and dance about Alain taking over as general manager. Ray intimated that if April was nice to him, her job would be secure."

Gaby struck the table. "That SOB!"

"I warned him he was flirting with a harassment charge."

"Did he back off?" André asked.

"No. Puffed up and blustered about what would happen to me when Margaret's dynasty took a tumble. April and I left soon after that." Crystal set her cup aside and stood. "Speaking of leaving, I've gotta run. I promised Nate I'd take Tanner to his physical-therapy appointment this afternoon, so I'm heading into work early."

André folded his napkin and climbed to his feet, too. "Crystal, when did that conversation with Raymond take place?"

"Don't worry about him, André. I can handle Ray. He suffers delusions of grandeur," Crystal said. "Alain, too."

"I thought all of that nonsense about me not being a Lyon had died," André murmured, beginning to pace in front of the sideboard. "Alain met privately with our family attorney after Papa's funeral. Yesterday Patton learned that Alain may contest Papa's will."

"On what grounds?" Leslie and Crystal said together.

"That I'm not his blood son, what else? Uncle Charles fueled that rumor years ago. Alain and Ray have always preferred to believe it. When I meet with David Patton today, I think I'll ask him to see if he can find out what's prompted the rumor to surface again.''

''No, André.'' Gaby clutched his arm. ''Let their jealousy wither away for lack of proof. Or tell Charles to quiet them. At Sharlee's christening I gave him copies of her baby pictures, Paul's and yours. Charles openly admitted the family resemblance. At Paul's funeral I heard him tell Margaret how Andy-Paul's the spitting image of your grandfather. Charles more or less apologized for the rift he'd caused. I gather your parents separated over it, or at least had a marital spat.''

''I've never known the particulars, but yes. What was Mama's response?''

''I didn't hear. I remember thinking how sad it was that your parents suffered Charles's wrath for so many years because your grandfather deliberately divided the business unevenly. I'd really hoped that with Charles softening, it'd mean Andy-Paul would have an easier time running WDIX. Will the family feud never end, André?''

He gathered Gaby in his arms and tucked her head under his chin. ''The week Mama went missing, I'd intended to broach the possibility of selling the whole shooting match. At our age, honey, I'm not sure we can cope long enough to groom Andy-Paul. He shouldn't feel obligated to take the helm like I did.''

A lump lodged in Crystal's throat as she listened, and her heart echoed Gaby's protests. It'd been no secret within the family that Gabrielle loved the business as much as Margaret did. Nor was it a secret that André had reluctantly stepped into Paul's shoes following his first heart attack. Crystal strongly suspected that André had stayed because he loved Gaby. Of course, he maintained a bond with his parents, but it was his commitment to

Gabrielle that set the course for his life. Crystal admired and envied it.

She cleared her throat, then whispered, "If Margaret had any inkling you were going to suggest selling, André, that could have caused her to take flight. Since the day Andy-Paul was born, she's been making plans for him to run the company one day."

André raised his head from Gaby's. "Mama couldn't have known, Crystal. This is the first I've breathed a word to anyone. I wouldn't have mentioned it even now, but I'm getting some really bad feelings about her disappearance. If David doesn't turn up something soon, I'm going to involve the police. I've reached the point of not caring if it shakes our place in the broadcast community. We've lost sponsors before, and they've always come back."

Gaby gripped her eldest daughter's hand. "That decision should please you, Leslie. I know you've thought from the beginning that we should call the police. Sharlee wishes she wasn't so sick with this pregnancy. I believe she'd come here to investigate, look into things." Gaby's voice shook. "For the sake of the business, I think we need to give Patton a little more time."

"Damn the business!" Leslie exclaimed. "I just want Grandmère found."

"I do, too," Gabrielle said, nervously fluttering her hands.

Crystal saw André blink repeatedly as he took one of his wife's hands and pressed his lips to her palm. Crystal, too, blinked back tears as she left for work.

It was as if a pall had fallen over Lyoncrest, and over the TV station, as well. Her world, which had turned upside down after the death of her mother, had seemed to right itself during these years she'd worked at Lyon Broadcasting and lived with the family. Crystal credited

Margaret's generous spirit for that. Now things had started to spin out of control again. She'd almost forgotten how family tension could cause her stomach to roll and pitch. It was terrible of Alain and Ray to have taken advantage of André and Gaby's unavoidable predicament at the board meeting. This was one of the rare times she regretted that her own grandmother had never had a vote. Today, Justine Lyon Jardin's stock would be hers to wield.

If Ray Lyon had been in his office, Crystal would have demanded to know why he and his brother were deliberately sowing discontent in the family again. As his area was dark and the door locked, her interrogation would have to wait.

Which was probably a good thing, she decided, stomping into her office. André wouldn't appreciate her fighting his battles. But dammit, she could imagine all too well how fast Lyon Broadcasting would decline with Alain as CEO.

At her desk the first thing she took from her briefcase was Tanner's budget worksheets. From what she'd gathered in their sketchy conversations, his life hadn't been any too easy. Then there was Skip and his pals. Skip, poor kid, didn't even know where he'd be living when he was finally released. It was enough to make her wonder if there were such things as totally stable households. Look at Rachel. And Jacob. They'd had to deal with broken families, too.

Crystal's dark mood prevailed all morning. It clung to her like the smell of fresh paint as she left the building at noon and drove to pick up Tanner.

He noticed the absence of her sunny attitude the minute he tossed his crutches into the back seat and heaved himself into the car.

"Rough day?" he queried.

"I guess," she said without inflection.

"You should've let me know. I'd have called a cab."

"Cab rides don't fit into your budget picture, Tanner," she said. Glancing at him fully for the first time as she eased away from the curb, Crystal saw the wink of a diamond in his ear. That must have cost a pretty penny. He could eat for several weeks if he sold it. But she'd tackle that later.

"I had some spare time this morning, Tanner, so I fed the figures we compiled last night into a basic computerized budget program. I got your exact salary figure from personnel and calculated withholdings. I used the difference for your monthly income. Then I plugged in your bills based on the expenditures for which I had receipts."

"And?" He arched a brow when she hesitated.

"And if the bills you gave me are correct and that's all you owe, it'll be tight, but if you're frugal you ought to be able to begin a small investment program six months down the road."

"Frugal?" Cale didn't like the sound of that.

She ignored his scowl. "Your credit-card debt is killing you, Tanner. For this plan to work, you have to get the cards back from your sisters and cut up all but one, which you'll keep only for emergencies."

"Now wait a damned minute. The girls depend on me."

"I allowed a reasonable maintenance for Jenny while she's still in college. Patsy is getting married next month, and you said Grace has started a good job."

He tugged at his earring. "I thought I'd subsidize Gracie's apartment in Austin for the first year. Just till she gets on her feet. How can I not buy them trinkets and things every month or so? I always have."

"Trinkets. Ah, yes," she murmured as she navigated a

busy intersection. "I suppose that's the stack of receipts I added up from various jewelry stores. How many trinkets do three girls need? You spent enough on baubles last year to buy a few pieces of prime Texas real estate."

"Uh, those weren't all gifts for my sisters," he muttered.

"Oh?"

"I do have a social life."

She felt the heat coil in her stomach. It wouldn't be the first time she'd imagined him with a bevy of beautiful women. "I, um...I'm afraid your social life will be greatly curtailed for a while."

"You'd better show me a copy of this budget," he said. "Did you allow me *anything* for entertainment?"

The annoyed bewildered look on his face provoked a wry smile from Crystal. "Entertainment is an occasional pizza and beer, or the cover charge at a jazz club in the Quarter. You may be reduced to picnics in the park, Tanner. Trinkets, as you call them, made of platinum, gold, rubies and pearls fall under the heading of major purchases. And you don't have the money for those, pal. In fact, to pay down your debt to where you're looking at solvency, you'll have to sell a few cars. I don't see any other way around it."

"Sell my cars?" he choked. "But I'm just getting a decent collection."

She backed neatly into a parking space in the hospital lot, then brought the car to a complete standstill before she answered. "Automobiles depreciate. You'd have been better off investing in mutual funds. Nevertheless it's a good thing you didn't throw all your money away. Selling some of the more expensive cars might get you out of the red. Bear in mind that if you sold the lot, you'd lop off what you're paying your uncle in storage fees, too."

"I've only sent him storage money for the last two years. Grace told me storms and drought played havoc with his bringing in a decent melon crop. He doesn't charge me rent. But he's a proud man, so I devised a method to help him out."

"And that's commendable," Crystal said gently. "According to notes made by your tax man, you've helped half the people in your hometown in one way or another. But your circumstances have changed. You can't be a one-man Salvation Army anymore, Caleb."

He gazed at her through those long dark eyelashes. Following a lengthy staring match, during which neither one gave ground, he smiled broadly, then leaned over and kissed her on the mouth. He took his time about it, too.

Crystal could hardly breathe. The cool minty taste of his lips sent shivers along her jaw. His aftershave, different from the one he'd used in the hospital, carried a subtle kick. She had no idea how long the kiss went on before she managed to extricate herself from his hold. "Wh-what was that for?" she asked.

"For using my first name," he said, hands still cupping the back of her head. "That's cause to celebrate." His thumbs traced lazy circles around the inner shell of her ear. "How about I take you out on the town tonight?"

Twisting her door handle, Crystal almost fell out of the car. She walked around the hood, jerked his door open and leaned over him to get his crutches. "I'm jamming with the band tonight. And, Tanner, nights on the town— the kind *you're* talking about—are something you'll have to eliminate."

He hopped on one foot, holding on to the door handle until she thrust the crutches into his hands. "Now I know why I never looked for a financial adviser before. They're a pain in the ass."

Crystal slammed the door after setting the lock. "Listen, Tanner," she said irritably, "my advice is free. You can take it or leave it. All you have to answer to me for is your company expense account."

"I was just mouthing off, okay? I appreciate everything you've done." His expression was suitably contrite. "It'll be a major adjustment. At least for a year, until I get in shape to play again."

As she watched him limping up the sidewalk on crutches, his one leg all but useless, Crystal felt a pang in her heart for him. He was so determined. She wondered how he'd adjust if he didn't recover enough to play again. Slowing her steps, she fell in behind him.

The automatic doors to the physical-therapy unit opened as soon as Caleb's crutches hit the corrugated rubber mat. Crystal didn't trail him into the building. "How long will you be? I want to run up and see Skipper while you're in your session."

"Then come on in. He and another kid are scheduled in my hour."

"Oh. Darn, I thought I'd have some time to spend with him. I wouldn't want to distract him or anything when he's trying to listen to his therapist."

"No sweat. We each have programs the therapists set up. We run through them at our own pace until they add new exercises."

"They trust the kids not to overdo it?"

"Why not? Kids aren't stupid. If something hurts, they back off."

She looked unsure. Seeing Skipper being wheeled over to one of the apparatuses, she excused herself and crossed the room.

"Hey, tiger. How's everything going? Sorry I didn't get to see you yesterday. I helped Tanner move."

The boy's face lit up the moment she came into his view. "Cale said you were going to drive him to therapy every day. That's cool. You wanna see what I learned to do yesterday?" he said in the next breath. Then before Crystal could respond, he grabbed eagerly for a set of metal rings that hung a foot or more above his head and hauled himself aloft by his arms.

Crystal's heart almost leaped from her chest as he swung back and forth, then twisted right and left. His paralyzed legs slapped the wheelchair, which he hadn't locked, and the force rolled it out of his reach. "Skipper, watch out!" Issuing a fearful cry, Crystal lunged for the chair. Because of its unwieldy bulk, it took time for her to maneuver it under Skip so he could ease into it again.

"Sweetheart, you could've fallen and hit this hard floor! What you did is terribly dangerous. I can't believe Mindy approves this sort of therapy."

"Crystal, stop mollycoddling the kid. If he doesn't push himself, he'll never get well."

She spun and faced Tanner, who, in the time she'd been with Skip, had strapped himself into an adjacent apparatus of wheels and pulleys. The machine worked rather like a bicycle, stretching the muscles of his injured leg. Sweat had popped out on his brow and his teeth were clenched.

Crystal glared at him until she saw Skip safely ensconced in his chair. Once the boy had wheeled a distance away to a table of weights, she turned and hissed menacingly at Caleb, "Maybe you aren't aware that Skipper's lost the use of both legs. He's here to improve the strength in his arms and shoulders. Obviously he shouldn't do that at the risk of further injury."

"So you're content to consign him to that chair forever?" Caleb used the tail of his undershirt to wipe his brow.

"It's not me! His doctor said the nerves in Skip's lower back didn't regenerate and—"

Cale cut her off with an impatient movement of his hand. "If I'd believed everything doctors told me about my injuries, I'd've been forced to quit playing ball five years ago. Doctors make mistakes. They aren't God."

"But if the nerves that supply feeling and mobility to the child's legs have quit working, it seems cruel to get his hopes up for any kind of recovery."

"One of the New York Jets linemen was paralyzed from the neck down. They shot him full of an experimental drug, and he's learning to walk again. Maybe they'll perfect the stuff and it'll work for Skip. Meanwhile, though, he's got to keep those muscles toned."

"You talked to Skipper about this drug?" She sucked in a huge breath. "How dare you? Even if such a drug were available to ballplayers who can afford them, that doesn't mean a boy in the welfare system has any prayer of getting it. Rachel told me the foster-care program doesn't even fund second opinions."

A smoky haze descended over Cale's green eyes. "Tough break for the kid. Still doesn't mean he should give up," he said stubbornly.

"I'm not advocating he give up. Under the best of circumstances, his life isn't going to be easy. Sooner or later he has to face reality."

"Reality stinks. Dreams are what make miracles happen."

Hearing Skipper call her name, Crystal gazed at Caleb's set features only a moment longer. Then she hurried over to spend her remaining time with someone who wasn't so hardheaded.

"Have you seen Sandy?" Skipper asked Crystal as he

hefted weights. "How long do chicken pops last, anyway?"

"Pox. It's chicken pox, Skip. And no, I haven't spoken with her recently. Has…hasn't Rachel been to visit you?"

"Yeah. A couple times. I thought if Sandy came and saw how good I'm doing in therapy, she'd call Ms. Fontaine or something. They won't really make me leave Sandy's—will they, Crystal?"

His words held such longing Crystal had to swallow and turn away. When she was finally able to speak, her voice sounded thick. "You'll have to take that up with Rachel, buddy. I know she cares about you, and she'll do her very best for you."

"Yeah, sure." He didn't seem convinced. "I'll tell you a secret if you won't snitch to the other guys. Every night I pray somebody'll show up who wants to adopt a kid like me. Randy says I'm crazy. He says God don't listen to kids. He said people who adopt just want babies. Is that true, Crystal?"

A terrible pain stabbed through her heart; another one behind her eyes made the room swim. Crystal bit her bottom lip until the fluorescent lights were no longer ringed by a misty halo. She'd just told Tanner to stop being unrealistic, and here she stood on the verge of doing the same. "Randy strikes me as a cynic," she said at last.

"What's a cynic?"

"A person with a gloomy outlook. Do you know what 'gloomy' means?"

"Yeah. But Randy's not so tough inside. He has nightmares, too. About his mom getting drunk and forgetting where she left him. His dad went out one day to get the newspaper, and he never came back. You wanna know what Randy likes best about the hospital?"

"The security? A clean bed?" she guessed, but Skip kept shaking his head.

"Nope. He likes getting three meals a day. He always had to scrounge for food unless he went with his mom when she cashed her welfare check."

The ease with which a child like Skipper meted out such sad information left Crystal speechless. Compared to Skip, who'd been abused in an earlier foster home, and his friends upstairs, her life had been a waltz through daisies. Luckily Skip didn't appear to expect a response. Instead, he'd moved to the next exercise on his list. Which was a relief, because Crystal wasn't sure she could have commented without breaking down.

As she continued to tail after Skipper and puzzle over where he'd go when the doctor discharged him, she found herself missing Margaret more and more. Margaret Lyon had a heart as big as the North American continent, and wisdom to match when it came to lost souls. If anything could be done for Skipper, Margaret would know where to start.

"I gotta go back to my room," he suddenly announced. "Did I tell you we got a new resident on our ward? His name's Mark. He plays clarinet. Nurse Pam asked if he played jazz and he said yes. If you bring your sax tonight, he'll do a few tunes with you."

"Oh, sweetie, I can't tonight. I'm spanging some new tunes with the band." When his face fell, she said quickly, "Tell him to bring it tomorrow. I'll run by after work."

"All right!" he shouted, punching the air. "Gibson's here to take me back to the room. See you tomorrow, Crystal. Don't forget."

"He's excited. Looks as if you made his day."

Crystal gave a start. It surprised her that she hadn't heard Tanner come up behind her. "I promised a jam session on his ward tomorrow night. Some new resident apparently plays jazz clarinet, and Skip's arranging for us to do a duet.''

Cale's smile took a nosedive.

"What's the matter?" she asked.

"Nothing. Just that you said you can't spend this evening with me. I thought I'd call your friends and make good on that pizza party tomorrow night.''

"Uh…I'd suggest I drop by after visiting hours, but Jacob probably has an early bedtime for Jordanna.''

"That's all right. You could still stop in after you finish here. We'll include Rachel and Jacob another time.''

"I don't know, Tanner. I should really eat at Lyoncrest before I go to the hospital. I haven't had dinner with the family in over a week.''

His downcast expression prompted her to say, "Tell you what. How about if I pick you up after work and take you to Lyoncrest? You can come to the ward while I play, and afterward I'll drop you at your apartment. You really ought to meet André and his family before you start work at WDIX.''

"I'd like that." He beamed. "Nate said André has plans for me to project an image out in the community. It'd be nice to hear exactly what he has in mind.''

"I recall hearing something to that effect. I can't imagine what you could do in the community, though. Maybe appear at high-profile fund-raisers. Mostly our team of newscasters does that, but who knows?" She shrugged.

"Fund-raisers. I'm having a hard time picturing what a news team would do.''

"Oh, you know, organizations like Kiwanis or Junior League might put on a circus in the park or something. Occasionally our newscasters help with MC duties. They give away mugs and T-shirts—stuff like that. It enhances the station's image with our viewers.''

"Hmm. Doesn't sound like my bailiwick."

"Well, don't worry needlessly. Wait until André spells out what he wants." They'd progressed as far as the car. Crystal stopped to open the passenger door and held Caleb's crutches while he eased into the seat.

"Did you hurt yourself at therapy?"

He leaned back and watched her from slitted eyes as she stowed his crutches in the back seat. "You know what they say. No pain, no gain."

"Fools say that, maybe." She sighed loudly as she closed the door. They'd covered that ground on the trip to the hospital. Belaboring her view of these punishing exercises when she had little hope of changing his mind seemed a waste of words. She took her seat, determined not to be drawn into an unwanted argument.

After looking in both directions, she pulled into the street. Half a block down, she turned on the radio. Her mind darted ahead to Skipper's quandary, Margaret's disappearance and finally the snarled traffic. She didn't glance in Caleb's direction again until he spoke.

"You're wrestling with a subject that must be mighty difficult."

"Why do you say that?"

He rubbed a thumb between her eyebrows. "Gee, I don't know. Maybe the frown?"

"Well, nobody's being square with Skip. His doctor isn't telling him the truth about his condition because he doesn't want Skip to give up on therapy. Rachel has to move him from his current foster home. It's not set up for use of his wheelchair. He overheard her talking to the nurse, but Rachel doesn't want to discuss placement with him until she has a new home lined up.'' She shook her head. ''I think it's crappy, all of it.''

''It is. I hate that system. I fought them for over a year, trying to keep them from making my sisters wards of the court when my folks died in a truck crash.''

''That's horrible! No wonder you do so much for the girls. You're like brother, Dad and Santa all rolled into one.''

''Yeah. Something I forgot to add to my list of expenses last night is their trip to visit me next week. I told them to put the airline tickets on my credit card.''

''Hmm. Well, it's not a long trip. Tickets on a commuter flight shouldn't break the bank.''

''Plane fare might not, but the shopping spree I promised them might.''

Crystal groaned. ''Tanner, you have to level with them.''

''What happened to you calling me Caleb?'' Extending his hand, he trailed a finger down her cheek. ''Here I thought we'd gone beyond friends, even.''

She felt the delicious aftershock of his touch all the way to her toes. ''Accountants are immune to sweet talk.''

He opened his mouth.

''And I don't take bribes,'' she added crisply.

He drew back as though stung. ''I wasn't going to bribe you.''

''That was a joke,'' she said, double-parking outside his apartment. ''Do you need help getting out?''

''I can manage.'' He stuck his crutches out first and used them as a brace to lever himself out of the seat. ''By the way, Leland is giving me a ride to PT tomorrow. What time shall I be ready for you? Is there a dress code at Lyoncrest?''

"No. Well, we'll probably be in work clothes. Why do you ask?"

"I can't recall ever being asked to eat at a house that had a name. I figured it might be classier than I'm used to."

"The house is beautiful. But a perfectly normal family lives there. André's parents used to change into formal dress for dinner, but we don't do that anymore."

"Will they be there tomorrow night?"

"What? Oh, no. Paul Lyon passed away last month. Margaret is…well, she's away at the moment. For dinner…don't buy anything special." She glanced at the worn jeans he had on and realized the shirt looked really battered. "Uh, you'd be okay as you are."

"I have decent clothes, sugar. No need to worry I'll embarrass you." He started to shut the door, and she leaned over to hold it ajar.

"Any concern I had was for you and your feelings." Averting her gaze, she muttered, "I'll pick you up at four-thirty, all right?"

"Fine. I'll be out here so you won't have to waste time finding a place to park." He did shut the door then, with a snap. Crystal's fingers tightened on the steering wheel as she heard the coolness in his tone. She wondered if she'd sounded condescending, but it was too late to apologize.

THE NEXT AFTERNOON, she was nervous about collecting Tanner, for a number of reasons.

She ought to have saved herself the worry. Caleb looked superb in black slacks and a khaki shirt. His dress shoes looked as if they'd been spit-shined. He had a smile on his face when he climbed in and tossed his crutches into the back seat. "I'm hungry enough to eat a mule. I hope they don't skimp on food at Lyoncrest," he said.

Crystal's heart surged happily. Another thing in Caleb Tanner's plus column—the man didn't hold grudges. "I guess you haven't lived in New Orleans long enough to hear the saying that we have two times here. Mealtime and in-between. It'll be your own fault if you go away from Lyoncrest hungry."

They laughed and talked about food likes and dislikes until Crystal drove through the wrought-iron gates that hid the house from the street. Caleb stopped talking and simply stared. At dusk, with the chandeliers gleaming behind the tall mullioned windows, Lyoncrest was a magnificent sight.

"We'll go in through the kitchen," she told him. "That way you won't have to navigate a million stairs.

Caleb was aware that the home where he'd grown up would have fit in one corner of Lyoncrest. His current apartment wouldn't even make a dent. She motioned him into an impressive entryway and beyond, to a dining room with walls of hand-rubbed cherry. Everywhere he turned, original artwork met his eye. Some old masters, some local painters. He recognized several by Rodrigue, a local artist who'd become famous for his paintings of blue dogs. Even the man's prints were expensive. Caleb suddenly couldn't believe he'd had the nerve to entertain the notion of starting a relationship with Crystal Jardin. She lived like a frigging princess. No wonder she'd frowned at his wardrobe yesterday. He studied the gleaming cream-colored place settings during the introductions and hoped to hell he wouldn't disgrace her—and himself—by using the wrong fork.

CHAPTER ELEVEN

CALEB'S UNEASINESS didn't last. Leslie Lyon McKay, her husband, Michael, chief of personnel at Lyon Communications, and their daughter, Cory, were home, too. Simultaneous conversations raised the noise level. Andy-Paul and his cousin, Cory, giggled and chattered. André and his son-in-law plunged immediately into the subject of football, pumping Caleb for details of Sinners games they'd missed.

It wasn't until coffee and dessert had been served that Caleb thought to ask about the job. "Nate said I'd probably be doing promotional work in the community, as well as handling football sportscasts. What will that entail?"

It so happened the women's conversation had fallen off. Leslie, newly pregnant, had asked to be excused, and Gabrielle had gone in search of unbreakable bowls to fill with bread pudding for Andy-Paul and Cory. As a special treat, the children were having their dessert in front of the TV. That left Crystal at the table listening to the men's exchange.

André passed Caleb a gravy boat filled with warm rum sauce after he'd ladled out his own. "Our recent demographic studies show that WDIX is losing the school-age viewing crowd—especially fourth grade through junior high. When I asked myself what most appeals to kids in that age bracket, I came up with sports and scary movies. It's our policy to not run horror flicks during family viewing hours. That leaves sports, my friend. It was Michael's idea to send you out to talk at schools.''

"I'm beginning to see. You want me to encourage a renewed interest in sports.'' Caleb handed Crystal the sauce before taking any himself.

"Right.'' André grinned around a spoonful of the rich dessert. "As soon as you feel up to it,'' he said after blotting his lips, "I'll arrange for you to go into class-rooms to chat informally about how team sports build healthy minds and bodies.''

Crystal almost dropped the heavy gravy boat. "André, no! I can't believe you'd condone such a program. Is WDIX ignoring the fact that some children suffer per-manent disabilities due to their participation in sports?''

André planted his elbows on the table and looked thoughtful. "Nate figured you'd come unglued. Michael ran statistics, Crystal. The percentage of kids who sustain permanent injuries from participating in organized sports' programs is tiny.''

"Tell that to kids like Skipper and Pablo and Randy,'' she said bitterly.

Glancing from Crystal's stubborn jaw to André's, Caleb laid out a plan he thought might let them compromise. "Coming off an injury myself puts me in a good position to talk about safety issues. More parents and teachers would give their stamp of approval on a presentation that included safety.''

André nodded. He and Michael broke into happy smiles. Only Crystal continued to scowl. "Ha! Like I'd trust someone who pushes injured kids to exercise beyond their endurance to promote safety!''

"Dammit, Crystal, I never suggested any such thing to your friend Skipper. You need to visit some football camps and see the positive effect of mind over matter.

Today I'm on crutches. Next time you see me I'll have progressed to a cane. A speedy recovery is ninety percent dependent on a patient's unwillingness to accept disability as his fate and ten percent on treatment prescribed by doctors.''

"Bravo!" Gabrielle exclaimed, returning to her seat at the table. "What a great motivational speech. Guys, Caleb's perfect for making the impact on young viewers we hope to make."

Leslie, who'd slipped back unnoticed, squeezed her husband's arm and echoed her assent.

André served his wife a portion of bread pudding. "I think it's how Mama would feel, too, if she was here. Crystal, I know how personally committed you are to the children who require long-term care. When you were in that situation, music was your motivator. Others are moved by a dream of returning to the very sport that struck them down. Shouldn't you support whichever method works?"

She looked carefully into every set of eyes trained on her. "Tanner said much the same thing to me the other day. I'll reserve judgment on your outreach program until I see how it's received by parents and educators. I won't make waves, if that's what you're worried about."

"I'm not trying to coerce you into changing your opinion," André said. "As usual, the Lyon dinner table invites an open forum."

They all smiled at that. Rising, Crystal began stacking empty dessert plates. "At *this* Lyon dinner table," she said, turning to Caleb, "perhaps we ought to warn Tanner it's not that way if he dines with the other side of the family. A week or so ago Ray took me to task because I opposed the addition of a soccer field with nighttime lighting to the community park in our parish. He said if

Alain had been general manager, I'd have been fired. They claim I jeopardized our sports-equipment advertising accounts."

Leslie straightened. "Ray pounced on you? I suppose he'd never admit we've lost local business thanks to rumors of his involvement in the black arts."

Gabrielle silenced Leslie's tirade with a sharp glance. "Let's not color Caleb's perception of the family, Les. We all have to work together."

"Right," Leslie drawled. "Mustn't let strangers think we aren't devoted, one and all. Well, I've detested Raymond since I was a kid, and he knows it."

Gabrielle settled into cool silence, and André rewarded Leslie with a surreptitious grin.

Leslie grinned back, then steered the conversation in a new direction. "Crystal, you keep looking at your watch like you're about to jump and run. Are we keeping you from something?"

"Yes, actually." Crystal handed the stack of plates to the cook and thanked her for a fine meal before elaborating. "There's a new orthopedic resident at the hospital who plays jazz clarinet. Skip and his buddies conned us into doing a few tunes together."

"Well, we all know better than to try and come between Crystal and jazz," Leslie joked. "I need to lie down, but before I go, I wanted to ask—Crystal, have you shown Mr. Tanner your collection of Mardi Gras masks?" Singling him out, Leslie added, "Her collection is fabulous. One whole wall of her bedroom."

"It's also upstairs. Tanner would be hard-pressed to navigate the stairs." Her blush said she didn't want him in her bedroom. She tapped her watch. "Anyway, look how late it is. Skipper's doctor might get tired of waiting, and the kids would be so disappointed."

"I think we have time," Caleb said, turning on his most charming smile. "I can hop pretty fast. Oh, and, Leslie, call me Caleb." He leaned toward her and whispered something that made her glance at Crystal and smother a giggle.

Crystal glared at him. "You haven't seen this staircase. Don't say you weren't warned."

He rose and shook hands with André and Michael. He thanked Gaby for allowing him to share their table and kissed her hand. The old Southern gentleman's gesture pleased her immensely.

"Don't be a stranger, Caleb," she said. "Drop by anytime. As you can see, we have plenty of room and enough food to feed an army." Since Crystal had already escaped the room, Gaby waved him off, too.

Hot on Crystal's heels, Cale took only enough time to lean his crutches against the newel post at the foot of the stairs. Bracketing Crystal's slender waist with his wide quarterback's hands, he surprised her by burrowing his chin into her shoulder and nibbling her ear.

She slapped backward at him.

"Tut-tut. I'm pretty rocky. You don't want me to fall, do you?"

Crystal's muscles bunched as his warm breath feathered over her cheek and neck. "What did you say to Leslie?" she demanded, pausing until he drew level with her on the step. She slipped over to his injured side and dipped a shoulder under his arm so that they now moved up the stairs together.

"I said you called me Tanner because it made you feel like a jock." He nuzzled her hair.

"Behave yourself. I agreed to show you a collection of masks, not etchings."

He laughed, then tightened his hold on her neck in a

jesting elbow lock. His laughter made him tilt his head back and for the first time Caleb absorbed the full impact of the winding staircase topped by a glass dome. He whistled through his teeth.

Crystal grabbed for the railing, afraid she'd somehow hurt his leg. When she saw what had claimed his attention—a full moon raining golden streamers through the glass dome—a fist clenched tight in her abdomen. Something about the moon combined with the warmth of his body made her wish they were going to her suite for reasons other than to look at masks. But they weren't. Sobered, she resumed their ascent.

"Now you see why I'm not in any rush to find a place of my own. We turn here," she said, bracing to take his full weight as they reached the second landing.

"Yeah, I see, all right, " he said as they entered what was most definitely her room. At least, he saw her mark in the bright alcove, whose walls bore jazz-concert posters. An array of expensive musical instruments filled the room. "Considering everything you have, why haven't you bought better treatment for that kid?"

"Everything I have? I'm not rich." She stopped short after leading him into a large room with high ceilings. To her left sat a huge four-poster bed, a vanity, a dresser and a desk. The wall on their right was a riot of colorful ball masks. Crystal frowned. "How can I, or anyone outside the system, help Skipper?"

"Seems to me anybody who has the resources to live here ought to be able to afford a couple shots of that nerve-regeneration drug I told you about. I called the lineman I mentioned. He said the stuff helped him. It's called Sygen." Cale's words trailed off as he stared at the wall. "Wow! I never had a clue they made masks out of feathers, leather, papier-mâché and clay." He let his fingers stroke a few. "Some of these suckers look heavy. Do people really wear them?"

"Yes," she said, pondering what he'd said about an experimental drug that might help Skipper walk again.

Caleb glanced around the room. His scrutiny lingered on a brocade canopy that topped a very inviting bed. For the first time he realized how secluded Crystal's room was from the rest of the house. It didn't help that the moon now filtered through tall glass doors leading out to a private lanai, which also beckoned intimately. Caleb cleared his throat. "I think we'd better go now or we're going to risk being really, really late."

If Crystal caught his meaning, she didn't let on. "Okay. Women love the masks. I suppose men aren't so fascinated."

With moondust sparkling in her hair and gilding her soft skin, Caleb found plenty that fascinated him in Crystal Jardin's room. Maybe too much. He wasn't in any position to dive into a relationship at the moment. And it was getting harder and harder to keep his hands off her.

They'd made their way to the bottom of the stairs, saying little. The doorbell rang as Crystal handed Caleb his crutches. "I'll get it," she called to André, who stood in the door of his study.

The caller was David Patton. He greeted Crystal, then asked, "No more odd activity in Margaret's bank account?"

She shook her head. "Do you have news?"

"I finally reached John Neville. He's been on vacation. He's appalled, as you can well imagine. He can't believe their computer system could be breached. He has no explanation for the missing codes. Apparently it's a sophisticated process that only a very clever hacker could break into. The man vouched for all of his employees."

"A hacker? That seems incredible. Um, are you here to report to André?"

"Yes. I haven't had any luck setting appointments with Alain Lyon or his brother, Ray. I'd hoped André could arrange a meeting. Other than them, I've interviewed almost everyone who attended Paul's funeral."

André stepped into the foyer. "I don't know what Alain and Ray could tell you that others haven't. Those two can be really unpleasant, but I suppose you need to include them."

"Sometimes people see things they don't realize they've seen. Experience tells me it's impossible to disappear without leaving some clues."

"I hope so," Crystal affirmed. "Please excuse us, Mr. Patton. We were on our way out." She introduced Caleb. The men shook hands.

"Ah. I thought you looked familiar," Patton said. "Damn shame you got hurt. Team's win/loss record will go to hell now." The P.I. turned back to Crystal. "Don't let me keep you. Nice meeting you, Tanner." He headed into André's den.

After Caleb and Crystal went out through the kitchen and climbed into the car, he slid an arm across the back of Crystal's seat and massaged her neck. "What was that about? If you get any tenser, you'll explode."

Crystal sighed. "I might as well explain. You'll hear, anyway, depending on how soon you begin work." In fits and starts she described Margie's disappearance. Caleb listened, his fingers stilling on her neck. He made no comment until she'd finished talking about the money evaporating from Margaret's bank account.

"If criminals hijacked her and they had this ability to tap into her funds, wouldn't they fleece her clean?"

"That's what I keep telling myself," she said, sighing

again. "On the other hand, while I know she misses Paul terribly, we're talking about a woman who pioneered WDIX-TV. Through fat times and lean, Margaret made tough decisions that affected the business and the family. She never ever shirked responsibility. Slinking off to lick her wounds without telling anyone doesn't really make sense."

Caleb traced the pattern on the silver clip that held Crystal's hair off her neck. "Three times over the course of talking about her, you've said how much she loved her husband. Facing life without him is probably daunting."

The eyes Crystal turned toward him shimmered with unshed tears. "Wouldn't you think it'd be easier to bear the loss surrounded by family who felt the same?"

"I'm no expert on love. But my folks had a great marriage. A special bond. They were like halves of a whole. Hard as it was to lose them both at the same time, I've always thought it's how they would have wanted to go."

Crystal parked outside the hospital. She was reluctant to disturb the tender feelings that poured from Caleb when he spoke about his parents. He'd described a love exactly like the love shared by Margaret and Paul. By André and Gabrielle. A love the likes of which Crystal caught herself longing for. Daydreaming about.

And on this warm moonlit night, she found it too easy to insert Caleb Tanner into the equation. His hand felt big and warm and comforting where it'd settled on the back of her neck. Too warm. Too comforting.

Shifting to break the unsettling connection of his touch, Crystal chided herself for drifting off like this. Caleb was just responding to her story. He'd probably die laughing if he had the slightest inkling of the direction her thoughts had taken.

"Thanks for listening. I needed input from someone

who doesn't know the family. Margaret will probably show up at Lyoncrest any day now, and eventually we'll all laugh about the scare she gave us.''

Reaching behind her seat, Crystal hauled her saxophone case into her lap. ''I'll come over to that side and get your crutches, Tanner.''

''What in hell does a guy have to do to get you to use his first name?''

''I'm sorry,'' she said. ''Tanner just slips out.'' She was half in half out with his crutches when he clamped a hand around her wrist and yanked her back.

''Let's call a spade a spade. You use it as a defense mechanism, a shield, anytime I get too close. I'd be interested to know why.''

''I don't know what you're talking about. You think I'm afraid of you?''

''Afraid of me? Or men in general,'' he muttered as he saw from the wariness in her eyes how his stab in the dark had upset her.

''That's nonsense. I work with a lot of men. And I don't take any guff. Ask Nate.''

He released her and when she came to open his door, he said quietly, ''Let's talk in terms of a nonwork environment. Did someone you had a personal relationship with hurt you?''

''Do all football players get hold of something and hang on to it like a bulldog? Or am I just unlucky enough to have stumbled on the only one who's a frustrated amateur psychologist?''

Caleb threw back his head and laughed as he climbed from the car. ''Now you sound like my sisters. At one time or other they've all called me a pit bull. And it's only because I used to ask their boyfriends a few questions. Well...they called it 'the inquisition.'''

Crystal surprised him. She didn't side with his sisters. "The girls ought to appreciate that you cared enough to worry about the caliber of guys who asked them out," she said as she opened the door to the hospital lobby and let him through ahead of her.

"When you were fifteen," he said, "did you understand your guardian's reason for thwarting your plans? Or in your case it was probably your dad."

Her voice sounded oddly shaky. "I...didn't date until I was a senior in college. I was engaged briefly that year. I can't recall how I told my father. He might've been drilling for offshore oil in Saudi at the time, or Chile, perhaps. My fifteenth and sixteenth birthdays he spent in Malaysia. I remember because he sent me the same jade pendant both years."

Cale heard the pain in her voice, though it was no more than a quivery inflection. Had they not stepped off the elevator outside Skipper's ward, he would have probed deeper. Obviously her life paralleled that of his sisters more closely than he'd first thought. Who had raised her? he wondered. Or maybe that was how she'd come to live at Lyoncrest. He didn't have an opportunity to ask. They heard the strains of someone running the scales on a clarinet.

"The doc has a swing in his tempo," Crystal whispered to Caleb as they entered the room. "This might be fun. Too bad you aren't proficient on that keyboard yet. We could have a real jam session."

When they met the young good-looking resident, whose eyes lit up the minute Skip introduced Crystal, Caleb wished he was proficient on the damned keyboard, too. Dr. Mark Wolfe had an abundance of pitch-black curls—the kind of hair women probably itched to run their fingers through. His eyes were a brilliant aqua—probably contacts, Caleb thought. The dude had more gleaming white teeth than any man had a right to. Caleb sensed an instant rapport between Crystal and the doctor. Left to his own devices while the two musicians talked jazz, Caleb pictured how the guy would look with half his pretty teeth pushed in.

Skip proudly introduced Caleb to each of his wardmates. It wasn't until Cale took a seat on the end of Skipper's bed and settled in to listen to the duet that he realized the tight nagging sizzle in his gut was jealousy.

He'd witnessed jealousy in many forms during his football career. Both personal and professional. He'd always considered it a wasteful emotion. It shocked him to discover such strong feelings in himself. Yet as the evening progressed, the more he watched Wolfe blatantly flirt with Crystal, the greater were Cale's primal instincts to stake his territory.

He ground his teeth and suffered through musical numbers he'd once liked but now couldn't hear through the angry static in his head. He couldn't begin to explain his relief when two of the nurses who'd stopped to listen finally said it was time to wind down.

"That was fun," Crystal told Mark as the two broke apart their instruments. "We'll have to do it again sometime."

"Gladly. Tell me when and where. If I can rearrange my duty schedule, I'll be there with bells on."

Crystal started to invite him to the club on Saturday night. Mostly because while they played, she began wondering if Dr. Wolfe could steer her in the right direction to get Skip tested for the drug Caleb had mentioned. She swallowed her invitation in surprise when Caleb muscled his bulk between her and the young resident.

"Time to leave," he snapped. "Need any help putting your sax away?"

"Tanner, what the—"

The young doctor moved back to keep from being stepped on. "Hey, man." The words were barely out before his face blossomed in awe. "Cale Tanner? Wow! I played a little high-school ball in Fort Worth the year you were on the Cowboys and brought the championship home to Texas where it belonged."

"High-school ball, huh?" Caleb growled. "Guess that makes you a young pup."

"Not so young. Twenty-six."

Cale shifted his crutches and looped an arm around Crystal's neck. "Young to us, eh, sweetheart?" He bestowed a smoldering gaze on Crystal. "It's a cinch we aren't walking backward through time. Another reason we oughtta hustle our old bones home to bed."

Crystal gaped, then blushed a brilliant fuchsia. "Caleb Tanner, what's gotten into you?"

Grasping her thick braid midway up her back, he twisted it gently around his wrist. With no forewarning, he closed off her question with a long-drawn-out kiss.

The room slipped into absolute silence. Seconds into the kiss, although it seemed to take longer, the nurses and patients in the room began to whisper. The boys, Skip and Randy especially, breathed out a collective "Yuck," and one of them, Randy probably, made rude sucking noises.

Dr. Wolfe apparently got the message Caleb had set out to convey. With little more than an accepting shrug, he closed his clarinet case and left.

Even though, on some level, Caleb sensed he'd driven off the enemy, he took his time ending the kiss. The dazed look in Crystal's blue eyes and the dewy swelling of her bottom lip accorded him immense satisfaction. It played hell with his equilibrium, but at least the fiery knot in his abdomen was no longer the result of jealousy.

And he didn't have to explain. For when he drew back and traced a shaking thumb over her lips, every adult in the room, including Crystal, understood that Caleb Tanner had placed his brand on her with that kiss.

The women envied her. The male patients who'd drifted by to hear the music wore looks that laid bets on the next step—whether or not Crystal would spend the night in Tanner's bed.

She knew the strange flutter in the pit of her stomach had sent all her good intentions of keeping Tanner at arm's length to hell in an Easter basket. And the way he continued to gaze at her with eyes that promised to eat her alive drove even the most basic thought from her head. The best she could hope for was to get out of here with as much dignity intact as possible.

"Most of my fans clap, whistle or stamp their feet," Crystal said aloud to a fast-emptying room. "Quite a few shake my hand after a performance. As you can see, a few are so moved by jazz, they…well, react more passionately." She walked to the bed and ruffled Skipper's hair. "That's when a musician knows it's been an exceptional session. Thanks, pal. See you tomorrow, okay?"

"Yeah." The worried look faded from the kid's eyes. "You and Cale aren't going to get so mushy and stuff that you won't have time to be my friend, huh, Crystal?"

"Oh, Skipper." Her voice broke. She smoothed back the lock of hair that had fallen into his eyes. "A friendship like ours isn't something anyone else can take away. I'm always gonna be in your corner, kiddo."

"I hope so." The child's somber green eyes sought out Cale and appeared even less reassured.

"I hate to rush you," Nurse Pam said from the doorway. "It's medicine time for these guys and then lights out."

Crystal frowned a bit as she gazed between the two males who had each captured a piece of her heart. She didn't understand Skip's sudden veiled hostility toward Caleb. She'd endeavor to sort out the reasons tomorrow. Returning to where she'd left her saxophone case, she led the way to the elevator.

Cale was strangely silent. The muted slap-slap of his rubber-tipped crutches kept Crystal from glancing back to verify that he still trailed at her heels. Maybe he hadn't meant that kiss the way she'd taken it—which might explain why he wasn't trying to engage her in any kind of conversation. If he feared she was so sexually repressed that she'd plaster herself to him because of one little kiss, he needn't worry. Even though it had seemed for a minute that they'd crossed an emotional line, she wasn't about to make a fool of herself and assume he was leading up to more than a simple kiss.

"Mouse got your tongue?" he asked after she'd unlocked the car, then tossed her saxophone case and his crutches into the back. She'd crawled into the driver's seat and left him to deal with settling his injured leg and shutting the door.

"Mouse? Since when doesn't that saying start with a cat?"

In the moonlight she saw his smile. "Why be predictable?"

"Don't you mean, why be difficult when with a little more effort you can become impossible?"

Crossing his forearms, he laughed heartily. "Should I stick out my chin, Crystal, so you can give me your best shot?"

After starting the car and joining the heavy traffic, she asked what he meant.

Uncrossing his arms, he ran a hand softly from her shoulder to her elbow. "I saw red when that young stud started coming on to you."

Crystal felt the power in his broad hand, but the sudden sensation in her stomach was pleasure, not fear that he'd unleash that power against her. She pulled her eyes from the road long enough to pin him with luminous eyes. "Why? What am I to you, Caleb?"

It was time to punt or pass on the ball. Caleb let her drive two more blocks and turn the corner near his apartment before he dragged in breath enough to answer. "I honestly don't know," he said gruffly. "What I do know is when I saw that guy making gaga eyes at you, I got angrier than when an opponent picks off one of my best passes."

Crystal thought it was a good thing a parking place opened up right in front of Caleb's building. Otherwise she would have been shaking too much to drive around the block again. She didn't have to know anything about football to understand his analogy. Because the tremor in his voice suggested he was serious about deepening their relationship.

If anyone were to press her later for details as to how they got out of the car and down the walk, into Caleb's apartment and then into his bedroom, she would be forced to admit she had a huge memory lapse.

Crystal did know that for a man with his injuries, Caleb moved awfully fast. Or else she was stronger than she'd thought. She might have heard his crutches hit the marbled entry shortly after he slid the dead bolt home. She may even have held him up as he started kissing her and more or less waltzed her backward to the bed she'd made up so reverently the other day.

The fine cotton that had felt cool to her fingers then now scorched her bare back. If the sheets were so hot, why did she shiver when their tongues met, dueled and teased?

Panting, Caleb broke away. He lifted his torso off her soft breasts and held himself there on unsteady arms. "Your last chance to call this off, babe."

Crystal arched against him. Parting her lips, she nibbled on his earlobe. Beyond comprehensible speech, she purred in his ear.

Shifting most of his weight to his good knee, Caleb whispered. "Reality-check time, little darlin'. Tacky as it sounds, I'm not hankering for another mouth to feed. Are you protected?"

Her gaze rose from the wide muscular chest to green eyes glittering coolly in a flickering moonbeam. "I'm not," she gasped, beginning to pull away. "Not in several years. There's been...no need."

Cale didn't even try to hide his heady smile. "That's nice. Real nice. Can you reach my wallet? You'll find a couple of useful packets behind my driver's license."

"A couple?" she asked, eyeing him with suspicion.

"My daddy had a long talk with me out behind the melon barn when I turned sixteen. He handed me a new box of condoms and suggested I never leave home without them. Stuff a few in my wallet, he said. Best advice Daddy ever gave me." Rolling onto his back, he tossed Crystal his pants.

She found the wallet and extracted the packets. She raised one eyebrow. "These look a little newer than that."

He blew out an exasperated breath and wondered if he'd have to end up telling her to just forget it.

"I guess that means they *are* new. If you're that active, maybe we'd better discuss getting blood tests."

Caleb didn't think he could discuss anything. While she talked in a breathy voice, she'd ripped open the foil and begun to sheathe him. He barely managed to moan her name and pull her astride him seconds after her fingers closed gently around him to make sure the condom was snug.

After that, neither one of them had anything to say for hours. Steam and passion and moonlight pulsed around them. Time and again Caleb thought he was about to either drift off to asleep or die a happy man. Then something would happen. Crystal would smile against his chest or his hand would streak across her satiny flesh. Either way, his desire for her would soar—as apparently hers did for him—and they'd lose themselves in each other again.

Each encounter was bliss. Which was why, when Caleb opened a sleepy eye around two in the morning and saw Crystal dressed and tiptoeing toward his bedroom door, he couldn't believe she was leaving.

He struggled to sit up, but his bad leg was tangled in the top sheet. "Crystal?" The sinking in the pit of his stomach abated only minimally when she blew him a kiss from the hall. He hadn't shared his bed with anyone who mattered in a long while. And sometime over the course of the evening, he'd discovered he wanted Crystal to fill that empty place beside him every night.

"I planned to leave you a note in the kitchen, Tanner. I've never not come home at night since I moved to Lyoncrest."

"Call them. I want you here—in my bed." Even before the shake of her head sent her hair flying about her face, Caleb knew the answer. If she was as committed to this relationship as he, she wouldn't be calling him Tanner.

"Under the circumstances, with Margaret missing, a call at this time of night would scare André and Gaby to death. Go on back to sleep. I'll see you soon."

"Tomorrow night?" he asked quickly. Then it struck him that this must be something of a role reversal. His partners on the team were famous for walking out on women in the middle of the night. He'd done it once or twice himself.

"Not tomorrow night or the next. I have dinner meetings with staff both nights. And then this weekend, I play at the club. Probably just as well. It'll give us some time to think about this. To see if we want to go forward."

"You may be right," he said reluctantly. "Day after tomorrow my sisters come to town for a visit. They'll be here a week."

"I'd like to meet them."

All at once, Caleb wasn't sure. His sisters were always trying to set him up, but he'd never introduced them to anyone he'd ever dated. When they'd seen newspaper photos of him with a woman, he'd told the girls they were all promo shots. "We'll see," he growled. "My brain doesn't function at this hour. Drive carefully, honey." He yawned and covered his mouth with his hand. "You want me to get dressed and ride with you? I can call a taxi to bring me home again."

"No. I'll be fine. I'm used to late hours and running around the city after dark." And that was the truth. Yet as she let herself out, Crystal wished he hadn't asked. She wished he'd just dressed and come with her, simply because her safety meant something to him. Although, she didn't know why she should expect that. No relationship lasted. She was wrong to dream this one would. She'd heard the gears begin to turn in his mind when she mentioned meeting his family; she'd felt him withdraw.

By the time Crystal reached Lyoncrest, she'd stemmed her tears and made a decision. Tomorrow she'd tell Nate Fraser to find a new chauffeur for his fledgling sportscaster.

CHAPTER TWELVE

DURING THE NEXT FEW DAYS Crystal kept busy enough to evade Caleb's attempts to reach her by phone. Gradually, the mention of his name stopped producing a rise of panic. If she'd hoped not seeing him meant forgetting him, though, she couldn't have been more wrong. He invaded her thoughts at home and work and everywhere in between.

So, on Friday night at the club, Crystal wasn't sure if the man who sat at a center table, flanked by three women, was real or a flight of fancy. Either way, she was so nervous she missed a cue. Something she'd never done before, not even when Margaret or others in the family came to see her perform.

"You appear to have picked up a special fan, Crystal." Sam, the band's horn player, muttered in her ear as they rested through a piano solo. "Guy looks familiar. He's only got eyes for you. Hey, maybe we oughtta spang out the song." Nudging her in the ribs with his trumpet, he waggled his brows and sang, "I on-ly have eyes for you." He was uncharacteristically off-key.

Crystal noticed that Caleb's presence created quite a stir. People ignored the music and crowded around him, seeking autographs.

"Who is that dude?" hissed Freddy, their group leader, midway through the next tune. "We might as well take a break until he knocks off holding court."

"Aw hell, I recognize him," said the drummer. "Caleb Tanner, former Sinners' quarterback. Where's a *Times-Picayune* columnist when you need 'em? If he's interested in jazz, it'll be good for business."

"I'd say his interest is in Crystal." Duke laughed, poking her with a drumstick. "Hardly seems fair that he wants to swipe our rose when he's brought half a dozen of his own."

"Three," Crystal pointed out dryly. "I thought drummers could count before they could walk." She was aware of Caleb's female companions, although they were cloaked in shadow while a spotlight played on his features.

As Caleb's attention still didn't waver from Crystal, the members of the band would not quit teasing. "Let's go check out his intentions. Say the word, Mama. Me and the boys will drop-kick the guy clean into the street," Sam promised.

"Don't you dare!" Crystal exclaimed. Then, realizing they were only trying to get a rise out of her, she busied herself unclasping the neck strap from her saxophone. The band had played together for several years, and she was the only woman in the group. They might tease her unmercifully, but they'd protect her at the drop of a hat. And they didn't know she was running scared after breaking every one of her self-imposed rules regarding men. Her friends only knew she always kept would-be admirers at bay. Or had—until she'd glanced up in the middle of that number and saw Caleb watching her with hungry eyes. She'd missed him, and the reality of that flattened her like a runaway eighteen-wheeler.

No two ways about it. She'd surrendered her heart again. Caleb Tanner held the whole thing in his two hands, dammit. A part of her had known it the other night.

The part that had sent her fleeing from his apartment. A part that cautioned her to back off. But one glimpse, and she was lost again.

Crystal considered going to the bar to get a soda. The bottom line—she didn't want Caleb to think she cared enough to avoid him. So she joined the crush of fans filing past his table.

Once she worked her way close to his party, she saw that his companions bore a striking resemblance to each other—and to him. Just then one of the women leaned back in her chair and laughed. Her mouth curved exactly like his. *Caleb's sisters!* How could she have forgotten he said they were coming to visit?

Caleb, glancing along the row of people requesting autographs, noticed Crystal at the end of the line. He had a few things to say to her for dumping him like so much garbage. Yet when she reached him, he didn't make any of the angry remarks souring on his tongue. Instead, he took her hand. "Crystal, come meet Grace." He smiled at the slender woman on his right. "Crystal Jardin." Unconsciously he entwined their fingers and gazed adoringly up at her.

Crystal met Grace's assessing eyes, a twin to Caleb's in color. The woman's hair was curlier than his and a darker blond. Next, he introduced Patsy, drawing Crystal's attention to his left. Her eyes were a pale jade, her expression chilly. Light blond hair framed her face. Of the three women, she had the lushest figure.

"And this is Jenny," Cale said of the young woman seated across the table.

Crystal immediately liked her breezy smile and no-nonsense handshake. Jenny's hair was sun-bleached and short. She wore little makeup. Her skin was beautifully tanned. "You're in college." Crystal released her hand, then gestured to each woman in turn. "Patsy is getting married soon. Grace took a job in Austin. Something with a computer company, right?"

Caleb grinned. "Our Gracie's going to come up with the next big innovation. Make a billion dollars." His comment earned him a punch on the arm from her sister, but he ignored it, his attention having returned to Crystal. "We came by WDIX this morning. You were in a meeting." His eyes were faintly accusatory. "You've been tied up all week. I guess you heard I'm starting work on Monday?"

"I saw from the personnel roster that you were scheduled for training films."

"I'll feel right at home. Half of football is watching training films." He pushed out the fourth chair at the table. "Do you have time to sit? The girls are champing at the bit to go shopping. I'd hoped you could direct them."

From his pleading look, Crystal deduced he wanted stores that wouldn't strain the budget she'd drawn up— although she'd explained that *any* extra expenditure would. "I doubt if our shopping centers differ much from those in Texas. If this is your first visit to New Orleans, you ought to soak up the history. Take a walking tour of the Quarter. Visit some of the plantation homes."

Patsy wrinkled her nose. "You've seen one musty museum, you've seen 'em all. I'm anxious to go to the boutiques at Canal Place and the Esplanade."

Crystal saw despair darken Caleb's eyes. So he hadn't told them of his plight. "Those places are costly," she murmured. "I'll give you a list of resale shops where they have really neat stuff." Taking a napkin and the pen Caleb had been using, she roughed out a map. She placed the last *X*, only to discover three women staring at her as if she'd just landed from outer space.

She studied the faces that ranged from curious to hostile. "I guess Caleb didn't mention that I'm his new financial adviser," she said lamely.

"No, I didn't," he murmured. "Am I still a...client? You left so fast the other night and you haven't returned my calls since."

Crystal groaned. Why didn't he take out a billboard declaring there was more than business between them?

His sisters' heads swiveled from her to Caleb and back. Grace appeared to make up her mind about something. "Hallelujah! Caleb's finally found a woman who's not trying to bleed him dry. Patsy, Jenny and I have worried for some time that this lunkhead's big heart would put him in the poorhouse. We've deposited half of everything he's sent us. This trip, Patsy's fiancé gave her money to buy some outfits for her trousseau. Otherwise we'd be first in line at the thrift stores."

"Wh-what?" Caleb stuttered his disbelief and choked on his response. "Wait a minute. Why did you all let me go on thinking you needed my help?"

Jenny squeezed his hand. "It seemed important to you, Caleb. You mean everything to us. We wouldn't hurt you for the world."

Speechless, all he could seem to do was swallow again and again.

"See there, Caleb? You don't need a financial adviser, after all." Crystal floundered, searching for a way to withdraw. Thankfully, she heard the band tuning up. "Break's over," she announced, and bounded from her seat. "Nice-to-have-met-you," she breathed, poised for flight.

Patsy stopped Crystal's retreat. "Caleb said you were going to drive him to my wedding but now you're probably not. If it's for lack of an invitation, let me say I would've mailed one if he'd mentioned it sooner."

Now it was Crystal's turn to gaze at Caleb in alarm. "But...but you're not using crutches anymore, and you're starting work," she blurted.

"What's that got to do with you driving me to the wedding?"

"I, uh, thought maybe you'd recovered enough to drive yourself."

Cale pulled a cane out from under the table. "I decided to try a walking stick. I thought Skip would tell you when you stopped by his hospital room."

"I...I...no, your name never came up."

Worry lines creased Gracie's forehead. "Caleb's pushed himself because Patsy wants him to walk her down the aisle. Please don't give him ideas about driving to Austin on his own."

"Do come to the wedding, Crystal," Jenny begged.

Folding his hands over the handle of his cane, Cale rested his chin on his knuckles and grinned unabashedly up at Crystal. He almost felt sorry for her. But not too sorry. He sensed the minute his sisters decided to hustle her on his behalf. Those rascals. They'd done this before, pushing assorted professional women in his direction. Usually he objected to their meddling on general principles. This time he intended to sit back and enjoy their campaign. "My leg's begun to throb," he murmured, taking pity on her, after all. "Play me a special song before I have to go?" He kissed Crystal's fingers.

She bolted and all but ran to the stage, where she disappeared behind the black curtains in back.

"Hmm." He shook his head sadly, playing on his sisters' sympathy. "Guess I blew it again, girls. We can leave any time you're ready."

"Crystal's really talented," Jenny said.

"Yes, and very pretty," Patsy ventured, carefully studying her brother.

"And levelheaded," Gracie added. "But who's this guy, Skip, she visits at the hospital? A boyfriend?"

Caleb, whose attention shifted to a stage gone suddenly dark, answered offhandedly. "He's a kid she cossets. Don't get me started on that subject," he said as from out of the blackness a saxophone began to wail. He didn't see his sisters exchange concerned glances. A spotlight sprang to life high above, spilling white light on a silhouette wearing a top hat. Slowly, by inches, the light increased its circle until it revealed Crystal Jardin and her saxophone to the audience. Cale's breath froze in his throat as the light climbed up Crystal's long bare legs, at last exposing a black sequined halter top and red satin shorts that barely covered her butt.

Goose bumps traveled up Caleb's spine as desire hit him in the groin. It was a damn good thing no one could read his mind. He wanted her naked and in his bed again—wanted it so badly the pain in his throbbing knee paled by comparison. The song had almost ended before he realized people were whistling, stamping their feet and pounding him on the back because she'd played a rousing rendition of "When the Saints Go Marching In." She played the last chorus like she was making love to her horn. Shivers rocked Cale to the soles of his shoes. He knew he had to leave the club now. It wasn't easy convincing his sisters to stumble out of the dark club with him.

No matter how embarrassed they claimed to be by his precipitous exit, it wouldn't compare to how red their faces would've been if he'd stayed until the lights came on.

Inside the club, near the number's end, Crystal's gaze

strayed to the empty table. She'd poured her heart into that solo, and Caleb hadn't even stayed to listen.

"Fine blowin', Mama." Duke crossed his drumsticks and held them aloft in a reverent gesture. Freddy and Sam, apparently sensing Crystal's distress, closed ranks around her.

"Tanner limped a lot as he made his way out," mumbled the ebony-skinned keyboarder. "Good thing he left when he did. Otherwise after hearin' that tune, the poor SOB would've been mobbed."

His words made Crystal feel better. She had to stop looking for slights from Caleb. Immediately after the song she'd told herself no way would she accompany him to his sister's wedding, but by closing time, she was asking Freddie to find a substitute sax player for the wedding weekend. She phoned the next day, reached Caleb's answering machine and left the message that she would drive him to Texas.

Over the next two weeks, she probably vacillated twenty times as to whether to stay home or go. Her waffling was due in large part to the major sensation Caleb became the minute he began his career as a sportscaster. Female employees who'd never shown any interest in sports mobbed his set. A studio assistant, normally outspoken about equal treatment for men and women, made sure Cale had a pitcher of ice water and a clean glass before every taping. The switchboard receptionist baked him chocolate-chip cookies. Talk-show hostesses argued over him. It seemed as if all the female staffers, single or married, fetched and carried for him, making a big fuss about his leg.

April abandoned her accounting class to run player-comparison stats for Tanner, which she claimed weren't available to him from AP and other sources.

Toward the end of his second full week, only Crystal—of all the women at WDIX, including Gaby—hadn't seen him in action. But she'd certainly heard about his exploits. Today she made her way to his soundstage because he'd sent word via April that he needed to talk to her before she left for the day. About their pending trip, she assumed. She'd received a nice note from Patsy inviting her to the rehearsal Friday evening and the dinner afterward. Otherwise she wouldn't be caught dead poking her head inside the door to his set.

Actually that wasn't true. She'd already decided to track him down, but for a different reason. She tossed an absent wave to Scott Lyon, Caleb's cameraman, as she entered. Last night Skip had moped for an hour. According to one of the physical therapists, Tanner had made arrangements to complete his therapy elsewhere. The boys felt abandoned. Especially Skipper. Crystal intended to ask Caleb about it. Surely he could find some time to visit the boys. Skipper was so quiet and depressed it worried her. She wished Rachel hadn't picked this week to be honest with him. It had been formally decided that the boy wouldn't return to Sandy's. The doctor, too, had compounded the problem. He hadn't said Skip would be confined to a wheelchair for life, but he'd hedged when Skip asked how long it'd be before he walked again.

She sighed despondently, then practically jumped out of her skin as someone with hot breath snorted behind her.

"Raymond!" she exclaimed as she whirled around. "Don't sneak up on me."

"I didn't sneak. You were so gaga-eyed over Tanner, you'd have missed a jet landing."

"For crying out loud," she scolded in a low voice, "I'm not gaga over anything. Tanner asked to see me.

Regarding his expense account, I imagine, since Nate's out of town.'' Crystal would walk barefoot over hot coals before she'd let Ray Lyon know she and Caleb were going away for the weekend no matter how innocent it was—and she intended that it *would* be for reasons that were increasingly evident. It had certainly become clear that Tanner could have any woman he wanted with little more than a snap of his fingers. She was beginning to think he'd dallied with her out of boredom. She could no longer conclude anything else.

"What are you doing here?" she asked Ray. "I left a stack of new collections at your door this morning. Did you get them?"

"I got them," he said sullenly. "Why don't you talk to the advertising staff about doing better credit checks before they run ads for so many deadbeats?"

"Gabrielle has. She cautions staff repeatedly, as I'm sure Jason tells you. Our percent of non-pays is lower than that of most stations. So why are you slinking around a sports taping, Raymond? Are you looking for your brother? Scott's working right now."

"Let him, the little squirt. I came to see Tanner. Alain has tickets to the Bronco-Steelers exhibition game that's going to be played in Denver this weekend. He asked me to invite Cale. Alain's got plans for Tanner. Big plans."

"Tough luck for Alain. I happen to know Caleb's sister is getting married this Saturday so he's not free. What plans?" she asked, trying to mask her interest.

"That's for me and Alain to know and you to wonder about, sweet cheeks. Too bad Cale's not available. By the way, I'm taking tomorrow off. Alain has a lawyer friend who's flying us to Denver in his six-seater Cessna." Throwing back his shoulders, Ray adjusted his jacket. "I'm going. That's all there is to it."

"Have fun." Clapping him on the back, Crystal edged him down the hall. She wanted him gone before Caleb finished taping and inadvertently mentioned their outing. She certainly had no problem with his taking a day off. Ray never did his assigned work, anyway, so she didn't think it would make any difference if he took a three-day weekend.

He studied her through narrowed lids. "What? No snide remarks?"

"Nope." She walked with him toward the elevators. "There's something refreshing about your honesty. As a rule you have Charles call in sick for you."

"Yeah...well, the old man's going bonkers."

"How so?" Crystal thought this might be news for André. Maybe Charles in his dotage had kidnapped Margaret. But no. He'd been genuinely distraught over his brother's death.

Ray stepped into the elevator and held the door as Crystal remained in the hall. "You think I can't see the wheels turning inside your head?" he muttered. "Declare my dad incompetent and knock him off the board. No, ma'am. I only meant he gets lost in his music and forgets the time. He'd be giving concerts if Grandpa had forked over his rightful inheritance, instead of tying Daddy to Lyon Broadcasting."

"That's an excuse, Ray. All of you blame Alexandre for having the foresight to keep the family fortune intact. In the last fifty years, your dad has taken enough money out of this business to buy the concert halls and launch a hundred piano careers. As well as Lyon money, he frittered away the Benoît wealth."

"Bull!" Ray released the door as he yelled at her. "Daddy didn't take anything but what was his, you stupid bitch. You'll see—Alain will prove once and for all that Tante Margaret's bastard son is not the legal heir.''

"You and Alain are the stupid ones," Crystal shouted back. "If not for Margaret and André, WDIX would have been gobbled up by a conglomerate years ago, and you wouldn't have a dime left. If you make trouble for André, maybe I'll hire a lawyer and press *my* claim to a share of the business." The door shut on her tirade. "Oooh, he makes me so mad!" It was all she could do not to stamp her foot.

Heads popped out of offices all along the corridor. Groaning, Crystal tried to smile and act as if nothing was wrong.

"Want me to put out a contract on whoever that was?" teased a deep voice.

Whirling, Crystal faced Caleb. His eyes crinkled at the corners. He appeared amused by her tantrum.

"He's not worth the price of a contract. Dammit, I hate that I let him provoke me into a shouting match in front of other employees."

"Is it the guy I saw you leave the soundstage with?"

"You saw us? I hope we didn't interrupt your taping. To answer your question, yes. I take it you haven't had the pleasure of meeting Ray Lyon."

"He wasn't in his office when Nate gave me a walk-through and introduced me around. Lyon, huh? Why were you yelling at a big cheese?"

"No big cheese. A fat rat maybe." She grimaced. "It's a long story. I shouldn't color your perception. He came up here to offer you a free ticket and transportation to the exhibition football game in Denver."

"Nate's covering that game. If it wasn't for Patsy's wedding, I'd have been the one representing the station, though."

"I didn't realize that, but I told Ray about the wedding. I walked him to the elevator because I didn't want him to know we're going together."

As a few curiosity-seekers still lingered in the hall, Caleb steered Crystal toward a quiet corner beyond prying ears. "Is this Ray the reason you've been deliberately avoiding me? Has he got some claim on you?"

"Heavens, no!" she denied with such vehemence Cale smiled and reached for a lock of hair that had escaped her braid.

"Glad to hear it." They continued down the hall, and Caleb stopped before they reached the door leading to the soundstage. Gazing deep into her eyes, he asked, "Why *have* you been avoiding me?"

"I've been busy." She stepped back. "This is quarterly tax time." Turning the tables, she asked, "What's your excuse for not visiting Skipper all week?"

"Skipper? Do I need an excuse? I barely know the kid."

"He and the other boys idolize you, Caleb. André arranged times for you to visit schools. Would it hurt to swing by the hospital after one of those trips?"

"And do what? Say what?" Caleb scraped a hand through hair that had been styled to look perfect for the cameras. "Why is it my responsibility?"

Crystal's eyes widened in surprise, then almost as quickly grew hurt. "Why did you suggest I try to get that special drug for Skipper if you don't care about him?"

"Just because I'm not treating the kid like he's part of my family doesn't mean I want to see him stuck in a wheelchair for the rest of his life."

"Is that what you think I'm doing? Treating Skip as a member of my family, I mean?" She placed more distance between them and shut down all emotion in her eyes. "Rachel called me last night. She told me to get a life of my own. She accused me of being a wanna-be mom. Did you put her up to calling me?"

"No. But I'm sorry I mentioned that drug to you. It's next to impossible to convince anyone connected to a foster-care program to listen. Give it up, Crystal. Someone with a heart as soft as yours will only get it smashed."

"I'll grant you the impossible takes longer," she said coolly. "But we're getting off track here, aren't we? April said you wanted to see me. What about?"

"We haven't spoken since that night at the club. I wanted you know I'm free to leave anytime tomorrow. How fast do you drive? Going to Baton Rouge and taking Highway 10 to Houston, then cutting off on 290, I've made the trip in four hours."

"I've seen it take two hours to get out of New Orleans. Are you a late riser or can we leave your place at six?"

Cale's lips curled slowly up on one side. "Depends on how much sleep I get. If you'd stayed around the other night, you might have a better idea of my habits."

Up till now, Crystal had not allowed herself to remember that night in his bed. Hadn't allowed herself to examine any part of it—because if she did, she risked opening her heart to total devastation. If she did she'd have to admit she'd fallen in love with Caleb Tanner.

For a long moment Crystal felt as if her body dangled from a rope left spinning in the wind. Then, burying her emotions, something learned through years of practice, she wiped away his smile with a harsh sentence. "A gentleman wouldn't remind a lady of her transgressions."

His humor returned. "I could put that night under a lot of headings, Crystal, but sin isn't one of them."

She glanced up and down the hall to see if anyone lurked nearby. No one did. "I'm quite sure you've had a rapid turnover in your bed, Tanner, based on the number of conquests you've made at the station since you started here.''

He crossed his arms and studied her. "Has someone claimed I slept with them?"

"Lower your voice," she warned, nervously checking over her shoulder again. "I haven't heard that precisely—no. It's only a question of time, considering how many women trip over each other to please you every day."

"That doesn't mean any of them follow me home."

"It doesn't matter to me," she said, sounding bored with the conversation.

"Why doesn't it matter?" Cale lifted his gaze from the soft hollow of her throat. "I thought something special went on between us the other night."

"Shh!" She put a finger to her lips. "We can't discuss this at work."

"Okay. I'll buy that. But get your pigeons lined up, Crystal, because we're going to talk about it tomorrow. I'll be ready bright and early." He relied heavily on his cane as he limped to the soundstage door, yanked it open and as quickly closed her out.

She mulled over their conversation all the way to her office. What did he mean when he said no other women followed him home? If he thought their lovemaking should matter to her, what was he saying about his own feelings? Good grief! If she didn't quit mooning about Caleb Tanner, she'd never get any work done. Then she'd be no better than Ray. Recalling Ray's parting shot, Crystal reached for the phone and punched in André's extension.

"André, Crystal here. No, there's no further activity in your mother's accounts. I'm calling because Ray, who's always shooting off his mouth, is getting more vocal and more obnoxious with regard to his family's claim to the business. Today he sounded as if Alain plans to make some kind of move to take over your job.''

From the other end of the line, André reassured her that any claim Alain thought he might have was bogus—whether Margaret was there to refute such claims or not.

''You're right, André. Ray's just a jerk who knows how to push my buttons.'' She paused. ''No word yet on your mother?''

''Nothing,'' he growled. ''It's beyond me how a high-profile woman could vanish without trace.''

She sighed. ''Maybe I shouldn't drive Caleb to his sister's wedding.'' She tucked the phone between her shoulder and jaw and listened. ''I know it's too late to back out. Promise you'll phone me, though, if you hear anything at all. You have my cell number.''

After she hung up, Crystal immersed herself in work. She still had to pack and do a million other things between now and six in the morning. First on her agenda was paying a visit to Skipper. She wanted him to know she wasn't forsaking him. She'd finally rounded up the musical instruments she had promised the boys.

Crystal left work on time and drove immediately to the hospital. She hurried down the hall toward the children's ward, lugging a guitar, a drum pad, a couple of clarinets and her saxophone. She stopped suddenly, surprised to hear her name called by a male voice.

''You are Ms. Jardin, are you not?'' asked a tall bearded man in a pale-blue lab coat. Folding a stethoscope, he stuffed it into an already overflowing pocket and stuck out his right hand. ''I'm Skip West's physician. Your request that we try Sygen on him landed on my desk last week. Oddly enough, the head of orthopedics has wondered about trying it on Skip. We'll begin testing him next week. If everyone on the team agrees, we'll meet with the manufacturers of the drug. You do realize it may not work, don't you?''

"Any chance is better than none, Doctor. I'd given up hope. In fact, I had words over that request with Skip's social worker just last night. She thinks I overstepped my bounds, writing the letters I did.''

"I probably shouldn't say anything, as you have no legal jurisdiction in his case. But you visit Skip more than anyone.'' He shook his head. "The ward nurses expressed concern for the boy's mental state. He's quite depressed about being removed from his foster home. I did discuss this with Rachel Fontaine. She hasn't been successful in finding him another foster parent. I know you can't do anything about that, but if you can think of another way to cheer him up, his chance of recovery, should we try the treatment, will improve markedly.''

"Thank you for telling me. I'll see what I can do to change his outlook.'' Crystal moved more slowly toward the room. Caleb's defection hadn't helped Skip's mood. They'd settled nothing during their earlier argument. Tomorrow she'd ask again. If only she could do more than play Skip and his friends a few tunes.

"Hi, guys,'' she said, poking her head around the door. Randy shut off the TV and greeted her with the sports news of the day. The others said nothing until she handed out the instruments and videos.

"You guys look like you can do with some jumping jazz tonight. The tunes will have to stay in your head until Tuesday. Remember, I'm going to Caleb's sister's wedding.'' She straightened Skip's covers.

"I wish I could go with you,'' he lamented. Frowning, he slapped at his legs. "I'm probably gonna be stuck in here forever. I don't guess I'm ever gonna play ball again." Tears made wet paths down his cheeks.

"Hey, there." Crystal set her saxophone aside to give him a hug. "None of that now. Think positive. Isn't that what Caleb told you to do?"

"Yeah." The sniffles eased some. "Only he don't care about me no more."

Crystal gazed at him sternly. "Of course he does. But remember what I told you? When a person starts a new job, life gets kind of crazy for a while. Besides, tiger, I care."

More tears squeezed past spiky lashes. "Enough to let me come live with you?"

His suggestion shocked Crystal into silence. Yet the whole time they stared at each other, a thought took hold. Why *couldn't* she be a foster mom? Lyoncrest had more than enough room. Andy-Paul and Cory would be good for Skip, and he for them. Crystal was almost certain Gaby, André, Mike and Leslie would agree.

"I'll ask," she told the boy softly, "but I can't make any promises." She handed him a tissue. "When I get back from the wedding, I'll look into the possibility, okay?"

Brightening, he nodded and snuffled back any lingering tears.

"All right. Then I want to see some smiles. Fluff those pillows, guys. Lean back and get set for some wicked bebop."

As Crystal ran through half-a-dozen catchy tunes, she laid plans to apply for foster-parent status. She couldn't believe Rachel hadn't suggested it—or that she hadn't thought of it herself.

CHAPTER THIRTEEN

STREAKS OF GOLD and lavender had barely begun to appear in the Friday-morning sky when Crystal stopped at a coffeehouse to fill a thermos. As she drove toward Caleb's apartment, the scent wafting from the sack of warm beignets she'd also bought was pure torture.

She noticed Caleb waiting at the curb, so she double-parked. A breeze ruffled his hair, newly cut for the occasion. The memory of how his hair and skin had felt under her hands was so real it caused a sharp ache.

Determined not to let plain old lust rise up and ruin an otherwise congenial weekend, she hopped from the car and opened the passenger door for him.

He stepped off the curb and almost took a header. She quickly grabbed the suitcase that had thrown him off balance. Reacting to the self-disgust settling across his face, she resisted trying to steady the cane he wielded in his other hand. "Do you need your case on the drive, or shall I put it in the trunk?"

"Trunk is fine. But I can do it." Caleb took back the bag and limped between the parked cars to the rear of her vehicle.

She winced each time he banged the suitcase against the car. However, she didn't say a word, just popped open the trunk lid.

"Ah, breakfast," he exclaimed, letting his nose follow the warm scent of the beignets drifting through her open window. After they'd claimed their seats, he rubbed a hand over his clean-shaven jaw. "I slept through the alarm and had a choice of fixing coffee or shaving. I'd kill for a cup of java."

"No need to be that extreme." Crystal pulled out a cup holder. "Behind your seat is a thermos and cups. Help yourself. I'll wait until we reach the freeway."

"A thermos, cups and beignets," he said as he poured. "Why is it women think of everything? Me, I'd have started out and had to stop at the first convenience store. I'll bet you filled the gas tank, checked air and oil, and had the wiper blades replaced, even though we probably won't hit rain."

She laughed. "Guilty as charged. I don't like stopping once I get on the road. Gee," she said sarcastically, "I never realized those are preparations I make because I'm a woman."

"Yep." He settled back with a smile, eying her obliquely. "The fact that you're a woman does nice things for that little romper thingy you have on, too."

Crystal glanced guiltily down at her short jumpsuit. "This is not a romper," she defended primly, knowing she might as well have saved her breath. Heat swept up her neck and into her cheeks.

"So, I'm not up on the technical names for women's clothes. Looks damned good on you, whatever it's called."

He looked pretty good himself in soft worn jeans and a knit shirt pulled taut over his biceps and chest. "Could we change the subject? This mutual-admiration chitchat gets boring fast."

"Do I look okay? Then please tell Patsy. She's gonna make me wear one of those damned penguin suits."

"A tuxedo? Um...nice. You'll look great."

"I told her it's not the Texas way. Any self-respecting Texan gets married in boots, new jeans and a ten-gallon hat. Leave it up to a damned car salesman to put on the dog."

"Patsy said he owns two dealerships. Does she know you don't like him?"

"I don't dislike him. He'd better treat her right, though, is all I've got to say."

A smile found its way to Crystal's lips. "You sound more like a father than a brother, Caleb Tanner."

"Watch who you're calling an old man," he cautioned. "Hey, how long have we been on the freeway? You haven't had any coffee. And I could use a second cup."

"Help yourself. You *have* served in the role of father. And served well from what I saw of your sisters. You should be proud. Which reminds me—as soon as we get back, I'm filling out an application to be a foster mom. So I can take Skipper," she added when frown lines marked his forehead.

Coffee splashed over top of the first cup as Caleb tried to pour. "Dammit to hell," he swore, juggling thermos and cup to try to keep from getting burned.

"Shall I find a place to pull over?"

"No." He sipped some coffee before setting his cup in the holder. Then he wiped his hand on his jeans and mopped up the spill before filling her cup only half-full. "How did you arrive at the stupid notion of taking in stray kids? Aren't you busy enough?"

She looked startled. "Why, I...expected you to understand."

"Well, I don't. Do you have any idea what's involved in raising a half-grown kid—especially a kid who's not your own?"

"No, but how is it different from raising a natural

child? At my age, most women have kids. Besides, Rachel hasn't found a foster family equipped to take Skip if he has to remain in a wheelchair. I talked to André, Gaby and the others last night. They're willing to add a few ramps. Other than that, Rachel's old room is perfect.''

"Providing a bed and bath is the easy part of the obligation, Crystal. Are you prepared to deal with unexpected illness, parent-teacher conferences, the onset of puberty and a million other problems that come up? What happens to your music career, to say nothing of your social life? When you sign on as a parent, every aspect of your life changes.''

"Were there no rewards in raising your sisters, Caleb?''

"What? We aren't talking about me.''

"I think we are. I'm contemplating one child, not three,'' she said gently. "I'm also not going to be on the road eighty percent of the time.''

"My aunt and uncle did a helluva job keeping the home fires burning. They handled most of the daily crises. Tough decisions still fell to me. You've got no idea of the worry. Especially when there's no one to talk to…''

"Didn't you ever consider getting married? That way you wouldn't have been alone.''

"If that's what you're counting on, I really hate to punch holes in your dreams. The opposite sex doesn't exactly line up asking for a crack at stepparenting. Mention it sometime, and watch how fast a date makes tracks in the other direction.''

Crystal almost lost her grip on the steering wheel. Just yesterday Caleb had alleged an interest in continuing—maybe even deepening—their relationship. Was he now telling her to deal him out?

She took a bracing sip of her coffee. "Maybe you dated selfish women, Tanner. I have role models with bigger hearts. Margaret, André and Leslie, to name a few. They all raised or are raising kids who aren't theirs.''

Caleb opened the bag with the beignets, wrapped one in a napkin and handed it to her. He polished off the one he took for himself, then reached for another, acting as if she'd never raised any issue at all. When he finally did respond, he dashed what few hopes she had. He looked so stern, she didn't mention the good news the doctor had given her about trying Skip on the experimental nerve drug.

''It's obvious that nothing I say is going to change your mind, Crystal. Might as well find a new topic. Better yet, do you mind if I turn on the radio? Last night I heard the Broncos' primary quarterback wrenched his throwing arm and might be pulled from the exhibition game. I want to see if it's been confirmed.''

''Be my guest.''

He scrubbed his hands along his jeans, leaving smudges of powdered sugar. ''Are you ready for another?'' he asked, extending her the bag.

Crystal shook her head. ''My cell phone is in a woven bag behind my seat. Would you hand it to me before you turn up the radio? I need to check with April and make sure the paychecks got run.''

''April? Snappy little redhead, right?'' Caleb twisted in his seat to find the phone. He missed the disapproving arch of Crystal's eyebrow.

''April has red hair. I guess you'd know better than I would about her being 'snappy.' There's something we need to get straight, Tanner. She's not your personal assistant. The sports department has a secretary—Rose Miller. She's worked there for eighteen years. Anything you want or need, place your request with her.''

He straightened and passed Crystal the phone. "I detect a note of censure. What crime am I being charged with?"

"It's not my place to reprimand you. That's up to Nate or André. April, though, works for me. I'd hate to come down on her for wasting time running your stats, instead of mine."

"Hey." He shoved a hand through his hair. "My first day on the job all these women came out of the wood-work. Every time I turned around there was a new one asking if I needed anything. Should I have been rude?"

Crystal let her shoulders relax. "No, but at a TV station, most jobs are independent."

"One woman, Nicole, brought me cookies. Obviously beyond the call of duty. But all the others acted as if they were *supposed* to bring me water, sharpen pencils, get me information I needed and make sure my tie was straight."

Crystal groaned. "You're new, good-looking and single to boot. In other words, fair game in the date market. I should think you'd see right through them."

"Guess I've played football so long I've learned to accept *and* ignore that sort of behavior. I never encouraged any of them, if that's what you think."

"Yes, actually I did, Tanner. Sorry." And she was. Jealousy was a new emotion for her. One she didn't like. Unsure what to say next, she punched in the numbers to her department and talked to April, extending the conversation as long as possible.

"You might have warned me what to expect," Caleb said when at last she disconnected.

"You never struck me as being naive. The opposite, in fact. When Nate, André and Michael first mentioned hiring you, I stopped by the newsroom and pulled a file on the Sinners. Quite an array of photos. Except for the action shots, you guys were always with some beautiful woman or other.''

"I don't deny it. PR usually likes to pair professional models with sports figures. Models have agendas, same as ballplayers do. But I didn't expect that would be true of sweet little ol' gals who worked nine to five.''

Crystal tossed her cell phone into the back seat without looking. "Pul-leeze, Tanner. You only talk Texas when you're trying to snow me.''

He laughed, and the warm deep sound caused Crystal's stomach to coil as tight as a clock spring.

"That's why I like you, darlin'. You don't take any bull,'' he said.

"Why do you keep handing it out, then? Bull and cutesy endearments. You know how I feel about those.''

He let his head fall against the headrest. As he faced her, the laugh creases faded from his cheeks. "It's habit. Starts in middle school. Guys trying to be cool in front of other guys.''

"Hmm. So, is there some way to keep Skipper from starting that disgusting habit? Assuming my plans to foster him work out.''

"You want the kid to grow up strange?''

They were on a flat ribbon of road leading from Baton Rouge to Lafayette. Crystal stepped on the gas. "No, I don't want him to be different from other boys. But—''

"Then get him out of that damned chair. Forget renovating the house to accommodate a wheelchair. Show the kid you expect him to walk and he will.''

Stricken by his bluntness, Crystal said, "You make it sound so easy. Now, here's the truth. The doctor said Skip's progress slipped when you left therapy. You inspired him to try harder. I'm not sure I can do that. I can't stand the thought of him hurting himself.'' Tears trickled from the corners of her eyes.

"Dammit! Why do women always cry to bring a man to heel?"

Crystal dashed at her cheeks. "I'm not! I hate it when I cry. I never used to."

"It's okay." He stretched to the limit of the seat belt and stroked her face. "I've already figured out how to juggle my schedule so I can visit Skip." His voice softened. "Did I mention that I see a lot of me in that little bugger?" Caleb tried to lighten the mood. "Which is the biggest reason you should think twice about taking him on. I was a pistol."

"That I believe." Crystal dried her tears. "Tell me about your childhood."

"Why?"

"There were no kids in the neighborhood where my dad's aunt lived. She raised me, remember? I went to a Catholic girls' school all the way through twelfth grade."

"No kidding? They still have such things? Half the fun in high school for guys was getting to fool around with girls. I think it was the same for girls."

"Yes...well, I was in college before I found out guys were *consumed* by that little pastime." She rolled her eyes. "That's not necessarily the part of your life I want to hear about, Tanner."

"Take out the X-rated parts and all you've got left is football." Happy to have cajoled her beyond tears, he launched into a tale of his life on the farm.

"I see a rest area with picnic tables over there," she said as he reached the point where he was drafted by the Dallas Cowboys. "I brought a cooler with fruit and cheese and stuff. What do you say to stopping for lunch?"

"Where are we? Man, we're already in Texas. I can't

believe I talked about myself for so long. You must be a good listener. Still got both your ears?"

After guiding the car to a stop, she patted her earlobes to show him she did.

"Turnabout's fair play. Next half of the trip I want *your* life story," he said as they climbed out and stretched cramped muscles.

Crystal retrieved a small cooler and a box of crackers from the trunk as Caleb got his cane. "I won't bore you," she said. "There's nothing much to tell. My childhood changed drastically when my mother died. Dad's secretaries sent cards from him occasionally. He was usually in some remote oil field. He missed my high-school graduation. Showed up for the one from LSU. Said he'd try to make my wedding. 'Try' was the operative word. Then I didn't get married." She invested a lot of time in slicing perfect wedges of cheese.

Caleb heard the pain in her voice. He knew she wasn't a virgin when they'd made love. He also knew it'd been a long time between partners for both of them. Now he had an inkling of just how long it had been for her. He wasn't sure why, but he didn't want to leave her with the impression that he was promiscuous.

"You're the only woman I've ever introduced to my sisters," he said. "And the first I've invited home to meet the people I consider my true friends."

The bite of cracker she'd taken went down the wrong way. "What will folks read into that?" she choked. "I never thought—will they all assume we're sleeping together?"

He handed her a bottle of water. "If I had my way, we would be. I wasn't the one who got dressed and tore out in the middle of the night."

Crystal heard his unspoken question. She carefully replaced what they hadn't eaten in the cooler. "I'm not as casual about sex as you are."

Caleb stood. Forgetting his injury, he jerked up the cooler. "I gave up casual sex quite a few years ago," he snapped. "We *made love* that night. Don't mix me up with whatever horny college kid promised marriage to get you in the sack, and then hurt you when he dumped you."

She handed him his cane and almost toppled him by yanking the cooler from his grasp. After returning it to the trunk and slamming the lid closed, she unlocked his door. "You got the horny part right. Ben put a ring on my finger and still slept his way through the club's chorus line. I did the dumping. None of which has anything to do with you and me."

Caleb pulled her tight against his body, gazed deep into her eyes and then kissed her. Deeply. By the time he let her go, she was fuzzy-headed and pliant. "We could debate how the rotten way he treated you affects your trust in me," he murmured, outlining her lips with the pad of his thumb. "But I want us to have a good time at Patsy's wedding. I propose we put all the messy stuff between us on hold until we get back home. By the way," he added, "you'll be bunking with Jenny at Gracie's apartment. I'll take the couch."

"All right." She floated around the car and got in on her side. After that she said little. It wasn't until they neared Austin that reality struck again. She'd let his kiss make her forget how vehemently he'd opposed her decision to foster Skipper. The truth was, Caleb had his own close-knit family and a cache of happy memories. Skip had no one except Rachel in his corner, and she was stretched thin with a caseload of other kids. Skip needed Crystal's love far more than this charismatic man beside her, who collected friends wherever he went.

Resolute in her decision, Crystal refused to examine the sense of emptiness deep inside. She pretended interest in the passing scenery to keep Caleb from reading the heartache in her eyes.

He seemed absorbed in the passing scenery, too. Either that, or he was lost in the pregame discussion he'd finally found on the radio.

Crystal could only take so much silence. "I told you Alain sent Raymond to offer you a ticket and transportation to this game." She hauled in a deep breath. "You accused me of not warning you about being pounced on by women at the station, Tanner. So let me warn you about Ray and Alain." She described their lifelong persecution of André. "They're trying to befriend you, and it wouldn't pay to get mixed up with them."

"Thanks for the tip." He flipped off the radio. "They aren't the only other Lyons involved in the business, though. There's Scott."

"He's okay. A decent guy."

"Then I met another. In advertising?"

"Jason. He used to be a jerk. He married a nice woman and has pretty much turned around. Although—" she frowned "—Jase hangs out at Chez Charles. The restaurant belongs to Uncle Charles and Alain manages it now. So I'm careful what I say around Jason in case it gets passed on. Gabrielle and André think he helped engineer some rotten stunts in the mid-seventies when André took over as general manager. Mischief that ended with a bomb hoax at the station. No one ever actually proved Jason and his brothers were involved—but no one doubted it, either." She gave a small shake of her head.

"Nice branch of the family tree. Consider me warned." He glanced at his watch, then out the window. "Hey, lead-foot, we're here early. Jenny is still in class. Gracie's at work. Patsy's spending the day with her future mother-in-law. Care to run out to the farm and take a gander at my cars? Last week I touched base with a country singer I know who's a car collector. He said he'd fly in sometime today, look over what I've got and maybe buy a couple. I'd like to see if he's interested.''

"Sure. I'm your chauffeur for the weekend."

He let that remark pass and gave her concise directions.

"This is beautiful country," she said of the lush green hills surrounding them. "I expected Texas to be hot, dusty and flat."

"Not in the hill country. When I was a kid, I couldn't wait to get out of the old hometown. After I saw the world, this farmland looked pretty fine."

"Maybe you'll come back here someday."

"I expect, in part, it will depend on my wife." He said it matter-of-factly, as if he had someone lined up to marry.

Crystal didn't look at him. Didn't dare. She steeled herself, thinking he might press the point. He didn't, but directed her through two turns. A short time later he announced they'd reached the farm.

The farmhouse was simple gray clapboard, but well kept. It had an inviting wraparound porch that overlooked a pond. Beyond, in a hollow, sat a barn and several outbuildings. As far as the eye could see lay fields of ripening melons. Behind the house sat two small airplanes, one under a lean-to, the other at the end of a packed-dirt runway.

"My buyer is here. It might be muddy down by the barns. You're welcome to come or you can sit on the porch. I won't be long. My aunt's in Austin helping with the wedding, but if you want, you can go inside to wait."

"I'd like to see that gold mine of cars. I'll brave the mud."

Caleb's cane sank into the muck and slowed his pace. "Damn, I hate being stove up," he muttered.

"The limp is less pronounced. You must be feeling some better."

"'Some' is the operative word. If I was a lot better, I'd never sell the cars. The consultant's verdict after viewing my X rays is that it's an injury that needs time to heal."

"More than the year you've allowed?"

He stared straight ahead, then said reluctantly, "The doc said more like two or three. The knee may never heal good enough to pivot for a long-ball throw."

"Caleb, I'm sorry." Sympathy washed over her and again dampened her eyes.

"Don't shed any tears for me, honey. I told the doc 'never' isn't in my vocabulary."

Crystal saw stubborn defiance tighten his jaw. Silently she rooted for him. If anyone could beat permanent disability, it was Caleb Tanner.

The door to the biggest shed opened and two men walked out. Caleb hailed them and paused while they approached. He introduced Crystal. The men greeted her politely. The older one, Caleb's uncle, inspected her thoroughly after Caleb and the singer returned to the barn. Feeling like an amoeba under a microscope, Crystal made small talk. She might as well get used to the scrutiny—if she really was the first woman he'd ever brought home. At last, though, she excused herself to go look at the cars.

Crystal didn't know what she expected, but it certainly wasn't this number of cars. She barely had time to admire the sleek lines of a vintage Rolls-Royce before Caleb beckoned her over.

"Crystal is my accountant," he informed the buyer, J. J. Grant. Placing a hand on her shoulder, he said earnestly, "J.J's offering three-point-five mil for the works. Should I accept?"

"Terms?" she asked, doing her best not to appear excited. Caleb hadn't estimated their worth at nearly so much.

"My personal check on the barrel today," the man promised. "And I don't send trucks to haul the cars to my place until you notify me the check has cleared."

"That's fair enough, Tanner. Your choice, though," she said, seeing the indecision that racked him.

With only minimal hesitation, he extended his hand to conclude the deal. In a surprisingly brief exchange, during which he signed an inventory list and an intent to transfer titles, Caleb tucked the check in his pocket and said goodbye to the singer. Moments after promising to see his uncle at the wedding, he ushered Crystal back to her car. "One of the girls should be at Gracie's apartment by now."

"You don't have to act like this is all in a day's work, Caleb. I know you sold a piece of your heart back there."

"No sweat." He shrugged. "Who needs cars when he has a chauffeur?"

"Hmm, yes. Well, in that case, Tanner—if you take the 'point five' from that sale to clear your debts and give me the three mil to invest and pay taxes, I'll earn you a monthly income that'll put a smile on your face again."

"A man would be a fool to turn loose of a woman who can do that." Caleb extracted the check from his pocket and carelessly shoved it into her handbag. His warm palm lingered on her arm.

"You shouldn't tease when it comes to money, Tanner."

"Who's teasing? But in the future when I introduce you

to friends as my accountant and fiancée, could you call me by my first name?''

His calm statement took Crystal's breath away. Her stomach pitched and her hands shook as she guided the car to a stop outside a modern apartment house on the outskirts of the city. The building bore the address he'd given her. Then of course the yellow and white balloons and wedding streamers tied to the balcony of an upper-level unit provided a pretty unmistakeable clue. ''You're asking me to *marry* you? You've gone wedding loco,'' she blurted. ''Weddings have that effect on people. So does making a lot of money.''

Cale unbuckled his seat belt, slid across and grasped her chin. ''It's neither,'' he said, forcing her to meet his eyes. ''When you raced out of my place the other night, I felt about as empty as I've ever felt. I let you go because I decided you didn't need a guy whose life was in shambles. Today I found out my life's not as much of a mess as I thought. More important, I learned I'm not empty when we're together. I feel like half of something good. I'm sorry it's taken me so long to put a label on what's been eating my insides. I love you, Crystal. I know it's sudden. Please don't throw it back in my face until you chew it over good. I promise you I've never said those words before to anyone outside my family.''

Those pesky tears filled Crystal's eyes again as she circled Caleb's strong wrist with fingers that were both clammy and unsteady. ''I said before and I'll say it again—you talk too much, Caleb.'' Straining against her seat belt, she brushed his lips lightly with hers. When he increased the pressure, their mouths opened and their tongues touched, tangled. Savored.

''Is that a yes?'' he breathed against her lips a moment later.

"What was the question?" Her eyes closed as she smiled and pressed her mouth against the pulse that bucked wildly below his jaw.

"Will you take that long walk through life with me? Will you have my babies?"

Crystal's eyes snapped open. Drawing back, she tried to see his eyes over his craggy chin. She finally felt free to admit she loved him. But, marriage? Dared she take that risk? She felt a sinking sensation harkening back to an earlier discussion. "Where does my decision to be a foster mom fit into this?"

He didn't look directly at her as he unclipped her braid and threaded his fingers through her tangled hair. "Marriage itself is a big adjustment according to the guys I know. They claim it takes time and patience to adapt to a mate's habits. Adding a third person into the mix is trouble newlyweds don't need."

She sat up, taking care not to touch him. When they touched, her mind didn't fire on all cylinders. "What if you'd fallen in love with me and Skip was my real son?"

"Why play games? He isn't. And you have no idea how hard it is to wake up every morning knowing you're responsible for the health and welfare of little people. As kids go, my sisters were good. Once I got them back and got them some counseling, their main ups and downs were the normal ones of passing through puberty. Skip has a physical handicap. And he's been in the system so long who knows what baggage he's carrying?"

"I have baggage, Caleb. So do you. You expect love to transcend our problems and fill our empty lives. Skip has empty spaces that need filling, too. He didn't ask for what he's had to endure."

Caleb reached into the back seat for his cane. What no one knew was how many football games he'd played on little or no sleep because he'd spent half the night worrying about some incident or other that had upset the girls. A bad grade. A slight by a friend. Crying jags over a crush gone sour. Granted, the separation of miles made the incidents seem bigger—colossal—but each had torn a huge chunk out of his heart. "I can't do what you ask of me, Crystal. I just can't." A shudder slammed through his body as he opened the door, stepped out and turned his back on his one shot at happiness.

She sat there stunned. *Why can't he do it if he loves me?* The pain went so deep she thought she might pass out.

She'd barely managed to hide her feelings when Caleb's sisters descended on the car.

"What's taking you so long? It's ol' gimpy here, I'll bet," teased Jenny as she made a show of helping her brother over the curb. The way the three of them laughed, chattered and hugged the newcomers, it was apparent they had no idea a storm had blown up between Caleb and Crystal.

She couldn't escape being pulled into the excitement surrounding the wedding. And she refused to wallow in self-pity. This was Patsy's weekend to be petted and pampered. Really, it was fun to involve herself in all the activities and pretend to be part of a happy family. Leslie had eloped and so had Sharlee. This might be her only chance to participate in the pomp and circumstance of a wedding. Rachel sure wasn't the type to indulge in all the trappings, assuming Jacob ever reached the point of asking her to marry him. Or she might turn him down, consumed as she was by her career.

Not everyone was destined to be married. The thought struck Crystal later that evening in the middle of the rehearsal dinner. Patsy and her fiancé were so wrapped up in each other they'd blocked out everyone else in the room. Crystal recalled being aware of every detail in the nightclub the night Caleb came to hear her play. Maybe she wasn't really in love with him.

She jumped when someone jabbed an elbow in her ribs. Jenny Tanner. Leaning close, she whispered in Crystal's ear, "Cale won't admit there's anything romantic going on between you two. But I notice he hasn't taken his eyes off you all evening. What gives?"

Crystal sought the man who sat across the table, flanked by his uncle and the groom's best man. He was indeed staring at her. Weakened by those incredible green eyes, she had difficulty answering Jenny.

"Maybe he's afraid you're telling me all the family secrets." As the feeble attempt at humor left her lips, Crystal faintly remembered hearing the term "family secrets" before. From Margaret. Yes. When she'd handed over a key to the safe-deposit box. What kind of secrets? Murder? Bad blood?

The room spun. To Crystal's knowledge, only she and Margaret knew the box existed. But given the mysterious manner in which she'd disappeared, should André be made aware? Was it up to her to tell him? It almost felt as if Margaret was reaching out to her.

Jenny shook Crystal's arm and urged a glass of water into her hand. "My aunt would say you look like you'd had a brush with a ghost."

"Excuse me, please." Crystal stood. "I forgot to call home. So much has gone on, I neglected to let my family know we'd arrived safely."

"The ladies' room might be the most private place to make the call. The restaurant's so noisy tonight."

Thanking Caleb's youngest sister, Crystal hurried off. Gabrielle answered on the second ring. "No, Crystal, not a word. André's decided to give Dave Patton two more weeks. Then he's contacting the police. Nothing we can do for now. So just relax. Go have fun.''

Crystal hung up, wishing she felt close enough to Gaby to talk about the latest turmoil involving her and Caleb. It was Margaret who'd listen, who'd discuss the situation endlessly, who'd analyze and comfort and advise. Decisions came easily to Gabrielle. Black or white. Yes or no. Crystal wished she could be that decisive.

Caleb accosted her the minute she returned to the dining room. ''Are you all right? Jenny said you turned white a minute ago.''

''I…you'll probably think I'm crazy. I felt a sudden weird connection to Margaret. I phoned home, but there's been no word from her. It must be the wedding hoopla. Margaret loves weddings, and she was terribly upset when both her granddaughters eloped.''

''Hmm. I've had too many premonitions to say you're crazy. Speaking of the wedding, the party broke up while you were gone. Everyone wants to be fresh for tomorrow. Run and catch Gracie if you'd like to be included with the group of women going to a beauty salon tomorrow. I'll meet you at the car. I've been on my sore leg too long, so I'll move slower than you.''

''You haven't reinjured your knee? Oh, Caleb.''

''I'm fine,'' he snapped, unable—circumstances between them being what they were—to bear her concern. Though he'd love to lean on her, to feel and accept the strength of her slender body.

Her lips quivered. ''I guess I don't have any pride. I don't want to lose your friendship.''

Several seconds passed before his body relaxed. ''I value yours, too. Don't you dare cry,'' he said as water pooled along the lower rim of her lashes. "Save the tears for tomorrow. Tears are acceptable at weddings."

AND SHED THEM, she did. Not only because Patsy was a beautiful bride. But because of Caleb. In spite of relying heavily on his cane as he escorted his sister down the aisle, he looked incredibly handsome in his tuxedo. Every aspect of the ceremony was moving and beautiful.

The problem, as Crystal defined it later, was that the day went by too fast. First the trip to the salon and all the morning's activities. Then, from the priest's first words to the singing of "Ave Maria" to the throwing of confetti at the getaway car that whisked the couple off on a two-week honeymoon—seven hours max.

"We're never getting married," Gracie and Jenny told Caleb the next morning as they sat around Gracie's small breakfast bar. "Months of preparation. Thousands of dollars. All over in a flash."

"I'll remind you of that one of these days. I can't see either of you spending the rest of your lives as bachelorettes." His laughter turned hollow as Crystal abruptly excused herself from the group.

"It's a long drive home," she said. "I'll load the car and leave you all to your goodbyes. Thanks for your hospitality Gracie…Jenny. Next time either of you comes to New Orleans, I'll take you out for dinner."

Caleb stood awkwardly by while the three hugged. He'd been taught that men didn't cry. But damn, he sure felt like it. This acute letdown was worse than what he used to go through after his team had played well, yet lost the game in the closing minutes.

Friends or not, he figured they were in for a long, silent drive home.

UNFORTUNATELY HE WAS RIGHT. And if he thought the tension had been bad in the car, it thickened outside his apartment.

"Well, so long," she said flatly. "See you at work."

"Yeah." He wanted to say something about getting together soon, but she didn't hang around long enough for him to get the words out.

As he stood on the stoop and watched Crystal nose her car into traffic, Caleb had a horrible feeling they were really saying permanent goodbyes. The night blackness swallowed the Caddy's glowing taillights. Caleb wanted to reach out and snatch her back.

Only once in his life had he felt this bereft. The day he'd lost his parents...

CHAPTER FOURTEEN

CRYSTAL FOUND CALEB'S CHECK the next morning when she was looking for her house keys. She realized he now had the means to hire a team of advisers if he wanted to. Which was fine by her. The thought of sitting down with him elbow to elbow as often as she did with family members whose investments she handled made her stomach jittery.

Leaning on her dresser, she peered into the mirror to inspect her bloodshot eyes. Bloodshot from tossing half the night, alternately staring at a dark ceiling and wishing things between her and Caleb had progressed differently.

But how could they? His heart wasn't big enough to include a small boy.

After showering, she dressed for work, tucked the check into a zippered pocket of her attaché case and left the house without speaking to anyone. The Caddy she'd borrowed for the trip was parked in the driveway. André, Gaby and the others would know she'd made it home. Crystal caught her regular streetcar and this time rode it to the stop nearest the courthouse.

Within minutes she sat in the bustling lobby of the Social Services office and filled out a foster-care form. She listed Rachel, André and the current attorney for Lyon Broadcasting as references. Carrying the form to the desk, she waited until a harried receptionist got off the phone. "I'm interested in fostering a child I've met through my volunteer work at a local hospital. Where, on the form, should I note that?''

"Why didn't you say that to begin with? This is the wrong form.'' The woman opened a different drawer and pulled out a packet twice as thick as the other.

Crystal knew she couldn't complete it and still get to work at nine. But she'd heard Rachel talk about how long it took for the wheels to turn in this office. Sighing, she sat down and telephoned André to say she'd be late. "The wedding was beautiful. I had a good time,'' she said in response to his first question. "I called to say I'm stuck in the foster-parenting office. I'm sure you're anxious to check your mother's bank record. I can give you directions on how to access the file.'' When he said he'd wait until she arrived, she signed off and started on the new forms.

An hour later she entered her office and skidded to a halt inside. André sat behind her desk and Caleb lounged in one of the other chairs. Both men hurriedly stood. Caleb wobbled without his cane until he steadied himself on the desk. Balancing there, he adjusted his tie with one hand and smiled crookedly. "Glad to see you aren't winging your way to Rio.''

She slapped her briefcase down next to his hand. He didn't so much as curl a finger, she'd give him that. "You're lucky I gave up forgery last week. You never endorsed the check, remember?'' Digging it out of her case, she watched him stuff the three million dollars plus nonchalantly into a pocket.

André glanced from one to the other. "Did I miss something? I came by to see if you were here yet and found Cale pacing the hall, wondering if you'd been kidnapped.''

"I suppose it's not smart to call my boss a liar,'' Caleb

said to Crystal. "Ask him what really happened. And by the way, the Rio remark was a joke."

André laughed. "Okay, I was the one anxious to see you, Crystal. I met Cale at the elevator and dragged him along to discuss Saturday's game. Hey, Cale, since you missed it, too, come to Lyoncrest for dinner tonight and I'll rerun the tape. Gaby and I took Andy-Paul and Cory to the movies so I had to record it on the VCR. I told her she chose a heck of a time to give Leslie and Mike a parenting break."

"That'd be great," Caleb said. "I tried to watch it, but I barely saw two plays. I told Patsy she could've planned her wedding better."

"I can just imagine the flak you took over that," André commiserated.

"Now that you have your social lives settled," Crystal said, sounding irked, "may I have my desk back? Some of us work for a living."

"Ouch. Someone got up on the wrong side of the bed," André said.

Caleb knew the source of her irritation. Plainly she'd prefer he decline dinner at Lyoncrest. *Too bad*. "One question before I go," he said. "How do I handle giving you the money we agreed I'd invest?"

She glanced up sharply. "If you still want my help, there's a form you sign at the bank. After the check clears, they'll transfer the amount you name to a holding fund. A money-market account. It earns some interest while I decide which stocks and bonds to buy. But we haven't talked strategy. You have a say in how you invest."

"I think *you* know I don't know beans about saving." The words were no more out than it dawned on Caleb that learning would be a way to spend time with Crystal. "Hmm, I suppose I ought to get a grip on my finances.

Tell you what. I'll check my calendar when I get to the sports room. I'll phone with a list of my free evenings, and you can pick a date that works for you.''

"As long as you're comfortable with the arrangement,'' she said stiffly.

"I'd be more comfortable if— Never mind.'' Caleb gave André a two-fingered salute. Leaning heavily on his cane, he left the office.

"You two on the outs?'' André asked after the door had shut behind him.

"A disagreement of sorts between two hotheads.'' She sighed. "If you'll move, I'll check Margaret's account. The withdrawal times have been staggered, but they've all been on Mondays. The bank's programmer wants to block the account. I can't authorize that. It's not my money. While something strange is obviously going on, Margaret may be involved. In any event, whoever's doing this has her bank card.''

André said little. He stood behind her as she struck the series of numbers needed to bring the account to her screen. Another three thousand winked at them ominously. They stared helplessly at the screen, then at each other.

"If this is Mama's doing and I ever find out, I may strangle her.'' André paced the small office, every so often jingling the change in his pants pockets. "I've tried to play this low-key in order to keep it out of the news. I wanted to allow Mama her privacy—and not throw employees and sponsors into a panic. But enough is enough. Did Gaby tell you I'm giving Patton to the end of the month? Then I'm contacting the police.''

"I'm sorry, André. I kick myself for not insisting on accompanying her to the cemetery that day. Leslie, Rachel and Gaby feel the same. This weekend I had a strange feeling Margaret was trying to reach us. I can't explain it. Did Gaby mention I called home to check?"

"Yes, and she dreamed of Mama that night. You ladies are scaring me. I wish you'd stop it." He shook his head in frustration. "I can't understand why she'd go off alone."

"André, do you believe there are secrets in this family?"

"How so?"

"Margaret has a safe-deposit box to be opened in event of her death. She acted really worried that it might fall into the wrong hands or something."

"I imagine her will has codicils on its codicils. I have a copy of Grandfather's will, and Papa's. They're pretty forthright with no twisted clauses. But I won't poke through her things until it becomes absolutely clear that's the only route left."

Crystal nodded. "Just remember, I have a key if it does turn out to be necessary."

André left her to her work. But Crystal didn't start right away. Her mind was too filled with disjointed thoughts of Margaret, Caleb and Skipper. Ultimately she set her thoughts aside and worked through lunch, then left early to visit Skip.

By that time, she was nearly caught up on the backlog that had accumulated the previous Friday. She left with a good feeling. No saxophone case to lug tonight since she was planning to visit with the boys, not entertain. She had slipped her laptop into her briefcase. There were family investments to check tonight. What she needed, Crystal decided, were more hours in a day. Lately it seemed she went everywhere at a dead run. Including this trip to the hospital.

Compared to the unhappy kids she'd encountered last

week, the boys she peeked in on now were laughing and talking boisterously.

"Hi, guys! Did somebody you know win the lottery?"

"Crystal, hi!" Skip shouted her name and motioned her in with both arms. "Guess what! Today Cale brought by a bunch of guys who play for the Sinners. Lookee! We all got jerseys with numbers, names and everything." He indicated the bright matching football shirts they all wore. Crystal hadn't even noticed.

The last thing she expected was to see Caleb's name on any of the shirts. Yet Skip wore number 22 and proudly showed her the "Tanner" printed on the back.

Randy kept pulling out the front of his shirt so he could gaze at the numbers. His secret smile said everything. Pablo looked like an elf in his oversize shirt. "Who dat player?" Crystal teased in Cajun street speak.

"Kenny Green's the Sinners' tight end." Skip acted as if no one could be that misinformed.

"Um...tight end. I've really gotta learn more about this game," Crystal muttered. "So, I hope you guys thanked Caleb for arranging such a special treat."

"Yeah, and you know what else?" Skip exclaimed. "He helped me with therapy, and I moved one leg. Not just my toes—my whole leg! Mindy says I got feeling coming back. I might not need that old shot they were thinkin' about givin' me."

"Skip, that's wonderful news!" Crystal gave him a hug.

"You're not gonna blubber, are you?" he asked warily, voice muffled.

Pulling back, she blotted her eyes. "I beg your pardon, buster. This lady doesn't blubber. But if I did, this would be the time." Crystal couldn't help hugging him again. This time when she let go, she reached for her purse. "I brought each of you a present from Texas. Nothing that compares to football jerseys, I'm sure. Maybe I should save my gifts for another time.''

''No, no,'' they all chorused. ''Wha'dya get us?''

''Four-color laser-light key chains. The Texas flag's engraved on one side of the barrel. It says 'Don't Mess with Texas' on the other. They're high-tech gizmos, fellas. So don't be shining them in people's eyes or I'll tell Nurse Pam to take them away.''

''They're cooool,'' Skip drawled. ''Thanks, Crystal.'' As she handed them out, the boys snapped them on and giggled gleefully as they pretended to duel with the light beams.

''You're welcome. Now I think you'd better try and calm down. You've all had a super-exciting day. I can't stay, but I'll be here for your therapy tomorrow, Skip. I want to see the progress you've made.''

''Crystal, this is the *best* day. If I can walk, I'll bet Rachel will let me live with Sandy again.'' He settled into his pile of pillows, a satisfied look on his face.

From the doorway, Crystal turned to frown vaguely. ''Did Tanner suggest that?''

''No. I just thought...'' He took a deep breath. ''I s'pose Sandy's already got another kid to take my place.'' His eyes dimmed with disappointment.

''You concentrate on getting well, tiger. When the time comes for you to leave, Rachel will have found you a nice home.''

''Sure,'' he agreed halfheartedly. The doubt in his voice stayed with Crystal even after she boarded the streetcar. All day she'd meant to call Rachel. To tell her she'd put in her application to foster Skipper and to ask if there was any way to speed the process so that Skip could feel secure and stop worrying. Crystal mentally placed calling

Rachel on a growing list of things to do after she got home.

She'd no sooner opened the front door at Lyoncrest than the sound of male voices mingled with the recorded roar of a football crowd.

"Crystal, you're late tonight." Gaby stepped out of the dining room. She held a stack of colorful napkins. "André forgot to let me know he'd invited Caleb to dinner. Not that I mind. It's no big deal to add or subtract place settings."

"And you didn't know I'd be late. I'm sorry. I went by to visit Skip." She set her briefcase and handbag in a corner. "Let me wash off the trolley grime and I'll fold those napkins. But why be formal? Feed the guys on TV trays in the family room. Tanner came to see the game."

Gaby nudged Crystal's ribs. "Not entirely. I've seen him looking at his watch and scanning the foyer. The game's a convenient excuse. He came to see you, lady."

"No. We had words over the weekend, Gaby. He doesn't approve of my wanting to foster Skipper."

"It is a big step, as André and I pointed out." Gaby trailed Crystal into the hall bathroom as Crystal washed her hands. "Are you sure Cale disapproved?" Gaby pressed. "André said Tanner took some of the Sinners players into classrooms with him today. I think he said they also visited the hospital."

"They did. I need to thank him. He made the boys' day."

"While you're doing that, tell them to put the game on hold and come eat."

The scene that greeted Crystal in the family room left her reeling. Andy-Paul was snuggled in Caleb's lap. Mouser was curled contentedly at his side. Such an inviting picture. What had ever made her think that she could ignore her feelings for Caleb Tanner and they'd simply go away? He looked right and natural holding a child. He'd be a wonderful father, a good family man. That thought had her sucking in her breath, scrabbling for something clever to say.

Just then, Caleb glanced over Andy-Paul's dark curly head and his lips parted in a huge smile. "Hi, there," he said, and his eyes seemed to grow darker, more intense. "I dropped by your office to see if I could catch a ride with you, but you'd gone. André gave me a lift, instead. I worried when we beat you home by so much."

"You worry too much. I went to the hospital." She stepped into the room and leaned down to hug Andy-Paul and then Cory, who shared a recliner with her father. Leslie dozed on the settee. Returning her attention to Caleb, Crystal said, "That was a nice thing you did today. Skip and his friends were so high I had to peel them off the ceiling."

André picked up the control and put the VCR on pause. "We're trying to watch a game here, Crystal."

"Yeah, Crystal." Echoing his dad, the boy waved her aside.

"Okay for you," she said, tickling the child. "That means more food for me and your mom. She asked me to tell you dinner's ready."

Andy-Paul, who loved mealtimes, was clearly torn. "What are we having?"

"Somebody's favorite," Crystal said, swinging away. "Ravioli filled with crawfish and crabmeat. Buttered summer squash and okra salad."

Hollering for his dad and Caleb to hurry, the boy scampered to the door.

André laughed and stood up. He lifted Cory out of the chair and left Michael to rouse Leslie. Caleb eased himself from the deep cushions of the leather chair, careful not to disturb the sleeping cat.

"Based on the rumble in my stomach, I vote we take a time-out," André said. "Cory, will you show Caleb where he can wash up?"

The girl bobbed her curly head.

Once they all met again in the dining room, they found Gaby had added a leaf to the table. She directed seating so that Caleb and Crystal sat beside each other. Quietly smug, she kept a straight face even when Crystal kicked her under the table.

André, apparently missing the undercurrents, continued to pepper Caleb with questions related to the first half of the game. A salad bowl exchanged hands without interrupting their banter. It was when Michael lifted a steaming dish filled with ravioli that the front door banged open, bringing all conversation to a halt.

Every jaw at the table dropped as Rachel Fontaine stormed into the dining room. Her fury stilled Leslie in the midst of a yawn.

Hands on hips, Rachel confronted Crystal. "What the *hell* do you think you're doing? First you write letters demanding experimental medical treatment for a ward of the court. Now you list me as the primary reference on a foster-parent application for a child in my caseload. Did you involve Skip in this scheme? Will I have to break his heart again?"

"No! I wouldn't do that." Crystal bunched the napkin she'd just stretched across her lap. "What's the problem, Rachel? I'm sorry I didn't call to discuss my plans with you in advance. That's hardly reason to rip me to shreds."

"The big problem is that my supervisor spent the last three hours flaying me for misusing my authority. She thinks I advised you to go over her head with that treatment request.''

''I'll phone her in the morning and explain it was my idea. And I'll tell her I listed you without asking. If you've just come from work, you must be starved,'' Crystal said. ''Let me set another place at the table.''

''I'll do it.'' Leslie rose. ''You two iron things out.''

''You still don't get it, Crystal.'' Rachel threw up her hands. ''You can't foster Skip. The rule at our agency is that parenting takes top priority. Even if you didn't play weekends at the club, you have a full-time job. The foster mother of a special-needs kid has to be able to adjust her schedule to the child's school hours. She has to be available for doctor and therapy appointments.''

Beside her, Crystal felt Caleb tense. She didn't dare look at him. She couldn't bear to see him gloat. It took every bit of her slim control to maintain dry eyes. She'd be darned if she'd let him accuse her again of seeking sympathy through tears.

''What's your plan for Skipper?'' Caleb asked Rachel in a low steady voice.

Rachel pulled out a vacant chair. Sinking into it, she propped her elbows on the table and rested her chin in cupped hands. ''I don't know.'' She sighed. ''After today, my supervisor will undoubtedly remove him from my caseload.''

''Why?'' Gaby asked softly.

''Caseworkers aren't supposed to get personally involved. The textbooks say it's detrimental for the child and clouds the decision-making ability of the person in charge of his or her welfare.'' She moved to let Leslie roll out a place mat.

''That's crap!'' Caleb's outburst shocked everyone. He, too, leaned an elbow on the table. His free hand found its way to the back of Crystal's neck, where he massaged her tense muscles. "Kids aren't cattle to be branded and marketed in a manner that happens to suit the bureaucrats. Parentless kids are scared spitless. They need the stability of familiar surroundings. They need to stay with people they know."

"Are you a child psychologist?" Rachel demanded.

"No, and I'm not a damned lawyer, either. I'm a man who spent half a million bucks fighting a welfare system that doesn't give a damn about kids, only about the rules. To hell with the kid's feelings. Mustn't bend or break any one of a gazillion frigging rules." Caleb pounded a fist on the table, and the silverware jumped.

"Sorry," he rushed to apologize as Cory edged closer to Mike, and Andy-Paul burst into tears.

Gaby consoled her son. Immediately afterward, a plate, glass and silverware appeared in front of Rachel. "We'll all feel better after we eat," Gaby said firmly. "Leslie, will you please pass the rolls?"

Crystal slid a hand to Caleb's knee. Squeezing lightly, she offered him a faint but encouraging smile. The gesture might have escaped some. It didn't get by Gaby. She let silence reign only a moment. "Rachel, André worked long hours when he brought you to live at Lyoncrest. So did I. Granted, we later learned that Leslie bore some resentment over spending more time with a nanny than with us. But I know you both had brighter futures because we made a few sacrifices."

Rachel pushed ravioli aimlessly around her plate. At last she lifted dark fathomless eyes. "You think that fact doesn't enter into every case I handle, Gaby? My hands are tied in this instance. Skip's file has already been red-flagged."

"Is he adoptable?" Caleb asked as he draped an arm

around Crystal's shoulders. All eyes were suddenly trained on him. He knew that without looking.

"Older kids are hardly ever adopted," Rachel snapped. "Especially boys. I thought everyone had read the grim statistics. And that's not even counting his condition."

"I didn't ask for statistics," Caleb said. "Is Skip in permanent foster care or not?"

"He could be adopted. But he won't be. There are recorded incidents of misbehavior at his first few foster homes."

"What if Crystal and I got married? Would we be eligible to adopt him?"

Crystal nearly swallowed her tongue, but outwardly she appeared less flabbergasted than the other adults at the table. Only the trembling hand that held her fork betrayed her.

Caleb gathered her nervous fingers with his free hand. "I've thought a lot about what you said when we drove to my sister's wedding. I want you and Skip in my life, Crystal. I know that now."

"You're not just agreeing to a package deal because you want me?"

He kissed her knuckles. "I want you as my life partner and I'll be proud to call Skipper my son."

Rachel dropped her fork with a clatter. "Is this a for-real marriage announcement? I assume so, since Crystal didn't fall off her chair in shock."

"The subject came up this weekend," Crystal assured everyone, though her gaze remained glued to Caleb, searching for clues to his change of heart.

"But earlier you said—" Gaby broke off as Crystal's foot connected with her shin a second time.

Caleb faced Crystal. Pulling her toward him, he kissed her once, twice, three times on her trembling lips. "I hope negotiations are still open," he said when she remained impassive. "Any breakdown in bargaining is my fault." He glanced briefly at those gathered. "I tried to place boundaries on my love. When Crystal dropped me off Sunday night and drove out of my life, I discovered my love has no limitations when it comes to this woman."

He gazed into Crystal's eyes until Andy-Paul clanged his silverware and said petulantly, "I want more ravioli. Why is everybody talking, instead of eating?"

"Good question." Face scarlet, Crystal stopped struggling with her confusion and dished up another mound of ravioli for the little boy.

"So is the affair one-sided?" Rachel tossed the candid question into the conversation that had resumed amid the clink of silver on china.

Crystal bristled. "We're not having an affair. Don't think you can discredit us by insinuating we are in your stupid report."

"Believe it or not, guys, I'm on your side. It's really romantic and brave of Caleb to bare his soul in front of your family, Crystal. And frankly…I never took you for a coward."

"So, you're all waiting for a public declaration of my undying love?"

André exchanged loving smiles with his wife. "To remain in keeping with Lyon tradition, we ought to alert a WDIX-TV reporter."

"I love him, okay?" Crystal admitted in a jerky voice. "It just happened. Don't ask me how. You all know I'm not very good at relationships."

Caleb tugged her out of her chair and onto his lap. His dazed but happy smile spread from ear to ear. Love shone from his green eyes.

Gaby mopped tears from hers. "This is marvelous,"

she said rapturously, jumping up and clapping her hands softly. "Fall weddings are so beautiful."

Crystal stirred in Caleb's arms. "Wait. We have to settle more than a date."

After kissing her silent, he drew back slightly. "Let's make it the first Saturday the church is available after posting banns."

"Yes, all right," she breathed, scattered, as always, by his kisses.

"Will you wear the Hollander gown?" Gaby put in. "Margaret wanted Leslie to, but she and Michael eloped. As did Charlotte. Margaret had so hoped one woman in the family would wear her mother's dress. Oh, I wish she was here. She gets so sentimental over weddings."

"I said that very thing this weekend!" Crystal exclaimed. "But, Gaby, I wouldn't feel right wearing such a special gown without Margie's express permission."

"Doesn't it strike you as really odd that Grandmère, Mom, Sharlee and I all eloped? That dress has been waiting for nearly seventy years."

André, who hadn't entered into the conversation, tilted back in his chair. "Think what a story that would make. Crystal, I'd be the last to turn your wedding into a media circus. On the other hand, if we made it the social event of the season and send pictures of you wearing that dress to the newspaper syndicates, it might be the very thing to bring Mama home."

"You still think she's staying away by choice?" Rachel asked.

"There's been no ransom request, no evidence of foul play," André said.

Andy-Paul stopped eating and wailed, "I want Grandmère to come home."

"We all want that, sweetie." Gaby smoothed tangled

dark curls out of his teary eyes. "I know what. You and Cory run get the scrapbook you and Nanny are putting together for Grandmère. Show Rachel, Cale and Crystal your drawings." As the children ran from the room, she lowered her voice. "They're making a daily log and pictorial account of their activities for Margaret."

"Margaret will treasure that," Rachel murmured. "She has a cedar chest full of artwork and sewing projects that Leslie, Sharlee and I made when we were younger."

Feeling weepy and sentimental, Crystal tucked her head into the hollow of Caleb's neck. "At the risk of sounding like Andy-Paul, I wish with all my heart that Margaret would walk through that door. She's the rock, the cornerstone, of this family."

"Nate showed me the fifty-year pictorial history of Lyon Broadcasting that Leslie assembled," Caleb said. "The statue of Paul and Margaret is impressive. I'd like to meet her. If she's not back in time for the wedding, maybe we can arrange a special album for her. Sort of like the kids' journal, only with photos of the ceremony and reception."

"What a great idea." Crystal threw her arms around his neck and kissed him so hard they almost fell backward off the chair. A telephone rang, putting an end to the kiss. Crystal felt dazed and Caleb was breathing hard. "Omigosh, it's my cellular," she said. Diving off Caleb's lap, she pawed through her bag, found the phone and flipped it open. "Hello," she said breathlessly. "This is Crystal Jardin. Hello, hello! Is someone there?" She plugged her free ear with a finger and listened intently. She realized her face must be undergoing a series of changes. "Margaret!" she gasped. "Oh, Margaret, is that you? Where *are* you?"

All chatter in the room stopped. Everyone around Crystal went still. They held that pose until she shook her head, frustrated, and pressed a finger to the disconnect button several times, trying to get the caller back.

"Tell us!" demanded André, a demand echoed by Gaby and Leslie.

Crystal's hands shook. "A voice. Very faint. A woman. It sounded like Margie. She said my name once. I heard a thump, like she'd dropped the receiver. Then a click followed by dial tone."

"It's a damn hoax," André raged, slamming one fist into the palm of his hand. "Somebody's playing with our minds."

Gaby slid her arm around his waist at the same time as Cale struggled to stand and do the same for Crystal. "Why?" she asked numbly. "Why would anyone call us tonight? Margie was in our thoughts. I know it sounds crazy, but maybe our...our energy somehow reached out to her."

"If so, she'll call back," André said with certainty. "In case it is as far-fetched as it sounds and we're dealing with a crank, let's have Dave Patton monitor your phone."

"Anything, André," Crystal replied. But she cradled the phone in both hands and cried softly, "I know it was her. Margaret will be here for my wedding. You'll see."

MARGARET HOLLANDER LYON, though still unsteady on her feet, had a sense of well-being for the first time in several weeks. Or was it longer? The pills made her so fuzzy she lost track of time. For two days now she'd managed to hide the pills and flush the damned things down the toilet. If she'd had the flu like some of the nicer nurses said, the pills should have made her better long before.

Just this afternoon she'd begun to wonder why no one in the family had come to visit her. Could her flu—if it *was* flu—really be so virulent that no one could be around her? That seemed odd, since the nurses who tended her didn't wear gloves or masks.

The disconnected feeling wasn't half as bad as the nightmares that plagued her. At least once a night she woke up in a panic, absolutely certain she was only heart-beats away from joining her beloved Paul.

And that prospect wouldn't be so bad except that she carried a burden, a secret, that had weighed on her for a long time. Fifty years. The precise nature of that secret seemed to hover just out of her grasp. Yet it shimmered there, like a barrier that kept her from going down the long bright hallway to meet Paul.

Twice he'd spoken to her. He'd said she must go back and tell André the truth. Who was André? she wondered as she finally made her way across the room, out the door and stumbled toward an office she remembered seeing at the end of this dim corridor.

Quiet. There is a need for stealth. I mustn't let the people who work here see me before I make my call. But who should I call?

The old woman was sweating profusely by the time she opened the office door and stepped inside. *There. On the desk. A beige telephone.*

Panic welled up again as she stared in confusion at the pad with the numbers. They had to be punched in a certain order. She knew that much. Suddenly a number hammered insistently in a head that hurt hugely. A number her fingers knew. One she'd used frequently in another life.

Another life. Hysteria rose almost rendering her cata-tonic.

Let your fingers do this. It was as if she heard Paul whispering in her ear.

Margaret lifted the instrument and felt better when

she'd listened to the reassuring hum. Her fingers carefully and automatically pressed out a series of numbers. The tone hammering at her ear changed. A ring, then emptiness, then a ring and emptiness. It seemed to go on so long that alarm overtook her again. Then a voice came through the plastic piece she held to her ear. A voice beloved, but sounding faraway.

Margaret's terror faded a little. She attached a pretty face to the voice, but her lips didn't seem capable of forming the name. And why would hearing that voice make her cry? Margaret didn't know, but her wrinkled cheeks were wet with tears.

"This is Crystal Jardin." The voice sounded warm. Familiar.

Crystal, yes. Oh, thank God, she knew that name. At last, vocal chords that had, out of necessity and pure stubbornness, remained silent for many days, responded in a tinny croak. "Crystal," Margaret said through the tears clogging her throat.

As she struggled to form other words, the door behind her opened and a cold wind from the hall numbed her shaking arms and legs. The doctor who'd visited her earlier batted the phone from her hand. While Margaret cringed and clutched the desk to keep from falling, the man in the white coat picked up the fallen receiver and put it back in its cradle.

This wasn't her trusted family physician, a nice softspoken man who'd handled all the medical crises in her life for almost fifty years. This man was slick and oily, and Margaret didn't trust him.

She struggled to avoid his hands, felt a sharp prick in her arm, then…nothing.

CHAPTER FIFTEEN

IN THE WEEK FOLLOWING the disconcerting phone call, Crystal's life skyrocketed in many different directions. Most of the time her orbits didn't intersect with Caleb's. Wedding plans were whisked away by Gaby and Leslie. In spite of lambasting Crystal for attempting to become a foster parent, Rachel had laid the groundwork for adoption. She'd hired an attorney, a specialist in difficult adoptions, to handle their case. Crystal, who still had some questions regarding Caleb's sudden decision to adopt Skipper, hadn't yet found a chance to ask exactly what had changed his mind. The day she received a letter saying the lawyer had filed a petition and a family-court judge had set a hearing date, she called Caleb and invited him to lunch. "Where have you been hiding? We have to talk."

"Believe me, I never planned to neglect you. My life's been a roller coaster, honey. I haven't had a minute to myself. You know I'm covering pro and college ball, plus we're setting the schedule for bowl games. I'll just tell Nate I'm going to take an hour today. Can we slip away without five nosy reporters following us?"

Crystal arranged to meet him at the back door. She was glad to hear she wasn't the only one who hadn't had a moment's peace since André released the news of their impending wedding.

"Whew." Cale pulled his cane into the car. "Take off.

The blonde who does the afternoon patter on the city's social scene spotted me. She yoo-hooed all the way down the hall. I pretended not to hear. She's like a hound on the scent of a possum."

Crystal pulled onto the road. At the first red light, she said, "André arranged for her to bring a video camera to the house to film a segment on the alterations we're doing to Margaret's mother's dress. Is that all right with you?" She took a deep breath. "Caleb, part of me feels like this wedding is a sham."

He reached over and coiled a loose strand of her hair around one finger. "I just want to kiss my fiancée without having to look over my shoulder to see who's watching."

She leaned toward him with parted lips, then had to pull back because the light had turned green. "What's happened here? How did we get lost in this media event?"

"I can't complain. At least I notified my sisters. Gabrielle told me your dad had to hear it on a national television report."

"Whose fault is that? *He* can't stay in touch? He's drilling in the Coral Sea. Doubts he can make the wedding. Offered to pay for our honeymoon if we'd come to Papua. So he can introduce you around—his son-in-law, the famous quarterback."

Caleb turned the curl loose and picked up her right hand. He brought it to his lips, burying a kiss in her palm. "I hope you told him no. I'd hate to spend my honeymoon in jail for assault."

"André offered to walk me down the aisle. I accepted. I've finally reached a point where I can say it's my father's loss. By the way, I told him about Skip—my dad, I mean. He thinks we're making a big mistake. He predicts you'll regret it and divorce me before the year is out." She glanced anxiously at Caleb.

"Damn nice of him to pass judgment on my integrity. Wait…" He tightened his hold on her hand. "Has he planted doubts in your mind?"

She shook him loose and grasped the wheel tightly. "The seeds were already there. Maybe he fertilized them. You objected so adamantly to my taking Skip as a foster child. We haven't had a chance to discuss what made you change your mind."

"Two things. When you dropped me at my apartment after our trip to Texas, it hit me how empty my life would be without you. And the next day I looked into the eyes of a scared little kid and discovered I didn't much like the man who had the power to take away that fear, yet did nothing." A grin frisked at the corners of Caleb's mouth. "You gotta remember, sweetheart, you're dealing with a backward guy from the hill country. It takes bein' smacked in the head by a two-by-four to penetrate this thick skull."

"Then I'd better buy stock in a lumber company."

"That's another thing I love about you, Crystal. Your quick feisty comebacks. You know…nothing in life comes equipped with guarantees. Humor is the best way to combat the tough times."

"Then laugh at this. We're stuck on a bridge crossing Lake Pontchartrain. Not only don't I know what possessed me to cross the bridge, I don't remember if there's a place to buy lunch on the other side. If that's not bad enough, we have less than half an hour left of our break."

"You don't think André and Nate will believe we got lost on the way to lunch?"

"They might. Life's been zany for all of us lately."

"I've been looking for the right moment to give you your engagement ring. I kind of like the idea of being able to tell this bridge-traffic story to our grandkids." He adjusted his posture so he could get a hand in the tight front pocket of his pants and came out with a sparkling ring. "Gaby and Rachel both said I should ask for your help in picking it out. My sisters hit on the idea of resetting the center stone from my mom's anniversary ring. I hope you don't mind that it's not new. But you sounded excited about wearing a family wedding dress and all." He glanced up and saw tears streaming down her cheeks. "You hate it," he said, wiping a nervous hand over his thigh. "What's wrong? Why is everyone honking? Crystal…?"

"Traffic's moving again and I can't see to drive, you ninny. I don't hate it Caleb. I love it—the ring and the sentiment. But if I wreck the car over this, your plan to tell our grandkids is gonna backfire big time."

"Here, let me steer while you mop up. You really like it, huh? The minute we find a place to pull off, put it on. I want to see how it looks on your hand. Gracie said I should tell you it's a blue diamond, not a sapphire. It matches your eyes."

"Which sister told you that?" she asked, starting to weep again. "About my eyes."

"None of them. That's my observation."

Traffic stopped again. Crystal strained to the limits of her seat belt to deliver a teary kiss to his lips. "Will you think I'm too old-fashioned if I ask you to slip it on my finger?"

"Don't ever be afraid to ask me anything, Crystal. I love you."

"Oh, Caleb, I love you, too." As the ring slid over her knuckle and settled into place, a sense of calm and well-being enveloped Crystal. And stuck with her throughout a hasty lunch of steaming Cajun shrimp they purchased at a roadside stand before making a U-turn and braving the bridge traffic again.

The languid sense of peace she'd acquired with the acceptance of Caleb's ring made it doubly hard to understand the chaos they walked into at WDIX-TV.

Anxious employees lined the hall leading to André's office. Angry voices and bitter shouts assaulted Crystal and Caleb's ears as soon as they left the elevator. "What's going on?" Crystal asked the vice president of engineering. Bruce Pritchard was a longtime employee whose office was separated from André's by a small room used to store outdated videotapes.

"It's just awful, Miss Crystal. I phoned Gabrielle and she's on her way. I can't piece it all together, but it's bad. A couple of us were coming back from lunch. Alain Lyon and some scuzzy character I've never seen before burst into André's office. Hot on their heels was that detective fellow André hired and John, our bank president. Two seconds later Raymond ran through here, knocking people aside and barged right in. The shouting's been nonstop ever since. André's going to have a heart attack like his daddy if they keep this up."

"Thanks for filling me in, Bruce. I'll go see if I can find out what this is all about. Do what you can about crowd control, okay?"

"I'll try," Bruce said. "Everyone's been edgy over Margie's disappearance. This is the last thing we need."

"At least the economy is stable and there's no shortage of headline news. You know Lyon Broadcasting has weathered worse storms."

"Maybe," he admitted grudgingly. "None quite this vocal."

Indeed the voices from inside the office had grown

louder. Caleb burrowed a hand beneath Crystal's hair and rubbed her neck. "Shall I stay out here and help Bruce?"

"You've never had a firsthand look at Alain and Raymond." Crystal nervously twisted the new ring on her finger. "You should probably meet the other branch of the family while there's still time to opt out of our marriage."

He kissed her nose. "The Tanners aren't lily-white, either. I guess no one at Patsy's wedding brought up Great-grandpa Carlyle. They hanged him as a horse thief. And one of my mother's uncles did time for printing counterfeit twenties."

Crystal leaned gratefully into Caleb's warm solid bulk. "Thanks. I needed to put this into perspective."

April sidled up to Crystal. "Before you go in there, boss, listen to this. Heather, the new accounts-payable clerk, told me at lunch that Ray was at a bar down in the Quarter on Saturday night. He was drunk and shooting off his mouth as usual." She frowned in the direction of André's office. "Ray tried to get the WDIX employees there to swear allegiance to his brother."

Crystal mangled her lower lip between her teeth. "That again. I hope nobody jumped on his bandwagon."

"Not that I know of. By the way, I noticed your ring. It's gorgeous," she whispered.

"Yes, I think so." Crystal slipped an arm through Caleb's and slanted him a smile. "The man who gave it to me is pretty gorgeous, too."

Not appearing the least self-conscious at hearing his attributes bandied about, Caleb still wore a grin when he yanked open André's door.

Talk fizzled out for a moment as all the men in the room turned to see who'd come in.

"Hi!" Crystal donned a brilliant smile. "Sorry we're

late. Gaby's on her way,'' she said, partly to warn André and partly to give the impression that they were all expected.

Alain leaned forward and planted both palms on André's desk. "Calling in reinforcements won't do you a lick of good," he sneered as the door banged opened again and a distraught Gabrielle wedged her way inside.

"Well," he continued, "since the gang's all here except my father—who's turned into a doddering old fool, anyway—I'll say this again so you all hear me loud and clear. After thirty years of digging I have proof that André's not a Lyon." Ignoring gasps from Crystal and Gabrielle, who had gone to stand beside her husband, Alain slapped the desk hard. "We knew ol' Margaret had plowed too close to the cotton. My father always said she'd blindsided Uncle Paul about his son."

"Quit maligning a woman who's not here to defend herself!" Gaby shouted. "And Charles *should* be here. He and Paul settled their differences. If your father's satisfied André's a Lyon, you should be, too."

"Bah! Tante Margaret probably bewitched him. I told you he's losing his grip."

"Show us this so-called proof!" Gabrielle cried.

Alain's demeanor changed. "Harlan served André a subpoena. I'll provide the judge with a copy of André's adoption papers as exhibit A. You're all welcome to take a look then. Prepare for a shock. And, André, prepare to pay my family full restitution for all the money you've stolen from us. The job as head of WDIX should and will be mine."

"Yeah," Ray put in, hitching his pants over a hefty stomach. "And we figure the humiliation we suffered, always having to come begging for a few dollars—or a crummy job—is worth a pretty penny."

Dave Patton gripped André's bowed shoulder. "I'm sorry I let Harlan Biggs get near you. Everyone in law enforcement knows what a jerk he is." Dave gave the lawyer a contemptuous glance. "I've dogged Alain for weeks, trying to ask him the questions I've asked everyone else. I finally followed him here. When Biggs popped up unexpectedly, I should've known something rotten was afoot."

Crystal walked quietly over to the banker's side. "Why are you here, John? Do you have information on the withdrawals from Margaret's account?"

"That's what I came to tell André, but I haven't been able to get a word in edgewise. Our computer expert camped on Margaret's account today. He watched the entire process. He doesn't think the card's been used. Instead, he suspects the funds are being transferred by computer. Tampering with bank accounts is a federal offense. It's only a matter of time till we get to the bottom of this."

Ray started edging from the room. Alain clamped a hand on his arm, holding him in place. But not before all eyes had focused on the two brothers.

André lunged across the desk and pulled Alain off his feet, holding him by both lapels. "You know something about Mama's disappearance, don't you, you bastard?"

Alain broke André's hold. "Huh-uh, cousin, stop wrinkling the threads. It's not *my* parentage in question. *I'm* not the bastard in this room. If Aunt Margaret shows up to testify about the validity of my claim, fine and dandy. If not, it won't make one iota of difference. Between now and the hearing, André old son, I suggest you watch how you spend Lyon Broadcast's profits. And don't sell Lyoncrest, either. I've always had a hankering to live in the old mausoleum." He removed a paper from an inside jacket pocket. "This injunction freezes all radio and TV assets." Snapping his fingers at his brother and his toothy process server, Alain strode from the room. The other two followed close behind, leaving the office in stunned silence.

Crystal fought a terrible nagging suspicion. Had Ray looked guilty? There was no question that he had unsavory contacts. Could he be paying someone to hack into Margaret's bank account? No. It was probably all in her mind.

André slumped into his chair and scraped his hands through his hair. Gabrielle wrapped both arms around him and cradled him to her breast. "There's some mistake, André. Alain's hired a forger or something."

"Can you get access to your original adoption file?" Dave Patton asked.

André rallied. His eyes flashed. "I don't know anything about an adoption. Years ago, when Papa was off reporting the war, Uncle Charles wrote to him, hinting that I wasn't his son. Mama forgave my uncle, said he hated being 4-F. I gather he felt second-best at everything. Grandpère's uneven split of the business only compounded the problem. I've always thought that was the basis for the rift. Maybe not. All I really know is that Papa made a point of taking me aside to tell me that I *was* his son."

"And he is," Gabrielle said staunchly. "Margaret has an album filled with pictures of Paul as a boy. Beside each is a picture of André at the same age. They're like two peas in a pod."

"Alain pulled this stunt on purpose while Mama's not here." André's dark eyes were furious. "Dave, she's the only one who can clear up this mess. We'll have to involve the police now." He shot to his feet.

Crystal finally put her worry into words. "Alain's blustered for years. But...he seemed awfully sure he's going to win this time. Could he and Ray know where Margaret is?"

Dave Patton began to pace. "Contact the family lawyer, André. Find out where you stand, what this adoption business is all about. No sense going off half-cocked unless we know for sure whether they've actually got something. Alain probably wants you to jump to conclusions. He probably *wants* you to accuse him of kidnapping Margaret. Then he could sue you for defamation of character. I recommend putting bird dogs on Alain and Ray. We need John's computer man to monitor your mother's account full-time. I think it's safe to assume she's alive and that wherever she is, it takes approximately three thousand a week to live. I'll check the more private resorts around the area."

Gaby straightened. "We have to present a united front if Alain decides to take this charge against André public. I'll notify Leslie and Sharlee. Crystal, will you phone Rachel?"

Sending Caleb a troubled glance, Crystal nodded. "I'll need to call her, anyway. This could scotch our chances of adopting Skip. I can imagine how Rachel's supervisor will receive a family scandal. Anyway, with this hanging over our heads, we'll be postponing our wedding."

Caleb pulled Crystal into his arms. As if the other people weren't in the room, he rocked her from side to side. "I know you hoped Margaret would show up for our wedding, sweetheart. But you always knew there was a good chance she wouldn't. What's changed, really? Except that Dave might find her. If you're so shaken by this, I'll agree to a delay of course. But remember, Leslie's in charge of invitations. She sent one batch out yesterday."

"She did," Gabrielle acknowledged. "Crystal, honey, it's your decision and I won't presume to make it for you. But I'd like us to hold up our heads and carry on as usual. Nothing will irritate Alain more. And angry men make mistakes. If he paid someone to forge papers, he may lead Dave to that person. I vote we act as though there's nothing wrong. And," she added grimly, "if we meet face to face, I'll spit in his eye."

André hooked an arm around his wife. Her outburst had brought his first smile. "Three cheers for the woman I married. Twenty-five years ago she and I let disagreements with Alain cause us to forgo the church wedding Gaby deserved. Because of them, we slunk into the bayou and said our vows in the dead of night. I want you and Cale to do as Gaby said. Make that walk down the aisle in the biggest church in town, in front of the biggest crowd we can assemble. Invite everyone who attended WDIX's twenty-fifth- and fiftieth-anniversary balls." His smile widened after Gaby bent and they shared a tender kiss.

Eyes bright with tears, Crystal rested her cheek on Caleb's solid comforting chest. "André's right. Family solidarity has always been Margaret's theme song. I love you, Caleb Tanner. Let the wedding go on and the adoption proceed. When it's all over, Alain had better watch out. There'll be two extra guys on André's team." Rising on tiptoe, she pressed herself against Caleb and gave him a kiss that left him aching below the belt and had his mind skipping to the honeymoon he'd already planned.

ON THE DAY OF THE WEDDING, St. Louis Cathedral, the oldest cathedral in the United Sates, rang out with the strains of a jazzy version of prewedding music. In black tails and snow-white shirts, Crystal's band looked more conventional than they usually did.

Huge white baskets of fall foliage lined the floor, yet they didn't detract from the beautiful stained-glass windows that glowed in the afternoon sun. But the attention of the well-dressed crowd was on the pretty attendants, who walked up the white satin runner, arm in arm with formally dressed men—veritable hulks who would have been more easily recognized in the player uniforms of the Sinners. Rachel, April, Leslie McKay and her sister Charlotte Oliver—the latter two pregnant and demure as Madonnas—were gorgeous in their floor-length jade gowns. Leslie squeezed her husband's shoulder as she passed his row. Rachel fluttered her fingers at Jacob Harris, her date for the event, and blew a kiss to his daughter, Jordanna.

Caleb, at ease in jade tails, smiled as he watched the unlikely parade. He'd ditched his earring for this solemn occasion. A shiny black cane, which he'd looped over one wrist, served as his only adornment. He awaited his bride standing firmly on his own two feet. But he sure wished the bridesmaids and groomsmen would walk faster. He hadn't seen Crystal in two days, what with all the added upheaval. Now he was impatient to look into her eyes. To touch her. To start a new phase of his life. Their lives.

The moody sounds of the horns had faded, to be replaced by the processional "Pachelbel's Canon." Silk rustled as everyone rose, signaling Crystal's entry. Like the invited guests, Caleb craned his neck to get a clear look at the lovely bride. *His* bride. Crystal had just begun her walk down the aisle, clinging to the arms of both André Lyon and Roger Jardin, who rose in Caleb's estimation because he'd come to see his daughter wed.

Caleb had recently been through his sister's wedding.

He didn't expect to be bowled over by the sight of the woman he was going to marry.

He was dead wrong. One hundred percent off base. Crystal was a vision, her skin warmed by the cream color of the brocade dress. His knees shook and his mouth went dry. *Good Lord!* What if he couldn't speak his vows?

Flashbulbs popped and videos whirred. Andy-Paul and Cory walked in front of Crystal, dropping aromatic rose petals on the satin runner. Andy-Paul looked bored. Cory was ecstatic. Only Gabrielle leaned out to snap pictures of the pair. Every other camera in the house was trained on the bride. Someone had patiently woven fragrant jasmine through midnight tresses so long they hid the bow that anchored a twenty-yard train to the Hollander-family dress. If Crystal Jardin—soon-to-be Tanner—cared that she'd be the city's most photographed and talked-about bride of the season, it didn't show.

She had eyes only for the man who waited for her at the front of the church. Huge eyes. Solemn eyes. Yet the steps she took to reach her intended were firm and sure. She wore no veil to hide the joy so evident on her face, the love that left her full lips trembling. By the time she reached her groom, there were few dry eyes left in the sanctuary.

Even hers overflowed when the priest called for the rings, and Caleb turned and handed his cane to Skip. Up to now the boy had sat quietly in his wheelchair at the end of the first row next to Caleb's sisters. Carefully balancing a lace pillow in one hand, on which symbolic rings were tied, the boy—their chosen son—took four tottering steps toward them. "Me'n Cale have been planning this surprise," he proudly announced.

Forgetting her unwieldy crinolines and her borrowed dress, Crystal dropped to her knees and gathered him in a fierce hug. Caleb followed her example. Amid a flood of tears, wrapped in one another's arms, the three ultimately managed to exchange the rings. They remained kneeling for the balance of the ceremony. Then, as if he'd never suffered from an injured leg, Caleb scooped Skipper into his arms and stood.

He even managed to help Crystal to her feet. He carried Skip back to the wheelchair, and after that, proceeded to kiss his new bride. Sensuously and thoroughly. *Before* the priest announced them duly married.

A ripple of laughter ran through the crowd. The groomsmen issued wolf whistles.

The priest gave up and simply made the sign of the cross above their heads.

The couple surfaced at last. As if they'd rehearsed it, Crystal and Caleb moved toward Skip and kissed him one on each cheek. "Yuck," he said, wiping his face. The crescendo of applause drowned out their *I love you*s.

Though his limp appeared more pronounced during the recessional, Caleb carried Skip all the way to the foyer. If Crystal hadn't already fallen head over heels for the man, his holding Skip for more than an hour in the receiving line would have gained him her heart. The only blight on her otherwise perfect day came when Charles appeared in front of her. Crystal felt the sharp pain of Margaret's absence. With each passing day, she'd expected Margaret to appear and denounce Alain and Ray as frauds.

She was incapable of hiding her disappointment. Especially when Charles whispered hoarsely, "That gown. Margie planned to wear it at her wedding." He clasped Crystal's hand between two that were blue-veined and shaky, and studied her through watery eyes. "Margie eloped with Paul. She deserved flowers, music and folderol," he said. Drawing back from Crystal, he wheezed and seemed befuddled and confused. "It isn't like Margie to miss a family gathering. She's not ill, is she?" He stumbled as if unable to get his bearings.

Jason and Scott rushed over to flank him. "Daddy is on a lot of asthma medication," Scott murmured, adding an apology to the bride and groom. "Mother's here somewhere. We'll run each of them home and then swing by the reception. That is, if we're welcome."

"Of course." Crystal pulled the lanky man toward her for a quick hug.

Scott lowered his voice. "Jase and I...well, we aren't part of Alain's scheme, whatever it might be."

Crystal took his hands. "I know. André, Gaby, Leslie— we're all aware. Alain and Ray want to split the family. I hate to ask, but will you interrupt our honeymoon if there's any news? I'd ask Gaby or Leslie to phone, but they won't. They're too sentimental."

Scott agreed before he escorted his father away.

"We can stick around town," Caleb said, catching Crystal's face between his hands. "The Sinners' owner will lend us his boat another time. His offer isn't contingent on whether I play for him again."

"You mean that? Oh, Caleb, you'd do that for me? You don't even know Margaret." Her hands stroked the satin lapels of his tuxedo jacket.

"I know *you*. And I remember how badly I played ball when things went wrong at home with my sisters." He curled his big hands securely around hers. "This pact we just made is for life, sweetheart. For better or worse." Blocking out the crowd, Caleb bent to kiss his wife.

"I want to go on our trip...but I feel this pressing need to stay," Crystal said in a shaking voice when he'd broken the kiss and set her back on her feet. "Am I being too paranoid? André and Gaby told me not to let Alain ruin our wedding plans.''

''I understand,'' Caleb said solemnly. ''You love Margaret. And from what I gather, she's put you in charge of keeping the family fortune intact.''

''Oh, Caleb, it's keeping the family intact that's important now. I have a horrible feeling that something's about to happen. I'd never forgive myself if Margaret or André and Gaby needed me, and I was off sailing in the Bahamas.''

''Then it's settled, sweetheart. Our honeymoon's on hold until Margaret shows up.''

''Only until then,'' she promised, her eyes glistening with love as she drew Caleb's head down for another long kiss.

Turn the page for a
preview of

FAMILY REUNION

by
Peg Sutherland,

the final story in

"THE LYON LEGACY" *saga.*

INSIDE THE conference room, Scott Lyon leaned against the wall closest to the door, one foot propped on an empty chair, arms crossed tightly over his chest.

He ought to resign from the station.

Hell, he ought to resign from the family.

The morning editorial meetings at WDIX-TV were wearing him down. These days, the time was rarely spent assigning stories and scheduling tapings, as it should be. Instead, the meetings disintegrated into bickering as everyone jockeyed for control. Scott should be used to it by now; it had been this way all his life. He'd been weaned on his father's bellyaching that he'd been robbed of his inheritance. Charles had always considered his side of the Lyon family a victim of greed and unfairness. Now, thanks to Aunt Margaret's disappearance and the injunction filed by Scott's own brothers, the ugliness simmering beneath the surface for as long as Scott could remember had exploded.

Jason, his loving brother and sales manager at the station, had obviously made it to the conference room first this morning. He occupied the chair at the head of the table, a seat usually reserved for the news director. But the news director wasn't family. To hear Jason and Alain tell it, even family wasn't family these days.

Bickering. Endless bickering. Scott slipped out and closed the door behind him as the words ''journalistic integrity'' and ''muckraking'' filled the air in the tense little conference room.

He stood in the corridor for a minute, working his jaw muscles and battling the urge to walk straight out the front door. He could dig ditches, for God's sake. Drive a cab. He didn't have to put up with this.

When he was calm enough to face the world again, Scott made his way to the break room. He inserted quarters into the vending machine and treated himself to a nutritious breakfast of hot, sweet coffee and two semi-stale sweet rolls.

His coffee had just gotten cool enough to drink when his cousin André walked into the break room. The low hum of conversation quieted with the presence of the station's embattled general manager.

André Lyon looked embattled, all right. At fifty-eight, he was still as tall and square-shouldered as he'd always been. But Scott thought his cousin's shoulders had begun to sag with the weight of everything that had happened since the station's fiftieth anniversary this past summer. First, André's father had died. Paul Lyon, together with his wife, Margaret, had been the cofounders of WDIX-TV in the late forties. Then, the day after the funeral, André's mother had vanished. At first, most people had assumed that Margaret Lyon simply needed to get away from the glare of publicity, find a quiet spot to grieve.

Then signs began to point to the possibility of foul play.

And in the midst of absorbing that emotional blow, the family had received another: Scott's brothers, Alain, Jason and Raymond, were challenging Paul Lyon's will in court. André wasn't a rightful heir, they claimed. He wasn't a Lyon, and they swore they had the documentation to prove it.

Scott was incredulous, and ashamed that his own

brothers would pull such a disgusting stunt. The rest of the family was equally stunned. And André, it appeared to Scott, had been nearly broken by the series of events.

Breathing out a heavy sigh, Scott took his litter to the trash bin beside the machines. André glanced up as he passed. His once-calm face looked weary, distracted.

"Oh, Scott. How goes it? News conference already over?"

Rising to the occasion, trying to sound normal. Scott had to respect that in his cousin. It was one of the things he'd always admired in Aunt Margaret, too. His own side of the Lyon family should take a hint.

"I slipped out," he said, hoping André wouldn't ask why.

André merely nodded, reached out and punched a button on the coffee machine. A cup dropped into the slot; coffee began to trickle.

"Any word?" Scott asked, knowing no further explanation was necessary.

André shook his head. "I'm afraid not."

"If I can help—" Scott almost hated to make the perfunctory offer. He doubted help from his side of the family tree would be welcome.

André put a hand on his shoulder. "I appreciate that, Scott. I know you're in an awkward position here."

"No. I stay out of it. And I mean what I say. If I can help, I want to. Aunt Margaret—" His throat grew unexpectedly tight at the mention of her name. He could almost see the grande dame of the Lyon family, marching purposefully down the corridors at Lyon Broadcasting in one of her severe navy dresses, head high, shoulders back. Being seventy-seven hadn't slowed her down a bit. "I think a lot of her."

HARLEQUIN®

SUPERROMANCE®

Join us in celebrating Harlequin's 50th Anniversary!

The LYON LEGACY is a very
special book containing *three* brand-new stories by
three popular Superromance® authors, Peg Sutherland,
Roz Denny Fox and Ruth Jean Dale—all in one volume!

*In July 1999, follow the fortunes of the powerful
Lyon family of New Orleans. Share the lives, loves,
feuds and triumphs of three generations...
culminating in a 50th anniversary celebration
of the family business!*

The Lyon Legacy continues with three more brand-new, full-length books:

August 1999—**FAMILY SECRETS** by Ruth Jean Dale
September 1999—**FAMILY FORTUNE** by Roz Denny Fox
October 1999—**FAMILY REUNION** by Peg Sutherland

Available wherever Harlequin books are sold.

HARLEQUIN®
Makes any time special ™

Look us up on-line at: http://www.romance.net   HSRLYON

Looking For More Romance?

Visit Romance.net

Look us up on-line at: http://www.romance.net

Check in daily for these and other exciting features:

Hot off the press

View all current titles, and purchase them on-line.

What do the stars have in store for you?

Horoscope

Hot deals

Exclusive offers available only at Romance.net

Plus, don't miss our interactive quizzes, contests and bonus gifts.

PWEB

"Don't miss this, it's a keeper!"
—Muriel Jensen

"Entertaining, exciting and
utterly enticing!"
—Susan Mallery

"Engaging, sexy…a fun-filled romp."
—Vicki Lewis Thompson

See what all your favorite authors
are talking about.

Coming October 1999 to a retail store near you.

Look us up on-line at: http://www.romance.net

PHQ4992

HARLEQUIN®
Makes any time special ™

WIN A DREAM

In celebration of Harlequin®'s golden anniversary

Enter to win a *dream!* You could win:

- A luxurious trip for two to **The Renaissance Cottonwoods Resort** in Scottsdale, Arizona, or

- A bouquet of flowers once a week for a year from **FTD**, or

- A $500 shopping spree, or

- A fabulous bath & body gift basket, including **K-tel**'s *Candlelight and Romance* 5-CD set.

Look for **WIN A DREAM** flash on specially marked Harlequin® titles by Penny Jordan, Dallas Schulze, Anne Stuart and Kristine Rolofson in October 1999*.

RENAISSANCE.
COTTONWOODS RESORT
SCOTTSDALE, ARIZONA

K·TEL

*No purchase necessary—for contest details send a self-addressed envelope to Harlequin Makes Any Time Special Contest, P.O. Box 9069, Buffalo, NY, 14269-9069 (include contest name on self-addressed envelope). Contest ends December 31, 1999. Open to U.S. and Canadian residents who are 18 or over. Void where prohibited.

PHMATS-GR

HARLEQUIN®

SUPERROMANCE

COMING NEXT MONTH